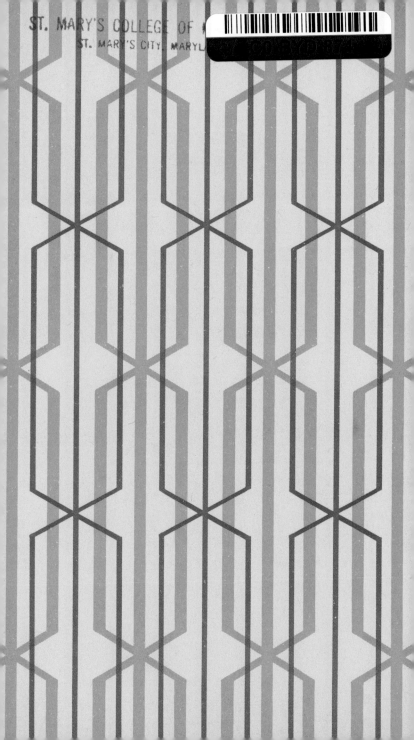

Later Pratt Portraits

Old Ben

" *Mebbe they don't wear bunnits up there,*" he hazarded.

Later Pratt Portraits

Sketched in a New England Suburb

By
Anna Fuller

Illustrated by Maud Tousey Fangel

Short Story Index Reprint Series

BOOKS FOR LIBRARIES PRESS
FREEPORT, NEW YORK

First Published 1911
Reprinted 1970

STANDARD BOOK NUMBER:
8369-3542-X

LIBRARY OF CONGRESS CATALOG CARD NUMBER:
79-122709

PRINTED IN THE UNITED STATES OF AMERICA

To
G. H. P.

CONTENTS

		PAGE
I.—OLD LADY PRATT'S SPECTACLES	.	1
II.—THE TOMBOY	.	39
III.—THE DOWNFALL OF GEORGIANA	.	76
IV.—WILLIAM'S WILLIE	.	112
V.—A BRILLIANT MATCH	.	149
VI.—JANE	.	190
VII.—PEGGY'S FATHER	.	226
VIII.—THE DEAN OF THE BOARDING HOUSE	.	267
IX.—THE DANDER OF SUSAN	.	304
X.—SHIPS IN THE AIR	.	341
XI.—THE PASSING OF BEN	.	378

CONTENTS

ILLUSTRATIONS.

		PAGE
OLD BEN	*Frontispiece*	
ALECK		32
THE TOMBOY		54
GEORGIANA		88
WILLIAM		118
ELSIE		166
JANE		208
PEGGY'S FATHER		246
ARABELLA		282
SUSAN		328
HAZELDEAN		368

LATER
PRATT PORTRAITS.

———

I.

OLD LADY PRATT'S SPECTACLES.

ALECK PRATT was a man of sterling
worth, and he was at no pains to
conceal the fact. On the contrary,
his every word, his every act, was redo-
lent thereof. Now self-righteousness, while
not as reprehensible a vice as many another,
is one which few of us can afford to indulge.
Not only does it warp the judgment, and
impede that growth in grace for which we
are taught to strive, but it repels one's
fellow-creatures to a degree quite out of
proportion to the intrinsic evil of it.

Of this very obvious truism no one ever

had a better understanding than Old Lady
Pratt, that wise old moralist who never
moralized, that keen philosopher who had
never read a word of philosophy, wherein she
was by just that much less befogged than
the average smatterer of a later generation.
She was the first to detect indications of
the aforementioned failing in her grandson
Aleck, and scarcely was that admirable little
person out of pinafores, than she made known
her discovery.   True to her principles, however, Old Lady Pratt—already at fifty-odd in
the enjoyment of that honorable title—reserved her criticism for the ears of those
most nearly concerned.

One pleasant summer morning her daughter-
in-law Emmeline, whom she greatly liked,
came running in, hatless and enthusiastic,
bearing a fresh-baked loaf of sponge-cake.
She found Mrs. Pratt and Betsy shelling
peas in the dining-room, the sun-light glinting
through the blinds and playing pranks with
the swiftly moving fingers.

"There, mother!" Emmeline cried, after
warmly kissing the two ladies, who had long
ago adjusted their minds to the highly
spontaneous caresses of Anson's wife, "I
believe we 've succeeded at last! It 's full

of eggs as it will hold,— and it has puffed out, and breathed in, and dried up, and moistened down, and done every single thing it ought to do, and so I just thought you and father might enjoy a loaf,—and Betsy too," she added, as she set her basket down on the dining-table and drew up a chair close to her young sister-in-law, who was so "hard-o'-hearin' " that she had long ago given up the effort. Emmeline Pratt, whose household duties were for the moment in abeyance, was capable of forgetting nearly everything that she ought to remember, but she had never yet forgotten to be kind.

"Did Alfred come in yesterday?" she asked, pitching her voice to an ear-splitting key.

"Why, yes!" Betsy was almost as proud of having understood the question as she was of the implication that young Williams's visits particularly concerned her. "He stayed to supper, and we had a game of six-handed euchre afterward."

"Who beat?" Emmeline inquired, with eager interest.

"Yes, it was,—very pleasant indeed!"— And Betsy, happily unconscious, relapsed into a contented silence, smiling softly to herself.

Old Lady Pratt meanwhile had stepped over to the table, where she lingered, "hefting" the cake with the air of a connoisseur. The small, wiry figure stood firm-planted as Justice with the scales,—differing however from its august prototype in that the shrewd black eyes had never yet been blindfolded.

"Yes," she declared, "you 've succeeded this time, sure enough. 'T ain't too heavy, and 't ain't too light, 'n' it *crinkles* jest right. I guess you made that cake yourself, Emmeline; you never could have taught that new girl of yours to do it."

"I 'm afraid that 's the trouble with me," Emmeline lamented, as she picked up a handful of peas and began snapping pods over the yellow bowl in Betsy's lap. "I never can make people do as I say,—anybody except little Aleck. He always minds."

"Minds better 'n Robbie, don't he?"

"I should hope so," \ s the laughing admission. "Robbie does n't mind much of any,—except when he 's sorry!"

Old Lady Pratt was shelling peas with great energy; the supply was getting low.

"I suppose Aleck knows what a good boy he is," she remarked casually.

"Why, how can he help knowing? The

child has n't had a bad mark in school, not since Christmas. He told me so himself."

"Seems kind o' proud of it, eh?"

Emmeline looked up quickly. She rarely fumbled over a meaning when there was one.

"Now, mother, what are you driving at?" she asked, desisting from her labors, as she had a way of doing when her thoughts were taking a turn.

"Well, Emmeline, if you want the truth I may as well speak out. We all know that Aleck is a good boy, but he 's gettin' to be a little prig."

"Oh, mother! Not really!"

"Yes, really. You ain't so much to blame. It 's his father that 's spoilin' him. Anson 's so tickled to have a boy that keeps his collar straight and don't slam the doors, that he can't conceal his admiration. Both those boys know jest as well as I do that Aleck is their father's favorite, and Aleck knows why, if Robbie don't. And so Aleck is gettin' to feel so superior that I would give ninepence to box his ears,—only he 's such a little deacon that he never gives me a chance!"

"And poor little Robbie always seems to be offering up his ears for boxing!" Emmeline sighed. "Why, only yesterday, when Mr. Fields was taking tea with us, Robbie—the little sinner never listens to him in the pulpit—got so interested in the talk that he flooded his plate with maple syrup, and half the tablecloth into the bargain, before anybody saw what he was doing! I have n't seen Anson so angry, I don't know when!"

"Well, I declare for 't! That *was* a bad mess!" the grandmother admitted, frankly aghast at thought of the trickling disaster. "And yet,—I can't think of anything that would do Aleck more good than to come to grief in jest that way! Mind you, I 'm not sayin' that the child *deserves* a spankin'. He 's as good a little boy as ever lived. But if he *could* deserve one, jest once, I do believe it would be his salvation."

But, alas, Aleck never did! Unspanked, unchidden he went his decorous way. He was never late to school, he never fell asleep in church; his sums always came out right, and he rarely tore his clothes, unless he was betrayed into a fight. For Aleck was a good fighter and got into more scrimmages than so proper a little boy should have done. Perhaps he was irritating; I am inclined to think he was. But he was a fair fighter, and it would be difficult to explain why lookers-on would have liked to see him whipped.

Robbie, for his part, was rarely among the lookers-on at such bloody encounters. He had an inherent aversion to black eyes, and would have no traffic in them. In fact, Robbie was singularly devoid of the evil passions which find their account in fisticuffs. But there were few other items in the childish decalogue that were not recorded against him. He could be frank to impudence, yet he was an adroit fibber. He had a dandified taste in shoes and collars, yet his pockets had to be sewed up to keep his hands out of them. He never mastered the multiplication table, but "Casabianca" and "A Soldier of the Legion" slipped off his tongue as easily as the Lord's Prayer, which he had repeated every day of his life since long before it dawned upon him that such words as "hallowed" or "trespass" had any meaning whatever. And so Robbie grew up an ingratiating ne'er-do-weel whom nobody loved the less for that, while Aleck, methodical, long-headed, irreproachable, did his duty in every relation of life, and nobody loved him the better for it.

In due course Aleck made a well-con-
sidered, advantageous marriage with a
warm-hearted girl, who, taking his handsome face for a cue, idealized him and prepared to spoil him in wifely fashion. But
Aleck was not to be spoiled; he was too well-
balanced for that. Nor did he prove in the
long run altogether stimulating as an ideal.
There was never any lapse of morals on his
part, never any parleyings with the tempter.
As husband and father he was above re-
proach, and Louisa never lost sight of his
many virtues. But after some ten or fifteen
years' experience of them, she used sometimes to catch herself wishing that he would
once, just once, have the grace to be in the
wrong!

Robert, on the other hand, who could so
abundantly have gratified a wife in this particular, had, for reasons best known to himself, remained single, and it was with the
detached air of a bachelor that he con-
templated his brother's achievements in the
domestic field, wondering idly at their un-
flagging excellence.

In the meantime Old Lady Pratt, balked
in a pet ambition, found herself obliged to
quit the scene of her long and beneficent

earthly activity without having once seen
her way clear to boxing Aleck's ears. Furthermore, such was the sheer weight of his
judgment and integrity, that she felt constrained to appoint him executor under her
will,—indemnifying herself, however, by
naming his mercurial elder brother co-executor, with equal powers. One may imagine
the sly satisfaction with which the old lady
inserted this thorn into her impeccable
grandson's flesh.

Now Aleck, who credited himself with all
the conventional sentiments, was under the
impression that he and his brother loved
each other,—an illusion, be it observed,
which the latter was far from sharing. Yet
it is but fair to admit that no brotherly love,
real or imagined, could have made Robert—
undisciplined free-lance that he was—tolerable as running-mate in any serious business.

"I 've half a mind to refuse the job," Aleck
declared, in a burst of conjugal confidence.
"It 's a paltry little property, anyway!"

Louisa's very needle paused in mid-air.
Such a word applied to any matter that concerned Old Lady Pratt bordered on sacrilege.

"Why, Aleck!" she protested, "what
would grandmother say?"

"I don't care what grandmother would say. It's what she has done that we've got to consider. I really thought she had more sense!" And Aleck stalked out of the room, conscious of that mild exhilaration which the righteous are prone to derive from a strictly innocuous profanity.

As he closed the sitting-room door, with due regard to the latch, Louisa gave a patient little sigh. It would have done him so much good to slam that door! Her very ears craved the sound of it.

As to Robert, if there had been nothing actually discreditable in his business career, beginning in his father's warehouse, of which he had soon wearied, and continuing at irregular intervals in one or another signally profitless commercial venture of his own, there had not been lacking evidence of an instability calculated to make the judicious grieve. His taste for horses, too, for cards, for harmless conviviality, all counted against him; while some there were among his sincere well-wishers who believed him to be seriously handicapped by his native predilection for music, play-acting, and the like, which, as every one knows, are at direct variance with such higher aims

as money-making and personal advancement.

Upon the still recent death of his mother,
who had survived her husband but a few
months, Robert, having thereby fallen heir
to a modest patrimony, promptly renounced
the pursuit of wealth in favor of his latest
hobby, the collection and earnest study of a
great variety of musical instruments. That
a man nearing forty should take to such
foolishness was a deplorable circumstance,
yet one which might have its uses. For it
was an open secret that Robert had at one
period allowed himself to be drawn into un-
holy and disastrous dealings on the stock
market, and the hope was that this new
vagary of his, developing at the critical
moment of his finding himself in funds,
might serve at least to keep him clear of
that pitfall. Better waste his breath on
wood-winds than his substance in gambling;
if he needs must choose between two evils,
better the fiddle than the ticker!

Great was Aleck's relief, then, when it
transpired that Robert, far from pressing
his authority as executor, seemed rather
bored by the honor thrust upon him, and
quite ready to leave matters in more com-

petent hands.   In fact, he let fall something
to that effect as the two brothers walked together to Old Lady Pratt's house in Green
Street the morning after the reading of the
will,—a function which had been postponed
several days, owing to the pathetic passing
of Aunt Betsy on the very evening following
her mother's funeral.   That unlooked-for
event, the only striking incident of a faithful
soul's career, had pulled sharply at the
family heart-strings; but now that the poor
lady had been laid to rest, close at her
mother's feet as beseemed a devoted slave,
she bade fair to be soon forgotten.   Even
Robert, who was rarely lacking in the finer
sensibilities, was already finding himself
more open to reminders of the imperative
little grandmother than of her meek familiar.

To-day, as the two executors sat before
the safe in the dining-room pantry, it was
with a curious compunction that Robert
watched his brother unconcernedly rifling
the miniature stronghold which none till
now had ever violated.   How often had he
seen Old Lady Pratt open the ponderous
little door to "get out" the silver for some
festive occasion,—jealously securing it again
like the good housewife she was.   Now and

then, when minded to be indulgent, she would draw forth some single object from one or another of the partitions, each of which the children believed to be the abode of priceless treasure; and trifling as the exhibit was,—her grandmother's wedding-ring per-chance, or her husband's masonic badge,—it served but to whet the childish curiosity. There was one drawer, having a key of its own, which the most favored child had never seen opened, and in this, as now appeared, were housed the handful of securities which had furnished means of sustenance to the thrifty old lady and her dependents. As it yielded up its contents, Robert could not forbear an only half-humorous protest.

"I say, Aleck," he exclaimed, "can't you almost hear grandma tell us not to meddle?"

"What puzzles me," Aleck remarked, with the fine disregard of other people's mental processes which had always char-acterized him, "is how those two women managed to make such a good appearance on a pittance like this."

"Well, they did n't live exactly like fight-ing-cocks, you must admit," Robert threw in, with a glance about the little interior in its Spartan simplicity.

"Here are six governments," Aleck went plodding on, wholly engrossed in his inventory, "and that Smithson mortgage. Twenty-five shares in the Dunbridge horse-railroad, — a gas-certificate, and — I'm blessed if they did n't do the old lady for a Realty Company bond,—and she never let on!"

"What 's that?" Robert inquired, with languid interest.

"Oh, a western mortgage swindle the Dunbridge National blundered into. Waste paper! Has n't honored a coupon in ten years!"

At the marked animus with which the offending document was tossed upon the table, Robert became gleefully alert.

"Did n't get scorched yourself?" he inquired, with a tender solicitude expressly designed to enrage the victim.

"Everybody got scorched."

"*I* did n't." Robert's modest disavowal was worth going far to hear.

"It was n't put on the market as a *gamble!*" Aleck flung back.

The co-executor raised his eyebrows and shrugged his shoulders. He had once taken lessons of a French violinist, from whom he

had learned certain foreign tricks not contracted for, and which Aleck especially
abominated.

"Shall we mark it 'insecurity' and pigeon-
hole it?" he inquired, tucking the bond into
one of the open partitions, cheek by jowl
with a bundle of family letters.

Aleck, with an impatient grunt that
might pass for acquiescence, proceeded to
gather up the other papers and restore them
to the locked drawer. Having made everything shipshape, and folded his inventory
to fit his wallet, he stood a moment irresolute,
fingering the bunch of keys which dangled
from a single ring.

"I suppose you'll have to have the dupli-
cate keys," he observed grudgingly.

"It *would* seem a painful necessity,—unless
you prefer entrusting them to Eliza!"

Whereupon Aleck, feeling in his heart that
Eliza, the "hired girl," who had served Old
Lady Pratt from time immemorial, would be
quite as available a depositary as Robert,
detached one set of keys and reluctantly
handed them over to his brother. As he
stepped aboard the horse-car a few minutes
later, on the way to his counting-house in the
city, the thought of that Realty Company

bond crossed his mind, and he took himself
to task for suffering his irresponsible partner
to treat it so cavalierly. Not that the bond
itself was worth its ink and paper; but, after
all, business was business, and it would
never do to encourage Robert in loose
views.

That his own judgment had been at fault
in this particular instance was brought home
to him in a manner not altogether painful,
when, only a few weeks later, there appeared
in his mail a notification from the Realty
people to the effect that a small payment
would be made on the bonds of the company
upon their presentation at a given office in
State Street.

Pending its final distribution, the little
property had been left in its accustomed
quarters, and thither Aleck repaired in quest
of the despised bond. To his extreme annoyance, it was not to be found; and after
diligently searching every nook and corner
of the safe, he set out for his brother's lodg-
ings in no conciliatory mood. The cheerful
warble of a flute which greeted him as he
mounted the stairs did not tend to allay his
irritation, and with only the pretence of a
knock he entered what Robert was pleased

to call his "workshop," and closed the door behind him.

The flute warbled blithely on, and Aleck stood a moment feeding his wrath on the sight of those inflated cheeks and grotesquely arched eyebrows.

"Robert!" he called sharply, when no longer able to contain his disapproval.

The performer merely changed the angle of his right eyebrow in token of intelligence, but not until he had finished the little roulade did he come to speech. Then, removing the instrument from his lips, and gravely drying the mouthpiece upon a silk handkerchief, "A pity you don't like music," he observed pleasantly. "It's a delightful resource."

"I have no lack of resources," was Aleck's curt rejoinder, as he seated himself face to face with the offender, whose countenance was gradually resuming its normal hue. "In fact, I'm rather too much occupied to be called upon to keep my co-executor in order."

"Your co-executor? Why, that's me! Sounds quite important! Well, what's wrong with the co-executor?" And by way of concession to the dignity of the office, Robert laid his flute on the table.

2

"I thought it was understood that the handling of grandmother's estate was to be left to me."

It was Aleck's most aggressive tone, and Robert was prompt to accept the challenge.

"Well, supposing it was," he mocked. "That's nothing to get mad about!"

"Look here, Robert, we're not in the grammar school!"

"Glad to hear it. Thought for a moment that we were! And now, what can I do for you?"

"You can tell me what you have done with that Realty Company bond."

"Done with it? I understood that it was done with us."

"What have you done with the bond?"

"I haven't done anything with it." And here Robert, as a delicate hint that he considered the subject exhausted, fell to fingering the keys of the recumbent flute.

"When did you take it out of the safe?" Aleck persisted.

"Didn't take it out of the safe."

"That's nonsense, Robert. The bond's gone, and you're the only person that has access to the papers."

"Really? How about yourself?"

"I'm a business man, and entirely accountable."

"Well, then; I'm not a business man, and I never assume any accountability that I can keep clear of." And from this point on, the flute was left to its own devices.

"Pity you could n't have kept clear of this, then!"

"Come, Aleck! Better go easy. You're running this thing,—that's agreed between us,—and you'll do as you please with the plunder. But you'll be good enough to let my character alone."

"Your character?"

"Yes, my character. It's a poor thing, but mine own,—that's Shakespeare, by the way,—you ought to feel complimented,—but such as it is, I really must ask you to keep your hands off it."

Perhaps the most exasperating thing about Robert was his entire absence of heat,— quite as if he did n't at bottom care enough about Aleck's aspersions to resent them seriously.

"I've not attacked your character," Aleck protested, yet in the perfunctory tone of one merely desiring to keep within the law.

"Indeed? And what is it that you are attacking? I state that I have n't touched your old bond, and you——"

"Can you state that you have n't opened the safe in my absence?"

"Assuredly not; for I did open it a day or two ago."

"Well, there we have it!"

"I went there to get a bunch of letters that mother wrote grandmother when I was a little shaver and had the scarlet fever. Grandma showed them to me after mother died, and I knew she had always kept them in the safe."

"Did they happen to be in the same pigeon-hole where you put the bond?"

"Might have been, for all I know."

"Hm! That explains it. You took the bond too by mistake."

"Nothing of the kind. I stopped and read the letters then and there, just where I was sitting when grandma showed them to me. There was no bond among them."

"Will you oblige me by examining those letters now?"

"No, I won't!"—And at last Robert did change countenance.

"May I ask why?"

"Because I have n't got them."

"Did you destroy them?"

"That 's my business."

"Ah! Then you did n't." Aleck eyed his brother narrowly, and a conviction of the truth seized him. "So—you lost them on the way home."

"Well, what if I did? I 've done what I could about it, for I valued those letters more than forty of your tuppenny bonds!"

"And what have you done about it?" Aleck probed.

"Advertised."

"And got no answer. Naturally! The man that 's got that bond is n't going to show up."

"I tell you there was no bond there, Aleck. I know what I 'm talking about. But those letters! Why, man, mother was a genius! I had forgotten how good they were. You see she was in quarantine with me,—I can see her now, moving about the room, her pretty——"

Aleck was on his feet.

"We 're not concerned about family letters just now," he broke in. "The bond is lost, and as you won't own to having lost it, I must make it good myself."

Robert's little burst of feeling had gone out like a flame.

"An inexpensive matter," he remarked dryly, "since it 's known to be worthless."

"You are mistaken," Aleck retorted, with injured dignity. "There is a payment to be made to-day."

"Indeed? How large a payment?—if the co-executor may be so indiscreet as to inquire."

"Fifty dollars."

"Hope it won't ruin you, though if you think it will——"

"It 's not this payment," Aleck made haste to declare. "It 's the bond itself. That will naturally rise in value, and I shall replace it with one of my own."

"Very right, I am sure," Robert chimed in, with a sententiousness copied after Aleck's own. "I hope it will make you more careful in future. Otherwise I might, as senior executor, find myself constrained to suggest your handing the keys over to Eliza."

And before Aleck was well out of hearing, the dulcet whistle of the flute was again audible in the corridors of the lodging-house.

As Louisa listened that evening to the tale

of Robert's dereliction, she was too dutiful a wife not to do justice to her husband's grievance. The attitude of the culprit was in itself trying enough, while the loss of a thousand-dollar bond, whatever its immediate status, was not to be regarded lightly. Old Lady Pratt had certainly blundered. Incredible as it must seem, even she, the ultimate authority, had suffered a lapse of judgment. Only Aleck had been right,—fatally, indisputably right,—as usual!

To this conclusion all were fain to subscribe when, in course of time, the family learned of the way in which Robert had again demonstrated his business incompetency. They took the matter rather seriously, these Pratt relatives. It was really mortifying that one of their number should be so slack as to let a valuable paper slip through his fingers. And perhaps the worst feature of the case was the indifference with which the delinquent himself persisted in regarding the affair. He would not even take the trouble to defend himself, but, coolly characterizing the matter as a bee in Aleck's bonnet, he went about his business, if business it could be called, as if nothing had happened. There was something so vexatious about this, considering too how ready every one would have been to pity and condone, that for once the family sympathy veered to Aleck's side.

The feeling against Robert reached its height when, after a few days, it came out that his precious letters had been restored to him and that he had let the finder depart without so much as asking his address,— let alone making any inquiry whatever for the missing bond. Why should he insult the man gratuitously, he would like to know? A pretty return that would be for a thumping great favor!

Now, such indifference savored of moral turpitude, or so his cousin Susan Leggett declared, and Susan ought to know, for she had married a professor of Christian Ethics. This sentiment about his mother was all very well. Aunt Emmeline had written a very good letter no doubt, even if her spelling had been a bit, well—old-fashioned, to say the least. But—"Really, Robert," the good lady urged, "you might have put the question, if only out of consideration for the family feeling."

"True, Susan! And while I was about it I might have inquired whether there did n't happen to be a diamond tiara under the strap. So easy to overlook a little thing like that!" With which arrant flippancy Robert dismissed the subject for the hundredth time.

Meanwhile, a very few weeks had sufficed for the settling of the estate, and to-day Aleck sat at his library desk, agreeably conscious of a task well done. At five o'clock that afternoon he was to preside at a meeting of the heirs, here in his own library, to render an account of his prompt and able stewardship, and to apportion to each his just share in the little property. Before him was his check-book containing checks drawn to the order of the several beneficiaries; here were the receipts awaiting their respective signatures; and there, in the yellow envelope where once had housed the goodly little company of "governments," still lingered that Realty Company bond which he had sacrificed on the altar of brotherly—shall we say exasperation?—and for which no market had offered. The envelope was of the accordion-shaped variety, designed to open out for the accommodation of a number of papers, and having once been taxed nearly to its capacity, it now presented a slipshod, overblown appearance which offended

Aleck's sense of fitness. He picked it up and inserted his fingers, with a view to removing the bond, which, however, seemed disinclined to come loose. Impatient of such contumacy in that particular paper, he gave the thing a shake, when lo, with a hitch and a flop, quite in character, there dropped on the desk,—his own broad desk, dedicated for years to conscientious and punctilious labor,—not his sacrificial offering alone, but its shameless double, none other than Old Lady Pratt's own bond!

For one bewildered moment Aleck believed that he was dreaming. He clutched the arms of his chair in the vain hope that they might crumble in his grasp. He lifted his head and glanced across the room, lest perchance the portrait of his father,—steady, incorruptible man of affairs whose mantle had descended upon him,—lest perchance the portrait might have melted away, as even more substantial things have a way of doing in dreamland. But alas, everything was in its accustomed place. The very canary-bird across the hall was singing at the top of its voice; he could hear his tomboy daughter Sophie whistling as she came in from school, and for the first time in his life he felt no impulse to administer a well-merited reproof. Yes, it was clearly he, Aleck Pratt, who had lost his bearings,—it seemed to him as if the whole fabric of his life were suffering disintegration.

Then, in a lurid flash of memory, he recalled the very act of placing that miserable paper there with his own hands. He remembered returning that same afternoon to verify his inventory, careful man that he was,—and that then and there he had half mechanically rescued the "insecurity," and tucked it in with the other bonds. What imp of darkness had impelled him to put it into just that envelope, the only one having inner folds to form a trap for its detention? And why, oh why, since it had remained in hiding through every previous examination, must it come to light now, when the mischief was done past remedy?

Past remedy? Was it then past remedy? And as the excellent man sat there in deadly consternation, the remedy he pondered was not of the wrong done Robert. It was his own personal straits that held possession of his mind, his own hideous discomfiture. Must he then face exposure, he asked himself, his heart hardening within him,—must

he produce the bond? Had he not made
good its loss? Had he not more than ful-
filled every obligation toward the heirs in
that as in every other particular? Why
take any step tending to lessen their faith in
him? Since he had made good that trifling
matter (how much more trifling it seemed
to-day than ever before!), why rake it up
again, at the expense of his reputation as a
trustworthy business man?

And how about Robert's reputation? The
thought gave him pause for a moment only.
Robert's business reputation! As if he had
ever had any to lose! It was not as if
Robert's probity had been in doubt. No
one had ever questioned that. But neither
had any one ever taken Robert's irregularities
seriously, least of all Robert himself! In
this very matter of the bond,—what had
Robert cared? The man was too indifferent to his own reputation to take the most
obvious measures for clearing it. Of course,
if Robert had cared,—if he had been distressed, mortified, even decently regretful!
But he did n't care! And whatever he had
lost in family esteem, it was a thing he had
not valued, while Aleck!—why, a doubt cast
upon his, yes, infallibility (he boldly used the

word himself), a doubt cast upon that would be a family misfortune.

Sitting there, motionless, still gripping the arms of his chair, head down-bent, eyes unseeing, thinking, thinking, thinking, Aleck felt himself becoming with every moment more strongly intrenched in his position. The family could not afford to lose confidence in him. They had been too long accustomed to turn to him for counsel in their business dealings. How faithfully he had served them, as executor, as trustee, as general adviser! Had he ever failed them? Never once. Yet did not the very stanchness of their faith in him render it vulnerable? Too strong to bend, might it not break under the shock of an unprecedented blow? It was surely not for him to deal that blow, not for him to imperil his own usefulness. A slight oversight must not be magnified into a damning misdeed. And with this forcible conclusion our hard-pressed sophist rose to his feet and continued his preparations for the impending formalities.

And when the family met in that very room a few hours later, there was naught in Aleck's face to betray the crisis through which he had passed. He sat, erect, authoritative, in his accustomed chair, giving his mind to the matter in hand, as untroubled by doubts of his own position as by misgivings touching the reality of the black-walnut furniture which he had regarded with such suspicion a few hours earlier.

Robert had declined the post of honor beside his co-executor, with the brief disclaimer: "Oh, no, Aleck; this is *your* funeral!" And so sure of himself was Aleck that he could contemplate without a qualm the grewsome truth that might have lurked in Robert's words had not common-sense taken command of the situation.

The ceremony of distribution was an affair of but a few minutes, for, aside from the checks in Aleck's book, there remained only the personal effects to be considered. These, under his practised and conscientious appraisal, had been collected in numbered parcels, to be assigned by the drawing of lots. Contrary to a well-worn tradition that has furnished grist to many a humorist's mill, the little rite was in this instance performed with a reverential quiet, eloquent of feeling. As one and another took possession of his small allotment, not all eyes were dry, nor was every voice quite steady, though we may be sure that no pains were spared to conceal such weakness.

While the others were comparing notes, or chatting in subdued tones, Robert sat, somewhat apart from the rest, studying a set of pink-lustre teacups which had, inappropriately as might appear, come his way. But he had no fault to find with Fortune's caprice. He had always loved those little shiny cups, whose natural claim to handles had been mysteriously denied them. As he lifted one of them in his hand, his mind was crossed by a curious analogy with himself. Was there not something akin to their ingenuous futility in his own equipment for life? He too had his shiny surfaces, oh, yes! and his ready receptivity. Was it perhaps the handles that he too had lacked? Was that why he had—well, spilled so much out of life? why the cup had so often slipped, just when the elixir was brimming? Across his fanciful reverie struck his brother's voice, harshly breaking in upon the lower murmur of conversation.

"I have something to say, that you must all hear."

To most of those present the accent was

merely a trifle more strenuous than usual.
But to Robert's ear, trained to the percep-
tion of undertones, there was a difference.
Nor did it escape Louisa's notice. She
glanced at her husband in quick anxiety.
Yes, his face was tense with suppressed
emotion, as she had rarely seen it. He
stood in rigid isolation over there by the
desk, the very picture of stolid self-sufficiency; yet in those square-set shoulders, in
that stiffly awkward pose, was something
that smote her to the heart.

In his hand Aleck held a pair of gold-
bowed spectacles. There was no one in that
little company that did not recognize them
at a glance, though none attached any
special significance to their appearance at
just that juncture. They had been included
in the little collection of valuables which the
Law of Chance—sometimes so curiously
relevant—had awarded Aleck. When he
had come upon them thus, a moment since,
he had suffered a severe shock. It was
not the peculiar shape of the heavy gold rims,
squared off at the corners, that appealed
with such poignant force to his memory,—
not the initials cut in the edge, recording a
gift from husband to wife. It was nothing

Aleck

He stood in rigid isolation over there by the desk.

less than a startlingly realistic vision of the
bright black eyes that had animated them
for so many decades,—of those eyes, so
shrewd, so humorous, so kindly, and always
so unerringly clear,—eyes before whose penetrating glance the boldest child had firmly
believed that "his sin would surely find him
out." What other articles might have
fallen to his share Aleck heeded not. He
had seen only those spectacles, and more
distinctly still the eyes of her whom he had
loved and reverenced all his life. And now,
as he stood before his kindred, with the
glasses in his hand, he was impelled to speech
by a power that he never once thought of
resisting.

"I have something to say," he declared,
"that you must all hear."—And in face of
the censure, the disparagement, the ridicule
he was inviting, his bearing only stiffened to
a greater tension, while a queer, discordant
break shook his voice. "The Realty Company bond which you have all heard about
has been found. Robert had nothing to do
with the loss of it. I myself had taken it in
charge, and then—forgotten."

A slight movement stirred the little company, but no one spoke, although all eyes

3

were fixed upon him, as he went on to the bitter end.

"I apologize to you all," he said, while a dark flush mounted to his very hair. "I apologize to you all, and most of all to Robert."

There was a second's embarrassed silence; then the click of a small tea-cup set in a saucer as Robert remarked, in a tone of easy unconcern, "That's all right, Aleck. I always told you the matter was not worth talking about!"

And at that the murmur of voices was resumed, and each member of the company fell to examining his newly acquired possessions with an exaggerated interest.

When the last guest had departed, Aleck returned from escorting his Aunt Harriet, now the senior member of the family, to her carriage. He walked up the path with dragging step, his head bowed, his hands clasped behind him, prey to a profound nervous reaction. They had all been very kind, oh yes. The Pratts were a good sort; not one of them all had shown the least disposition to exult in his downfall. Uncle Ben, to be sure, who must have his joke, had poked him in the ribs and said something quite

inoffensive about humble-pie; but Uncle Ben's
jokes never rankled. A cousin or two had
gone so far as to give his hand a significant
squeeze under cover of the general leave
taking, which was a long sight worse than
Ben's pie. But they meant well. Yes,
they had all been very kind,—especially
Aunt Harriet, who had leaned from her carriage to say, "I think mother would have
been pleased, Aleck," adding,—the better
to point her allusion,—"I wondered whether
you realized that you were holding her
spectacles in your hand all the time."

Realized it! As if he had realized anything else! And he did not, even now, regret
what it had driven him to. No, he did not
regret it,—except for Louisa. It had hurt
at the time, hurt atrociously, but now that it
was over, the only person that really seemed
to matter was Louisa. Louisa had always
respected him so. He had always been
aware of her respect; but only now did he
perceive how much it had meant to him
all these years. He somehow could not bear
to step down from the pedestal which he felt
assured that he had occupied in her esteem.

As he entered the house, in gloomy self-
absorption, and drew near the library, his

attention was arrested by a muffled sound. He stayed his step, embarrassed and alarmed. There, in the chair where he himself had sat enthroned an hour ago, in fancied security, was Louisa, her arms resting on the desk, her head upon them, sobbing gently. The lamp shone full upon the pretty hair, striking its decorous brown plaits into bronze. Had they been less severely disciplined, those heavy plaits of hair, they might have got entangled in the gold-bowed spectacles, so close did these lie, there where they had dropped, when their brief mission was accomplished.

A quick compunction seized Aleck. He had not thought that she would take it this way; he had only imagined her thinking less highly of him. But that she should feel it like this, that she too should be mortified and distressed,—on that he had not reckoned. He could not remember that he had ever before seen her cry since their little Emmy died. Why, this would never do, never in the world!

He crossed the room, with a curious hesitancy and self-distrust, and stood beside her, deeply troubled, not on his own account, but for her.

"Don't take it so hard, dear," he begged. When before had he ever called her "dear"? "Nobody's going to think the less of you."

"Of me?" she sobbed. "Of me? Oh, Aleck!"

He began patting her shoulder rather awkwardly.

"Don't cry!" he entreated. "Don't cry, —*dearest!*"

At that reckless, that incredible endearment, Louisa lifted a face, radiant through its tears.

"I'm not taking it hard," she gasped, with a blissful inconsequence. "I never was so happy in my life before!"

"Happy, Louisa? Happy?"

"Yes, happy! Ah, don't you understand? You've been wrong, wrong, outrageously wrong!—and you've owned up like a splendid great hero, and—oh, Aleck, *I adore you!*" And, seizing his faithful hand, she pressed her face against it in an excess of joyful emotion.

Then Aleck, grown old before his time on a diet of respect and esteem and such-like sober fare, took his first draught of adoration like a man. What if it did go to his head a bit? Louisa would have been the last to mind that. For suddenly she felt herself caught up into her husband's arms in a swift embrace which was quite the most delectable thing she had ever known. And as she hid her face against the familiar waistcoat, on which she had that very morning sewed an unconscious button, "Louisa," she heard him declare, with an uncontrollable throb of feeling, "Louisa, I don't care what they say about me, now that I know you are on my side,—and grandmother," he added, under his breath.

Whereupon those same gold-bowed spectacles might have been seen to twinkle more knowingly than ever.

II.

THE TOMBOY.

BY the time Sophie Pratt had got to be twenty years of age, her father had all but given up hope of her ever getting married. This not because she was unattractive,—quite the contrary in fact,—but because he could not conceive of any man in his senses marrying an incorrigible tomboy.

The young lady herself, however, entertained no such misgivings. From childhood up she had looked forward with cheerful confidence to the married estate, to which she felt herself distinctly called by reason of her strong preference for playing with boys.

"As if getting married was games and stunts!" her brother Sandy used to argue, with much heat and no little show of reason. For Sandy, in whose mind weddings were

fatally associated with velvet jackets and
patent-leather pumps, cherished a deep-
seated aversion to matrimony and all its
attendant ceremonies. But to Aleck, their
father, that sacred institution offered the
only prospect of relief from a well-nigh in-
tolerable cross.

Some there were who held that the in-
tentions of Providence, usually so inscrutable,
were never more plainly manifest than in the
bestowal upon Aleck Pratt of a tomboy
daughter. For while the good man would
have been properly grieved had this eldest
child of his developed some physical infirmity
or moral twist, the circumstance could hardly
have furnished that daily and hourly flagella-
tion of spirit commonly regarded as bene-
ficial, and which was mercilessly inflicted
upon him at the hands of his innocent child.
The sight of a little girl—anybody's little girl
—walking fences or playing hop-scotch, was
an offence to his well-ordered mind. Inso-
much that when his wife Louisa sought to
placate him by the confession that she herself had been something of a tomboy in her
day, he could only render thanks that he had
not been earlier made aware of the circumstance, since the knowledge thereof must

inevitably have deterred him from what had been on the whole a very happy marriage. This guarded admission, made in the secrecy of his own consciousness, was characteristic of Aleck. His feelings of satisfaction were habitually under better control than his sense of injury.

In this, as in nearly every particular, little Sophie formed a sprightly antithesis to her excellent father. The delights of life it was that she keenly realized,—the joy of living that sent her scampering along the decorous thoroughfares of Dunbridge, that gave her the catlike agility which made nothing of the most contumacious apple tree or the dizziest barn-loft. It was sheer bubbling spirits that set her whistling like a bobolink under the very nose of her outraged parent. Scant comfort did Aleck derive from his brother Robert's assurance that the little bobolink whistled in tune.

"Might as well swear grammatically," he would declare, in cold disgust; thereby causing Robert to rejoice mightily at thought of the salutary discipline in store for the tomboy's father.

Nor was Robert alone in his unchastened triumph. Old Lady Pratt herself was not above breathing the pious hope that Aleck had got his come-uppance at last. And although she was forced to depart this life before the situation had fully developed, she did not do so without many a premonitory chuckle at her grandson's expense.

"You 'll never fetch it over that girl of yours," she assured him more than once. "You might as well try to make an India-rubber ball lie flat."

And Aleck's handsome, clean - shaven mouth would set itself in a straight line indicative quite as much of martyrdom as of resistance.

Little Sophie, meanwhile, who could no more help being a tomboy than she could help having curly hair and a straight back, took reprimands and chastisement in perfectly good part, all unconscious of that filial mission from which her elders hoped so much. For herself, she had but two griev- ances against Fate: namely, the necessity of wearing hoop-skirts, and the misfortune of having been christened Sophie,—a soft, "squushy," chimney - corner name, ludi- crously unsuited to a girl who could fire a stone like a boy. But, after all, there was compensation in the fact that she *could* fire a stone the right way, and not toss it up like an omelette as most little girls did; while as to the hoop-skirts, whatever their iniquities (which were legion), they had never yet deterred her from any indulgence of her natural proclivities. Why, there was a tradition in the neighborhood that the first time Sophie Pratt stuck her feet under the straps of her brother's stilts, she had walked off on them as a calf walks about on his legs the day he is born.

After which exposition of the child's quality it is perhaps superfluous to state that she was famous for hairbreadth escapes, or that she had a way of coming out of them with a whole skin. She was indeed a living witness to the efficacy of that spontaneous order of gymnastics which is independent of rule and regimen; for, now that she was past her teens, she could recall having been so much as ill-abed only once in her life, long, long ago, on which memorable occasion the doctor came and stuck a spoon down her throat and nearly strangled her. But he was so firm about it that she never squirmed at all, and when it was over he called her a good girl. She used in those childish days to wish it might happen again, just so that

she might hear him call her a good girl. For
the doctor had a beautiful voice, low and
wise,—oh, very wise,—but somehow it went
straight through you, and Sophie did like
things to go through her. But she was in-
curably healthy and got no more compli-
ments from the doctor, who never took the
least notice of her when he came to attend
the interesting invalids of the family. This
was of course quite natural, since the doctor,
being even then an elderly widower,—going
on for thirty!—with a little girl of his own
to look after, could hardly be expected to
bother with a small tomboy who never had
anything the matter with her.

Then all of a sudden, before anybody
knew what she was about, the small tomboy had grown into a big tomboy,—a gay,
flashing, exuberant girl of twenty, who could
out-skate and out-swim the best of them, or
ride bareback when she got the chance,—
who could even curl up in a corner, if circumstances favored, and pore over her
Shakespeare by the hour together,—but
who was never to be caught sewing a seam
or working cross-stitch unless upon compulsion. And Aleck wondered morosely
why he of all men should have been singled

out for this particular penance, and why on
earth some misguided youngster did n't
come along and take the girl off his hands.
Youngsters enough there were, dancing attendance upon the young hoyden, but so far
as Aleck could discover, all had heretofore
warily avoided committing themselves.

"I doubt if she ever has an offer," he declared impatiently, as he and Louisa were
driving together behind old Rachel one day
in early spring. The outburst was called
forth by the sight of Sophie, tramping
across-lots with Hugh Cornish, pitcher on
the 'Varsity Nine.

"But you surely would n't want her to
marry young Cornish," Louisa demurred,
"seeing how you feel about college athletics."

"I should be thankful to have her marry
anybody!" Aleck insisted, treating Rachel
to a sharp flick of the lash, which caused the
good beast to jerk them almost off the seat.

Whereupon Louisa, in the interest, not
only of corporal equilibrium, but of marital
harmony as well, allowed him to have that
last word which he looked upon as his in-
alienable prerogative.

After that they were silent for a time,
while the excellent Rachel drew them at her

own pace along the quiet highway. Sophie and her stalwart cavalier were long since lost to view, yet Aleck's mind still dwelt upon the picture, harassed perhaps by a gnawing conviction that the girl had not got into that field by the legitimate ingress. And presently Louisa, divining her husband's mood as a good wife will, cast about for a palliative.

"In some ways," she remarked, "Sophie is a good deal like your mother, Aleck. The dear woman was perhaps not quite so domestic as some, but there never was her like for rising to an emergency."

Here Aleck, as in duty bound, emitted a corroboratory grunt, though it must be owned that he had never more than half approved of his charming but undeniably erratic mother. And Louisa, encouraged by that grunt of acquiescence, deemed the moment favorable for pursuing her theme.

"Just think," she urged, "what a tower of strength the child was when little Henry was so ill last winter. After the first week the doctor was quite willing to have her left in charge for hours at a time. That was a great compliment to pay a girl of twenty."

"Hm! He did say she was a good nurse," Aleck admitted; for he was a just man.

"Well, he ought to know, for he was watching her as a cat watches a mouse. Especially that night when we were all so frightened, the night he spent with us. You remember?"

But Aleck, not to be drawn into any more concessions, abruptly changed the subject.

"What's become of that girl of his?" he inquired.

"Lily? Why, she has been abroad with her aunt this last year. Dear, dear! I often think how hard it was for the poor man to be left a widower so young!"

At which the talk trailed off into harmless gossip, and Aleck's face cleared, as a man's does, when he transfers his attention from his own perplexities to those of his neighbors.

Fate, meanwhile, was doing its best to set his wisdom at naught, and we all know Fate's resourcefulness in such matters. For at that very moment Hugh Cornish, fresh from an intercollegiate victory, was bracing himself for that categorical proposal which Aleck, too faint-hearted by half, had prematurely despaired of.

Sophie was as usual in high spirits, none
the less so, if the truth be known, because of
the glory inherent in the attendance of so
distinguished a personage. As they tramped
along together over the broad expanse of
turf, elastic with the forward pressing of a
thousand hidden, mounting urgencies of
spring, she was deterred from challenging her
escort to a race only by the well-founded
conviction that he would win. She gave
him a sidelong glance, of which he appeared
to be quite unconscious—a man accustomed
to the plaudits of the multitude might well be
oblivious of such a little thing as that,—and
she concluded that she would have liked the
inarticulate giant well enough, if it had not
been for his ill-judged zeal in the matter of
helping her over stone walls. She supposed
it was his nature, however, as it was the
nature of the silly tie-back skirt she wore
to dispute her freedom of movement. Almost as bad the thing was as those hoops
which had been the bugbear of her childhood.
Only a few minutes ago, as they were scrambling through a thicket, that absurd skirt had
twitched her backward so viciously that she
had been caught taking Hugh's great offi-
cious paw in spite of herself. Neither of

them had said much since then, though
Sophie had by this time quite recovered her
temper, while Hugh, for his part, had been
too much preoccupied to observe that she
had lost it.

Presently, after a somewhat prolonged
silence, Sophie, at sight of a pair of horns
over yonder, was so magnanimous as to own
that she was afraid of cows. One must
find something to talk about, and Hugh's
resources might be trusted to fall short even
of the bovine level.

"I 'm glad there 's something you are
afraid of," he remarked, in his stolid way.
Whereupon she had immediate resort to
hedging.

"Oh, well," she explained, "I 'm not
afraid, really. Not with my brains, you
understand. Only with my elbows."

"With your elbows?"

"Yes, it 's only that when a cow stares at
me, or waves her horns ever so little, I get
the jumps in my elbows."

"You mean your nerves. I 'm glad
you 've got nerves."

Hugh was apt to be repetitious, but then,
he was a personage, and fairly entitled to
indulgence. So——

4

"Why are you glad?" she inquired, willing to humor him for the battles he had won.

"Because," he answered, standing stock still and squaring himself for the attack, "a girl who's got nerves needs a man to take care of her. And—and—Sophie, what I want is to take care of you—for always."

And before she could get her breath he had added something fatuous about a strong arm, and Sophie, to whose self-sufficient spirit other people's strong arms were a negligible quantity, felt herself easily mistress of the situation. Good gracious, she thought, was that the way they did it? Well, there was nothing very alarming about that! And she rashly undertook to laugh it off. Upon which the popular idol, inured only to that order of opposition which may be expressed in terms of brawn and muscle, came suddenly out of his calm stolidity as he was said to have a way of doing when the game was on.

Then Sophie sprang to her guns, and so effectual was the repulse that, next thing she knew, she was climbing a stone wall to the road, quite unassisted, while Hugh stalked in great dudgeon toward the woods. And her silly tie-back skirt played her one of those scurvy tricks that are in the nature of petticoats, and somehow or other a small stone tilted, and a big stone shifted, and there was her right foot caught in a kind of vise, and to save herself she could n't wriggle loose without danger of bringing the whole thing down on her ankle. It was not doing any harm for the moment, but it was ignominious to be squatting there like a trussed fowl. She only hoped Hugh would not look round and catch her in such a plight. She shuddered to think of his triumph. But he never once turned his head, as he went stalking away toward the woods. Well, so much for Hugh!

And here were wheels on the road,—not her father and mother, she hoped! But no, it was nothing but the doctor, the very man she would have chosen for the emergency. It was not the first time he had caught her climbing stone walls; in fact he had once picked her off one and given her a ride home, telling her that he was to be put out to pasture himself in a day or two, going up with Lily to see the colored leaves. With this reassuring recollection, and reflecting also that he would understand how to get her loose without pulling her toes off, be-

cause he knew just how they were stuck into
her foot, she promptly made a signal of
distress.

'Then the doctor drove on to the grassy
border across the road, and making fast the
weight, came toward her, looking exactly as
he had looked years ago, when he stuck the
spoon down her throat and called her a good
girl,—wise and firm and very professional.
Somehow, in spite of their later intercourse,
much of it so important, and in which she
was aware of having played a creditable
part, Sophie always thought of the doctor as
sticking a spoon down her throat and calling her a good girl, in a voice that went
through her.   How nice to be Lily and have
a father like that!

The doctor meanwhile was finding it a
ticklish job to lift that stone without hurt-
ing the foot.   He said afterward that it was
one of the most delicate operations he had
ever been called upon to perform.   When
it was accomplished, and the foot drawn out,
the impromptu patient said, "Thank you,
doctor," very politely, and stood up on top
of the wall to stretch herself.   But as he
extended a hand to help her down, she
jumped lightly off to the other side.

"Still the tomboy!" he remarked indulgently.

"Yes," she retorted; and then, with an exultant thought of her late encounter, "Father says I shall die an old maid if I go on like this!"

It was a very flighty thing to say, but Sophie was feeling flighty, as a girl does after a first offer, especially when it has been based on the strong-arm plea. As if she were to be the beneficiary indeed!

"Should you like that?" the doctor asked, studying the vivid young face with amused attention. She looked anything but a sick-nurse, the little fraud! A reversion to type, he told himself, complacently misusing the familiar phrase. He remembered having once stated in a moment of inspiration that a tomboy was an organism endowed with an overplus of vitality. Well, here was vitality with a vengeance! It emanated from her every feature, played in her lightest movement. It quite made the good doctor's nerves tingle! Nor was it all a question of youth, either. One didn't lose that sort of thing with the years. And it crossed the doctor's mind, parenthetically, that he was himself on the sunny side of forty. He had just saved a man's life with a quick operation. He could never have done a thing like that in his early twenties, when he was a hot-headed medical student, making a runaway match with Jennie, poor child! Oh, yes, vitality had staying power, and this little friend of his certainly possessed it to an unusual degree.

"And how would you like that?" he repeated, a quizzical look gleaming in those wise, kind eyes of his.

"Oh, that would depend," Sophie answered, with a little toss.

"On what?"

"On Mr. Right, I suppose."

Old Mrs. Inkley was expecting the doctor that very minute, but, after all, there was nothing really the matter with her but temper, and if he found her more spicy than usual, all the better for him. So he lingered a bit, and remarked, in his fatherly way,—at least Sophie supposed it must be fatherly, since he had a sixteen-year-old daughter of his own,—"I wonder what a young girl's idea of Mr. Right is, nowadays. A baseball hero, I suppose."

"A baseball hero!" she flung back. "Anything but that!"

The Tomboy

" Perhaps you would like to know more about Mr. Right,"
she remarked, with a saucy challenge.

"You don't say so!"

"They think they are so strong," she explained. "They want to take care of you."

"Oh, that's it! I never understood before. I've got a daughter just growing up, you know, so I gather data where I can."

Upon which, abandoning for the time being his strictly scientific investigations, he turned to regain his buggy.

But Sophie, tomboy to the last, was over the wall in a trice.

Coming up behind him,—"Perhaps you would like to know more about Mr. Right," she remarked, with a saucy challenge,— "on account of your daughter."

Startled to find her so near, he turned sharp about. But the quizzical eyes met hers with an answering gleam that was entirely reassuring. So, without a misgiving, and thinking to please the kind doctor,— "Do you remember sticking a spoon down my throat years ago?" she inquired.

"I'm sure I don't," he laughed. "I've stuck spoons down the throats of half the youngsters in Dunbridge."

His calling her youngster settled it. "Well," she observed demurely, "I made up my mind that day that I should marry somebody exactly like you!"

Exactly like him! He looked into those dancing eyes, he felt the tingling contagion of that vitality he had been philosophizing about, again he remembered that he was on the sunny side of forty, and his heart leaped.

"Why not marry me?" he cried.

And Sophie's heart, being all unpractised in the most primitive motions, knew no better than to stand still.

"Oh,—*could I?*" she faltered.

"Would you?" he urged vehemently, seizing both her hands.

But she snatched them away.

"How ridiculous!" she heard herself say. And the next instant she was over the wall, and speeding across the pasture, to the tune of a heart that had caught the rhythm at last.

With a long look at the flying figure, the doctor turned away and went back to his buggy. There he picked up the weight, climbed in, and drove straight to Mrs. Inkley, who lived in a boarding-house, where he was quite likely to find other patients with nothing the matter with them. But there was something the matter with the doctor himself this time, and later on he should have to take up his own case.

His case did not lack attention, for his friends and patients took it up with great vigor. One and all declared it to be a headlong affair; quite what might have been expected of Sophie, but so unlike the doctor, who had always been accounted a model of caution and good judgment, and of touching constancy to the memory of his first love. Old Mrs. Inkley went so far as to assert, as any Mrs. Inkley, old or young, might be depended upon to do, that there was no fool like an old fool. In this case, considering that she might have been the doctor's grandmother, the stricture savored of hyperbole.

But, for the culprits themselves, they were chiefly concerned to make excuses to each other,—Sophie declaring that she had not been headlong, for she had been in love with him ever since he stuck that spoon down her throat,—only she did n't know it. While the doctor, for his part, strenuously maintained that he had never given her a thought until the very moment that she offered herself to him! Naturally he declined to admit, even to himself, that he had been thinking about

anything but his patient during those long
hours of the night when it had been pro-
fessionally incumbent upon him to keep a
close watch upon the interesting young
creature whose overplus of vitality was
standing them in such good stead. It had
certainly been a revelation of the girl's character, in which he had taken a keen psychological interest,—but purely psychological,
he would have himself understand. A pretty
state of things it would be if a doctor were
to go about falling in love with his nurses
while they were on duty! He hoped he was
old enough to know better than that!

And, after all, the one thing that really
mattered was to get the consent of Aleck and
his wife to hurry up the wedding so that they
might have a chance to get sobered down
before Lily got back. For really, the situation was too surprisingly delightful just at
present for reasonable behavior. The doctor
was so far gone in recklessness that more
than once he caught himself smiling at the
way he had stolen a march on Lily. Lucky
that she was the kind of girl she was, by the
way, for if she had been a less vigilant guardian all these years, who could say what
might have befallen him before ever Sophie

thought of proposing! And that admission, that there might perhaps be other marriageable young women in the world than Sophie, if he had but chanced to observe them, was the only indication the doctor gave of having passed his first youth.

They had their way, of course. For when Aleck tried to conceal his satisfaction under cover of the perfunctory argument that a man who had once made a runaway match could not be very dependable, Sophie retorted that she thought that was the way such things should always be managed, and she did n't know but she and the doctor might decide upon it themselves. At which Aleck was so scandalized that he felt, and not for the first time, as we know, that he should be lucky to get her married off on any terms. And when her mother asked how she could ever expect to cope with a grown-up stepdaughter, she said she was glad of the chance to show that a stepmother could be a real mother to a girl! And she said it with such ingenuous good faith that Louisa did n't know whether to laugh or cry.

And so the doctor and Sophie were married, and lived happily ever after,—until Lily came home.

Sophie had essayed a correspondence with her stepdaughter, but she had made little headway, though the letters were punctiliously answered.

One morning in early September, as she sat behind the coffee-urn, doing her prettiest, and very pretty it was, to look matronly, she glanced across the table and observed doubtfully, "I've just had a letter from Lily. Would you like to read it?"

"Oh, I know Lily's letters pretty well," was the lazy response. "Can't you tell me about it?"

"Well, there's not much to tell. That's just the trouble. I wonder—do you think it possible that she may be afraid of me?"

And the doctor, who knew his Lily quite as well as he knew her letters, replied, with a somewhat artificial cheerfulness,—for the day of reckoning was at hand,—"Oh, that will pass off. Just you see if it does n't. Shall you feel like driving me round this morning?"

"Feel like it!" the formidable stepmother cried, falling joyfully into his little trap; and straightway she forgot all about Lily.

This driving the doctor round was in itself a delectable function, and it was astonishing how quickly the rounds were made, and how often the busy practitioner found time for a spin out into the open country. He said it was because Sophie was a so much better whip than he, and also because he did n't have to bother with the weight. But it must be confessed that those of his patients who had nothing the matter with them were inclined to feel neglected. Old Mrs. Inkley said that she had half a mind to send him about his business, only that nobody else understood her case!

And then, by the time these two young people—for they certainly felt near enough of an age to be twins—had ceased to be an object of interest to the community at large and were settling down into that state of homespun content which is about the best weave there is,—especially when shot through with flashes of something keener and more stimulating which a youthful dynamo of Sophie's stamp may be trusted to set in motion,—the inevitable occurred, as the inevitable is forever doing, and Lily arrived.

Her father met her at the dock and brought her home, and Sophie was at the open door, her hands outstretched in eager welcome.

And Lily was so polite, and so disconcert-
ingly self-possessed, that Sophie instantly
experienced that fatal sensation in the
elbows which heretofore only one created
thing had had the power to induce, and
would no more have dared kiss her than—
well, it would not be respectful to the doctor's
daughter to pursue the comparison.

Thoroughly unnerved, and for the first
time too in a career that had not been want-
ing in adventure, Sophie dropped the neatly
gloved hand and took refuge in a conventional observation which smacked so strongly
of her father that it gave the doctor quite
a turn. To his intense relief, however,
this proved but a passing seizure, and before
the day was out, Sophie was her own spontaneous, irresistible self. Irresistible that is
to Lily's father,—a fact which Lily was quick
to perceive and to resent. That there was
something seriously amiss, Sophie became
aware to her cost, if not to her complete en-
lightenment, when rash enough to venture
upon non-debatable ground.

Coming into Lily's room next morning,—
"Won't you let me help you unpack?"
she had the temerity to ask.

"No, thank you," was the crisp reply.

"I don't like to have a stranger handling my things."

And Sophie, rarely at a loss for a retort, bethought herself just in time of the peculiar obligations of her position, the which she so misconceived as to rejoin, with preternatural good humor, "I hope we shan't be strangers long, Lily."

"In a way, I suppose not," Lily parried, while she measured her stepmother with a hostile eye, "since we 've got to live in the same house."

Whereat Sophie, still rather new to the exercise of angelic virtues, made as dignified an exit as circumstances would permit.

"And I meant to be kind to her!" she gasped. "I meant to be such a good stepmother! And I will be, too,"—this with an accession of high resolve, materially reinforced by a pinch of the Old Adam, "I 'll be a good stepmother, *whether or no!*"

Now Sophie was a young woman of strong will, unschooled to reverses,—had not everything always come her way, even to the most adorable of husbands that she had got just for the asking?—and she certainly had no mind to be thwarted by a snip of a girl like Lily. And thus put upon her mettle,

and erroneously concluding that Lily's hostility was but an instance of that oft-incurred
disapprobation of which her father was ex-
ponent-in-chief, she unhesitatingly launched
out upon the doubtful emprise of changing
her nature. She would be a tomboy no
longer, but, mindful at last of her father's
long-suffering admonitions, she would im-
mediately institute a thoroughgoing reform,
in deference not, alas, to her own filial
obligations, but to those parental respon-
sibilities which she herself had so confidently
assumed. Above all, she would be invariably kind to Lily. And it never once
dawned upon her that nothing in the world
could have been so exasperating to the little
rebel as this conciliatory attitude. She had
come home armed to the teeth against a
tomboy stepmother, and here she was confronted with a pattern of good manners and
good temper, in face of which the poor
child, at her wit's end, relapsed into a
smouldering suspiciousness which found its
account in the most pertinacious chaperoning
ever administered to a pair of properly ac-
credited lovers.

The doctor meanwhile had been not unprepared for trouble; for, young as he claimed

to be, and as he firmly intended to remain, he had seen something of human nature in his day. If he was rather taken aback to find his daughter turning the tables on him in this highly original fashion, he was too fair-minded to begrudge the child any small indemnification she could devise for herself. What did bother him was the unlooked-for transformation in his wife, which he was inclined to regard as a violation of contract. He took her point, however, for he had had his misgivings touching the effect of her innocent but spirited lawlessness upon the discreet Lily. And he also entertained the hope that so precipitate a reform might prove short-lived.

"Could n't you relax a bit?" he inquired, at last, with a whimsical supplication difficult to withstand.

"But I simply must win Lily over," was the ardent, not to say obdurate, protest.

"And how about Lily's father?"

That expressive voice of his could be perilously appealing. But the young enthusiast was on her guard.

"Oh, he 's too dead easy!" she retorted wickedly.

In which lapse from grace the doctor

was obliged to find what consolation he could.

It was but a week after the reign of decorum had set in that they repaired to the mountains for the doctor's autumn holiday, Lily in assiduous attendance. The self-constituted chaperon had heroically sacrificed a seashore invitation, with all its allurements, to a sense of duty second only to Sophie's own; and this although she had been urgently admonished not to take the others into consideration at all. And so it came about that the proverbial three, almost as abhorrent to Nature in certain contingencies as the vacuum she more consistently repudiates, went to see the colored leaves. These latter did all that could be reasonably expected of them. They glowed and they gleamed and they shimmered; they splashed the mountain-sides with bronze and carmine; they spread a gold-embroidered canopy overhead and a Persian carpet under foot; and Sophie, who had never seen their like, found it difficult to refrain from an unbridled expression of delight.

Thanks, however, to Lily's repressive influence, she succeeded in keeping her spirits in check,—to such good purpose indeed that, when one day the doctor was summoned in consultation to a remote farmhouse, no child delivered into the hands of an unscrupulous stepmother could have felt the sense of utter abandonment that overwhelmed poor Sophie, as she turned from bidding him good-by and confronted the coldly critical eye of Lily. True to her colors, however, she made a valiant rally.

"Shall we go for a walk later on?" she asked, with unflinching affability.

"Whatever you wish," was the crushing response.

And accordingly just at the perfect hour of the day, they started on one of Lily's conventional promenades. Thus they circumspectly followed the dusty highway, though fields and woods were beckoning; and very rough going it would have been for Sophie, only that she was walking in step to that trumpet-call of color, and her thoughts were not of Lily, but of Lily's father.

Perhaps Lily suspected as much, and it may have been with a view to discountenancing the indiscretion that she remarked brusquely, "I wish you would n't race so."

"I beg your pardon," said Sophie, bringing herself up short in more senses than one. "I was n't thinking."

"You appeared to be," Lily observed, with veiled satire. After which brief dialogue, conversation became if anything less animated than before.

Presently Lily announced, as if she had really come to the end of her endurance, "I 'm going back across the fields. It 's shorter."

"Good!" cried Sophie, literally jumping at the chance. "Here 's a gate."

A gate, indeed! Did Lily know how to estimate the concession?

"Oh, you 'll not care to come," she demurred, with a too palpable satisfaction in the circumstance. "You 're afraid of cows, you know, and there are sure to be some over the hill."

And Sophie, yielding to the spirit rather than to the letter of the argument, meekly acquiesced.

"I 'll meet you on the lower road," she said. And then, having taken down the bars and put them up again,—for Lily was peculiarly liable to splinters,—she stood a moment, watching the slender figure as it progressed, straight and stiff, across the field, the silk skirts swishing audibly from side to side.

Poor Lily! It *was* hard upon her, very hard, to be possessor of an incomparable father like the doctor, and then to have another girl, a perfect outsider, come along and insist upon going snacks. She only wondered that Lily bore it as well as she did. And, speaking of fathers,—what a pity that her own was not there to see how she was beginning to profit by his excellent bringing-up. He would certainly have had to approve of her at last. And somehow that reflection, which ought only to have confirmed her in well-doing, worked just the other way about, and in a flash she was all tomboy again.

Lily had disappeared in a hollow, and the general public seemed to be represented for the moment by one old plough-horse, temporarily out of business, and a vociferous flock of crows. Perceiving which, and shaking her head in a characteristic way she had, as if her mane of hair were loose and flying, the model stepmother caught at the chance for a run.

Then off came the scarlet jacket that the doctor thought so becoming, up went the tie-back skirt to her very boot-tops, and away went Sophie down the road. Oh, but it was good to run,—it *was* good! As she raced along the road,—really raced this time,—the swift motion going to her head like wine, she felt herself purged of alien virtues, as irresponsible as any young animal, bounding over the good friendly earth for the sheer joy of it. If only she might run like this forever! If only she need never arrive anywhere! If only——

She had rounded the great rolling pasture, and as she approached the lower gate, she slackened her pace. There were cattle, as Lily had predicted, scattered about the field, grazing quietly, or standing here and there under an apple tree, switching at belated flies. It was all very peaceful and rural, save for the intensely dramatic setting of the autumn foliage, and Sophie smiled to think that she could ever have imagined herself afraid of an innocuous cow. She did not know much about real life when she thought that!

And there was Lily now, a natural sequence in her train of thought. As she watched the sedate figure, appearing at the crest of the slope, she only hoped that there was nothing in her own aspect to suggest that she had been guilty of anything so undignified as a run, with skirts picked up and hat on the back of her head.

And still Lily came sedately on. Already Sophie could hear the swish of silk skirt and overskirt. She would never have ventured to question their appropriateness for a cross-country stroll,—so had the day of the stepmother waned,—but she was glad that she herself knew the comfort of jersey and corduroy. And Lily, giving no more sign of recognition than as if the waiting figure had been clad in a garment of invisibility, came sedately on, while the skirts swished from side to side, and—What was that?

A low rumble as of distant thunder,—then louder, and louder still. Good heavens! *There* was somebody disapproving of those swishing skirts who was not afraid to say so! One of the cows, her horns lowered,— no, no!—a cow did n't do that! It was a bull! And look, he was charging, head down, tail up, straight across the field at the unconscious Lily!

"Run, Lily, run!" Sophie screamed, vaulting over the bars, and tearing across the field in the general direction of the bull, who, fortunately, had yet much ground to cover. "Run! Run!"

And Lily gave one glance over her shoulder, saw the awful brute bearing down upon her, and stood rooted to the ground, stiff with horror. Run? She could no more have run than she could have flown!

And Sophie, wildly waving her scarlet jacket, and yelling with all her might, dashed straight for the bull. Perplexed, not to say annoyed, he halted an instant. Which should it be? That mean-spirited blue thing just in his path, that was showing no fight at all? or that maddening red thing over there, flourishing defiance in his very eyes, and daring him, with vociferous insults, to come on? With a blood-curdling bellow he announced his choice, and as Sophie turned and fled before him,—"Run, Lily, run!" she found breath to scream.

Then Lily looked again, and the horror lifted,—the horror that was paralyzing her. But in its place came another horror that lent wings to her feet; and, espying a passing team, she picked up her swishing skirts, higher than Sophie's had ever gone, and flew over the ground, shrieking, "Help! Help!"

But in her heart was a deadly fear, and she did not dare look back.

The men were at the gate, and making her a clear passage. And as she stumbled over the lowered bars aslant, "Save her, save her!" she choked. "Oh, save her!"

Then one of the men laughed. Was he mad? Was all the world mad? Or was she mad herself?

"I reckon she don't need no savin'," he opined, with slow deliberation fitting the bars back again,—for he was himself not over-anxious for an encounter with a bull on the rampage. "Look, Sissy; she's up in the gallery, 'n' he's doin' the bull-fight act for her, all by himself. Ain't that pretty, now?"

Then Lily looked; and there among the higher branches of a low-spreading apple tree, sat her pattern stepmother, quite at ease, while the bull, with deep growlings and mutterings, trampled and tore the offending jacket into flinders.

Such was the bucolic scene that met the doctor's startled eyes as he came driving home along the quiet country road, discussing congenital errors of circulation with his professional colleague.

"It was really great fun," Sophie declared, with easy nonchalance, when, the
bull having been subjugated and led away,
she found herself at liberty to resume com-
munication with her agitated family. "For
I had my eye on that apple tree from the
start, so that I knew there was n't the least
danger."

This with a tentative glance at the doctor,
who struck her as looking not quite himself.

"But you are afraid of cows!" Lily stammered, still rather white and breathless.
"You said you were."

"Yes; but you never heard me say I was
afraid of a bull!"

With which gallant disclaimer, the heroine
of the hour took on an air of buoyant un-
regeneracy, which proved so reanimating
to the doctor that he was able to observe,
with only a slightly exaggerated composure,
that the tomboy had won out at last.

And yet,—was it then the tomboy, he
asked himself that same evening, when,
coming out on the moonlit piazza, he caught
sight of two girlish figures on the steps over
yonder, leaning close, in earnest talk,—
Sophie's voice low and caressing, Lily's subdued to a key of blissful surrender. Was it

indeed the tomboy that had won out? Or was it that other Sophie,—the Sophie he had seen brooding over her little patient, mothering him so tirelessly through the long night-watches,—the Sophie whom the doctor had made such a point of not having fallen in love with?

A vagrant whiff of cigar smoke betrayed his presence, and instantly the two were on their feet and coming toward him,—Lily a bit shamefaced and disposed to reticence. But Sophie could brook no secrets from the doctor.

As they came up to him,—"Only think," she announced cheerfully, yet with a just perceptible vibration of feeling, "Lily says she will have me for a mother after all. And, do you know,"—the shy note of feeling hurrying to cover,—"I did n't have to offer myself, either!"

But there was no trace of banter in the doctor's tone, as he drew Lily to him and said, with a look that Sophie put away in her heart to keep there forever, "It 's what we 've been in want of all our life; eh, little one?"

And at the word, that primal and essential three which Nature in her wisdom prefers above all others, came quietly into its own.

III.

THE DOWNFALL OF GEORGIANA.

GEORGIANA RICE, daughter of Anson and Emmeline Pratt, had been married some fifteen years, and no one who enjoyed the advantage of her acquaintance could have failed to note that she had the situation well in hand. Indeed, the passing stranger, had he been endowed with the most rudimentary perceptions, might have been trusted to reach the same conclusion. Georgiana's countenance was set in firm, reasonable lines; no evil passions had pulled it out of drawing, neither had it been blurred by any least laxity of temperament. One saw at a glance that this forceful, self-possessed woman was complete mistress of herself and of her environment.

Perhaps one reason why Georgiana had turned out such a capable manager was that her mother had been so poor a one. Every other quality had Emmeline Pratt possessed, to make life charming for her family,—good taste, good temper, good spirits,—but she had never had the ghost of a faculty as housekeeper. Nor had she any realizing sense of the importance of the function. She could not conceive why good Mother Earth, for instance, universally esteemed as she was for her many benefactions, should, when venturing in the form of desultory particles upon surfaces of man's contrivance, be condemned as dust, and regarded with inappeasable animosity. Nor did it seem to Emmeline that her little daughter's embroidered frock was any less a thing of beauty, because a too impetuous firecracker had chanced to burn a hole in the flounce,—around at the back too, where nobody need ever see it! That the small Georgiana herself, aged six, was unable to take her mother's view; that in fact she was caught making an earnest though futile effort to repair the damage with her own tentative little fingers,—this instance of misguided zeal was fairly to be laid at her father's door. For Anson Pratt, as none could deny, was nothing more nor less than a born housewife, whom a caprice of Fate had imprisoned in the frame of a man. Small wonder that a child possessed of so shining an example in the one parent, and so signal a warning in the other, should have made out to steer a straight, not to say narrow, course. Much as ever, if she escaped becoming a pattern of all the virtues,—a really serious handicap in this queer old world of ours.

All this however is neither here nor there, since what we are concerned with is less the origin of Georgiana's qualities, than their effect,—upon her immediate family, and primarily upon that good man, her husband. For be it known that well as this admirable mother loved her little brood of children, her husband it was that formed the very pivot of that energetic, unswerving activity which constituted her daily life. That David should be well-fed, well-clothed, well-housed, that his children (she never thought of them as her children, in that grasping way that some mothers have) should grow up a credit to his name, in short that she, Georgiana, should prove in every particular a model wife,—such was her ruling passion.

Yet if the root of it all was a surpassing love for David, this was something so wrought into the fibre of her being that she did not give it very much thought. Who ever stops to consider the good red blood that keeps his heart going? What healthy person, for the matter of that, ever stops to consider that he has a heart? There it is, that funny, lop-sided organ, pumping away for dear life,—literally for dear life,— all day and all night, and there at the centre of Georgiana's ceaseless activity was her love for David. There was no need of coddling it, no need of making any talk about it. There it was; and it made of life the entirely satisfactory thing she had found it ever since the day on which David had mustered courage to tell her, what she had been perfectly well aware of for a month of Sundays, that he loved her.

But Georgiana was not like her cousin and special intimate, Lucy Enderby (she that was a Spencer), who was always bubbling over with wifely enthusiasm.

"Is n't Frank adorable?" Lucy had exclaimed, only the other day, apropos of a red rose she was wearing. For some reason, known only to themselves, Frank kept her supplied with just that kind of rose, in season and out. Such lovers as those two were, after eighteen years of it!—for Lucy had married when she was still in her teens.

"I'm glad you find him so," Georgiana had replied, with becoming reserve. "But you know, I'm not one of the adoring kind."

"But you adore David; now you know you do, Georgie dear."

"I'm very much attached to David, of course. But,—well, you know I'm not an emotional person."

And to her credit be it recorded that there was no assumption of superiority in the disclaimer. It was as if she had said,— "My eyes are gray, you know; not black, like yours." There was no implication of superiority in the possession of gray eyes —nor of black ones either, as far as that went. She was very much attached to David, of course, but he had never struck her as being adorable. Indeed, to Georgiana's thinking, the term smacked of idolatry. Her affair was to do her duty by David, and no nonsense about it.

The cousins were sitting in the Rice family library, so called because of a tall book-case behind the glass doors of which

housed sets of the classics in elegant desue-
tude. Yet not more orderly were they in
their seclusion than were the contents of
Georgiana's work-basket over yonder, in
the decorous precincts of which no spool
nor roll of tape was ever known to overstep
its appointed inch of space; where the very
emery-bag, though fashioned in the genial
guise of a strawberry, had been taught to
mind its manners, and would never have
thought of such a thing as lying down in
company. The points of Georgiana's scissors were stuck into corks, her little cake
of wax dwelt in a small bag lined with oiled-
silk,—for well she knew the susceptibility
of its too yielding nature to contaminating
influences. Only the needle and thread in
immediate use were enjoying some freedom
of action.

"I declare," Lucy exclaimed, in admiration tinged with an envy which no playful-
ness could conceal, "I call it positively
deceitful to darn a table-cloth like that, so
that no one would suspect there had ever
been a hole! I wonder that your conscience
allows it."

Lucy was a pretty woman, a trifle faded
perhaps, but only the dearer for that. It 's

6

not the look of newness that we prize in the things we love, but rather that blending and softening that the hand of Time alone knows the secret of.

Georgiana however was even less alive than usual to subtleties of this sort. She had something on her mind which had got to be got off.

"Lucy," she broke in, without the least attempt at a natural transition from one subject to another. "Lucy, I 'm told that your Richard has been seen smoking a cigar."

"Trust him for that," was the tranquil rejoinder. "It 's just what the silly boy does it for,—to be seen!"

"But, Lucy! Don't tell me that you are going to let your boys contract the smoking habit!"

There was condemnation in the very phrase.

"Oh, but that 's something for their father to decide."

"But surely you would n't wish them to!"

"I don't know about that. I think I want them to grow up just as much like Frank as possible."

Was there a hint of stubbornness in the

movement with which the speaker settled back in her chair, sending its mahogany framework perilously near the wall-paper? And was it a slight nervousness on that account which sharpened Georgiana's accent as she returned,—"I suppose if Frank squinted, you would n't want the boys to copy that!"

"Oh, but Frank could never squint! His eyes are straight as a trivet." Lucy had a disconcerting way of evading a point by cutting round the corner!

"Well, Lucy, I must say that I 'm surprised at you!" And if the statement needed confirmation, it was not far to seek in the momentarily suspended needle-work. "I 'm not disputing Frank's good qualities. Every one knows that he is an excellent husband, and a clever architect, and all that,"—"all that" might have stood for some such quite extraneous accomplishment as piano-playing, or agility on the flying trapeze,—"but you must admit that smoking is a vice."

"Indeed, but I 'm not admitting anything of the kind. I should n't think it polite to David!" This with a touch of gentle malice.

"David only smokes one cigar a day,"

Georgiana affirmed, loftily,—for here was
something she was really conceited about.
"And he never scatters ashes on the floor."

"Seems to me," Lucy ventured, generously
ignoring the little thrust,—for Frank did
have an absent way of flicking the ash off
into space, with what his wife considered
a quite inimitable movement of the little
finger—"seems to me there must have been
some adoring on foot the time you and
David made that compromise. It was such
a sacrifice to you both."

"It was no sacrifice to David. He agreed
to the arrangement only too willingly,
because he recognized the wisdom of it.
And I will say that he has carried it out
to the letter."

"He smokes half a one on his way to
town, does n't he?—and the other half in
the evening?"

"Yes; excepting when he forgets himself
and finishes it in the morning."

"But does n't he miss it dreadfully after
supper?" Lucy persisted, as she fastened
her tippet and rose to depart.

"Yes, he does get pretty fidgety, I must
admit. But it 's better than having his
constitution undermined, and his manners

demoralized." And as the two friendly disputants parted company, it is fair to assume that each was more firmly entrenched than ever in her own position.

How thankful Georgiana was that she had had the foresight and the resolution to exact that promise of David at the very outset. She often thought with pride of his ready acquiescence; a quite pardonable pride, too, since she was conscious of having acted solely for David's best interests. If she had been glad to concede that one cigar a day,—for it would be no exaggeration to state that she was even then very much attached to David,—she had not done so until assured on the highest authority that smoking was injurious only when carried to excess. And she had so expressed herself that she felt that no reasonable man could have refused her; little dreaming that the success of her plea depended solely upon the well-established truth that a man in David's position never is reasonable.

"I don't make this a condition, David," she had said. "I only ask it as a favor."

And David, who in his then state of mind would cheerfully have renounced the use of drinking water, or have foregone his pinch of harmless, necessary salt for the term of his natural life, had said,—"Yes, dearest, I promise."

It is safe to opine that Georgiana would have been very much put about, had she guessed that David was at the moment far more mindful of the hue and texture of that cheek which his rapturous lips had touched for the first time, than of the fateful pledge so lightly given.

Having then espoused his best good before ever she had espoused the man himself, Georgiana proceeded to fulfil her marital obligations with a completeness and efficiency which was the admiration of all beholders. No house in Dunbridge was better kept than hers, no husband and children in all the community more wisely and devotedly cared for. Truly David Rice had every reason to consider himself a fortunate man.

Now David was not only grateful for the excellent wife that had been accorded him, but as time went by he grew more and more instant in telling himself how grateful he ought to be; a circumstance which, had he been of an introspective turn, might have led him to question the spontaneity of the sentiment.

He was a kind, shy man, just turned forty, who had that in common with his more aggressive helpmeet, that his chief aim in life was to do his duty by his family. Politics did not interest him, nor theology, nor modern science, then in its adolescence; while what is known as conviviality was as foreign to his retiring nature as battle, murder, and sudden death.

He was in the real-estate line, and such was his prowess in the matter of leases, mortgages, debentures, and what not, and such his reputation for scrupulous honesty, that much business came his way, first and last, and many a bill-board, on many a vacant lot, bore the somewhat startling legend:

FOR SALE

AS A WHOLE OR IN PARTS

DAVID RICE.

If the ambiguous wording of the announcement caused such of the ungodly as were blessed with a sense of humor to chuckle furtively, we may be sure that Georgiana was no such purist in her mother tongue as to take exception to those signs, which were really the pride of her heart.   Indeed

she was as unmoved by the gruesome suggestion that David held himself ready to
dispose of his own component parts under
a deed of sale, as by the cold-blooded notice,
"Lobsters: alive or boiled," which at that
period decorated one of the palings of the
long bridge.

On a day when the true purport of those
equivocal bill-boards had been triumphantly
demonstrated,—and few working days went
by that David had not carried through
some profitable transaction in his own line
of business,—he would come home to his
well-ordered house, his well-behaved children, his handsome, efficient wife, and tell
himself that he was a fortunate man.

Now it chanced that on a certain afternoon
in early spring Georgiana might have been
seen in the full exercise of her housewifely
authority, having the dining-room set to
rights after a severe dispensation of spring-
cleaning and carpet-turning. Mrs. Lufkin,
her mouth full of tacks, was still on her
knees, grubbing after possible derelicts,
cook and housemaid were shoving ponderous
pieces of black-walnut about, while Georgiana
kept a watchful eye upon the proceedings, lest
a stray nail-head or scrap of thread should

Georgiana

In the full exercise of her housewifely authority.

elude Mrs. Lufkin, or lest the middle of the sideboard should get pushed a quarter of an inch beyond the middle of Grandma Rice's portrait,—that portrait which Robert Pratt, Georgiana's irreverent brother, had accused of having been painted with a flat-iron. Of course, as everybody knows, you can't paint an oil-portrait with a flat-iron; yet it must be admitted that Grandma's hand, with its incredibly tapering fingers, certainly did have the appearance of pie-paste at the rolling-pin stage of its development.

Just as the six-barrelled, silver-plated castor, which passed its leisure hours in the precise centre of the top shelf, had achieved a position exactly under Grandma's wedding-ring,—the fingers, by the way, could not have been quite as tapering as they appeared, for although they sloped down with studied carelessness that ring had stayed on for more than half a century,—the sound of David's latch-key sent an electric thrill through Georgiana's veins. Her heart had been set upon getting the job done before David got home, and done it was; so that, ambition being thus appeased, the heart in question found itself free to thrill as electrically as it would.

"Well, David," was the cheerful greeting, as she met him in the front hall, "the carpet's down, and you *will* be glad to know that we are to have supper in the dining-room. We've got a power of work done since morning, Mrs. Lufkin and I."

"I'll warrant you have," he answered, with a somewhat forced enthusiasm; for David was not feeling quite himself this evening. The worst of Georgiana was that you never dared stand out against her. When she demanded admiration,—not for herself, dear no! but for a good job done,— you trumped it up at any cost, even at that of scrupulous veracity.

"Yes," she reiterated, briskly. "We've got that carpet all turned and down. It's good as new."

"Well, I call that pretty smart," was David's dutiful rejoinder, as he made for the staircase.

"Stop a minute, David. Come and look at it before the daylight goes."

It was a good firm kidderminster, which had worn like iron. Being however but a mortal fabric after all, the exposed side of it had succumbed to adversity in the shape of sundry stains and fadings-out which had long rendered it an eyesore to the mistress.

"There!" was Georgiana's confident challenge. "Would n't you say that was a brand new carpet?"

"Yes, I should," David testified, truthfully. "I never should know it for the same carpet."

Nor would any one else have surmised its identity. From a dull red surface, with a sprangly pattern of unobtrusive yellow, it had become an uncompromising yellow, sparsely decorated with red; from an inoffensive groundwork which no one ever noticed, it had turned (in more senses that one) into a staring apparition that hit the eye, square and relentless as a sand-storm.

David could remember how they had chosen that carpet together, he and Georgiana, fifteen years ago,—the air of competency with which his young wife had examined the warp and the woof of it, testing its quality, appraising its value. He could even recall the pungent odor of the dye, as the big roll let go some yards of itself, with a view to compelling admiration. Georgiana's judgment had been justified in this as in other instances. David had

never had any fault to find with the carpet,
—nor with Georgiana either, as he would
have assured himself, had he been capable
of raising such a question. All the more
was this revelation of the under side of that
particular carpet a distinct shock. It was
like discovering concealed hostility in a
familiar friend; one could n't tell what might
happen next.

He turned away, with rather a spiritless
air, which his wife failed to observe. It was
not the first time that she had been too
much occupied in making David comfortable,
to perceive how uncomfortable he really
was. On this occasion she detached her
mind from the matter in hand long enough
to call out,—"Don't forget to brush your
coat, David!"—but not long enough to
notice that David did not answer. And
David mounted the stairs with dragging
steps, wishing that he might be let off this
once.

Early in their married life this fortunate
husband had learned that his wife could
not understand a man putting on his coat
without brushing it; and although there was
almost always something he would rather
do than brush his coat, he had a very well-

defined impression that it would be quite too dreadful to be the sort of man Georgiana could not understand.

As he stood, a few minutes later, in the waning light, and feebly plied a stiff whisk-broom of Georgiana's providing, he was conscious of a sickly longing, for what, he could not have said. Not for that cigar which he had improvidently smoked in the morning—he felt curiously indifferent about that; not for the pleasant red carpet whose face he was never to see again; not even for the wife of his youth, who had made him forget carpets and eschew cigars; for, bless you, she had n't changed a mite, in all these years. Yes, she was the same Georgiana, precisely the same, that he had fallen in love with such ages and ages ago. A good wife she had been to him, if she *had* made him toe the mark a bit. And at this point, the stiff whisk-broom slipped from his fingers, and he became aware that he could not for the life of him have stooped to pick it up. Yes, a good wife Georgiana had been to him. Should he ever see her again, he wondered, vaguely, as he staggered across the room to the big four-poster, trailing the coat by one sleeve behind him.

The bed looked inviting; he wished he could remember how you set about it to get aboard. Oh, yes; this way. And, with a sudden lurch, he tumbled over upon the immaculate counterpane, which had never before been so profaned, and lay there shivering, and telling himself that Georgiana was a good wife.

And when the last tack had been apparently eaten by Mrs. Lufkin, and the last dining-room chair had found its exact position in the scheme of the universe; when the children had been gathered in from play, and tidied up,—not without careful scrutiny of that elusive spot in behind the ears, which no child ever voluntarily scrubbed,—Georgiana, all unprepared for the shock which awaited her, went to her own room to change her dress.

On the door-sill she halted, rigid with horror, at the sight, not, alas! of her prostrate lord, but of her desecrated counterpane.

"David!" she cried. "Your boots!"

That purely automatic protest of the outraged housekeeper was scarcely uttered, however, than she had grasped the situation. There lay David, his eyes closed, shivering miserably, but still clinging to the sleeve of the coat, which hung limply over the side of the bed, while on the floor a few feet away lay the whisk-broom, mute witness to the effort he had made in his extremity to do her behests.

Georgiana's heart smote her at the sight, but she did not flinch. Now, if ever, there must be no weakening. David was ill, apparently very ill; he must be got into bed. Bobby must run for the doctor. Maggie must fetch the hot-water bottle. Cook must have supper served for the children; nurse must come down and keep the younger ones quiet. And John, man-of-all-work, must n't go home for the night until they made sure there was nothing the doctor wished him to do. It was like the winding of a well-regulated clock. A turn of the key, which was Georgiana's brain, and all the wheels were running accurately, and the hands pointing to—what? Was it high noon with poor David, as it ought by good rights to be? Or did that shadow on the dial mean the close of such brief day as is the life of man?

Not that Georgiana could have put it fancifully, like that. It was grim reality to her. David was ill, ill for the first time in

his life. David might die. But she held
it at arm's length, that thought; not an inch
would she yield to its importunity. For
Georgiana was first of all mistress, not only
of her own actions, but of her own emotions
as well.

The sick man roused sufficiently to be
got into bed before the doctor arrived, but
almost instantly he sank back into that
half-torpor which had overpowered him
at the outset. And so the doctor found
him.

The malady was pronounced to be an
attack of influenza, a virulent form of which
was going the rounds; "la grippe" they
called it over in France. A chancy customer
at best; never any telling what turn it might
take. The stupor might last all night, or
high fever might set in. There would no
doubt be pains in the back and in the bones.
The patient might be in for a pretty tough
siege of it, or the thing might peter out in
a few hours into a heavy cold in the head.
Mrs. Rice wouldn't have a nurse? Very
well, then. It would be hard to find her
own match in that line. Better lie down
though, on the couch over yonder, when she
got the chance. She had probably a wakeful

night before her. And now, good-night, good-night. And the doctor was off.

Well, Georgiana told herself, there was nothing the matter with David after all but influenza, and thank heaven there was no need of calling it by the ghastly name those excitable Frenchmen scared themselves with.

She sat beside her patient, her fingers at his wrist, noting each smallest variation in the pulse, until she heard the children on their way to bed. Upon which she stepped to the chamber door and kissed them good-night, charging them to say their prayers to nurse,—who, it was to be hoped, showed herself graciously inclined to "keep" their little souls, and to bless "pupper" and "mummer," and other beneficiaries enumerated with childish explicitness.

Then, when a bowl of ice, cracked in carefully graduated sizes, had been prepared, and the spirit lamp made ready; when John had fetched the prescription, when the entry lights were turned down, and all the household presumably wrapped in that slumber which the responsible head must so frequently forego, Georgiana permitted herself to think of her own comfort.

7

Taking off her gown, and slipping into a
fresh white dressing-sack, she proceeded
to brush out her hair, which was long and
abundant, and inclined to curl. She always
brushed it very thoroughly, and never
without annoyance at its tendency to wind
itself around the brush, or about her dexter-
ous fingers. Under certain conditions of
the barometer those locks had to be sternly
coerced, before they would lie flat, as well-
conducted hair ought to do. She was about
to subject them to severely repressive
measures, when a slight movement over
in the great four-poster gave her pause.
Swiftly she crossed the room, and stood
beside the patient, watching for a sign.

He did not move again at once, but she
was quick to perceive that the stupor was
yielding. She seated herself beside the
bed, quietly alert.

The house was so still that David's deep,
regular breathing sounded fairly stertorous.
The tinkle of a distant horse-car seemed as
detached and inconsequent as a street-cry
intruding upon a cathedral service. For,
to Georgiana, upborne on the very flood-
tide of wifely devotion, the whole great
dreaming, waking, revelling, suffering world

outside was but as the shingles on the beach, the mists on the far horizon. How thankful she was that this privilege of service was all hers; that she, and she alone, held David's welfare in the hollow of her hand! Never had she felt more adequate, more truly equal to an emergency.

As she sat there, wrapped in the consciousness of her high mission, David moved again, and instantly she was all attention.

The room was mostly in shadow. A single gas-jet illumined the white figure of the watcher, the strenuous, capable face, the billowing hair, that was making the most of its little holiday.

Suddenly David opened his eyes, which looked unnaturally large. Was it because the outline of the face merged into the circumambient tract of pillow? Or was it that some sentiment of wonder or admiration had set them wider open than usual? Presently he spoke, in a low, awestruck tone.

"I see," he murmured. "I see; you are an angel."

This tribute, though superficially flattering, smacked too much of adulation to be altogether pleasing to its object.

"There, there, David," she admonished. "You'd better not talk." And as she leaned toward him, her hair fell over on either side of her face. She essayed to gather it back, but——

"No," he begged. "Leave it be. Leave it be." Then, with a remote, puzzled speculation in his eye,—"My wife had hair like that."

"Your wife?" she echoed. "Why, David! Don't you know me? It's I,—Georgiana."

"Yes," he concurred, gravely. "Georgiana. That was her name. A good woman. Mind you, I'm not finding any fault with Georgiana."

Finding fault with her? She should rather think not! When had he ever found fault with her? What occasion had she ever given him? And, patiently disengaging the errant locks, which he had begun fingering, dubiously, she essayed again to gather them up. Whereupon he broke out with—"Let that be; let that be! Georgiana was always sticking it up, so you couldn't half see it!"

"Do you like it better down?" she asked, with unwonted indulgence.

"Of course I do!" Adding, irritably,—

"Georgiana could never let well enough alone."

Troubled and perplexed, she let her hair loose again.

"There, David," she said, soothingly. "I am Georgiana, and I am letting my hair be, just the way you like it. But,"—and here spoke the responsible sick-nurse,— "you must keep your arms covered up, or you'll take cold."

The familiar note of authority seemed to disquiet him.

"No," he protested, anxiously. "You're not Georgiana. You're only trying to bulldoze me!"

"To bulldoze you? David! What do you mean?"

An ominous misgiving had assailed her, and no wonder; for that ugly word, as Georgiana knew it, stood for nothing short of the intimidation of negro voters in the South!

"I don't want to be made to do things," he declared. "I've had enough of it!"

"But, David," she remonstrated, in keen distress. "I never ask you to do anything that is not for your best good."

"There! Now you are talking just like

Georgiana," he fretted. "I wish you'd
go away."

"And you would n't want Georgiana
here, beside you,—now, when you are ill?"
There was a sharp physical pain at her
heart, as she held her breath for the
answer.

"No," he insisted, stubbornly. "I want
a little peace."

And at the word, the very edifice of her
life, sapped already by that insidious misgiving, came tumbling about her ears.

He wanted a little peace,—he did n't want
Georgiana. It was impossible to misappre-
hend the animus of his speech. With all
due allowance for fever, for delirium, it was
an arraignment, and Georgiana did not for
a moment deceive herself.

David had subsided again; his eyes were
closed, his breath came evenly, but the
fever was still upon him.

Quietly, efficiently, she tended him. She
gave him his drops, she bathed his brow;
from time to time she refilled the hot-water
bottle, or shifted the pillows, to give him
ease. But all the while her lips were set
in a thin, straight line of endurance, and
those fine brows of hers, drawn to a poignant

angle, made dark the eyes, where gleamed a really tragic light.

And when she had exhausted her resources, and David seemed at last to be resting comfortably, she arose, and, fetching a ribbon, tied the rebellious hair back, just enough to keep it out of her eyes, but not enough to trouble David. And then she returned to her post, and sat there, seeking to measure the wreckage of her house of life.

A less intelligent woman than Georgiana would not have been so quick to grasp the true significance of David's random insinuations. A woman of conscience less alert than hers would have repudiated them altogether. But Georgiana not only understood this impeachment of her conduct, but unerringly she perceived the justice of it. Strong, self-reliant, autocratic, too often had she appealed to justice as against her fellow-sinners, not to recognize its countenance when turned upon her own shortcomings.

"You're not Georgiana. You're only trying to bulldoze me." This was what her fifteen years of confident endeavor had come to; this was the upshot of her tireless devotion,—tireless but, alas, too, too despotic. "I 've had enough of it. I want a little peace."

A more violent denunciation would have been far less crushing. It was the perfect naturalness, the homely truth, of David's phraseology, that carried conviction. She had not made him comfortable, she had not made him happy. It had all been a sickening failure.

"Georgiana could never let well enough alone."

Yes, she *had* bulldozed him, she *had* tyrannized over him, though always for his best good as she understood it. Without a qualm she had seen him "fidget" for that second cigar which she had pledged him to forego; like the veriest marplot she had frowned upon such small lapses of conduct as conflicted with her own ideas of propriety. No genial disregard of meal-hours had there ever been for David, no romping with the children beyond limits set, of time, of place, of decorum; no dozing over his paper into the small-hours, and creeping up to bed, his heart in his mouth, like any dissipated young blade. What coercion she had practised in the matter of muddy boots, of indiscreet neckties, of sensational literature! The works of Mrs. Southworth and her school had a fatal fascination for David.

With few words her ascendency had been established, for Georgiana was no termagant. A look, an inflection of the voice, had sufficed. But in all those hard and fast ordinances of hers, no slightest allowance had been made for differences of temperament, for differences even of conviction. Unwittingly, perhaps, she had played upon the too pliable nature, the too sensitive conscience of a good man, and held him subject to her arbitrary will. That she had not forfeited his allegiance, that his loyalty had never swerved was no credit to her. It was in the nature of the man himself, the quiet, unpretentious man, who would have given his heart's blood in her defence, but who would not lift a finger to defend himself. Her rights had been secure in his keeping, but never had he deemed his own rights worth asserting.

As the night wore on, and Georgiana kept her place beside the bed, ministering from time to time to the patient's needs, marking every least change in his aspect or condition, she felt no doubt whatever of his ultimate recovery, of her own ability to pull him through. All the rest had been a mistake, a lamentable, an egregious mistake. But here, in her battle with the enemy, she was in her full rights, and never for a moment did she doubt a triumphant issue.

The little flame of fever had quickly burned itself out; only the ashes of it rested upon him, holding him in a stupor which was not really sleep. Then, toward morning, a change came, a change for the better, and Georgiana perceived that it was to be a light case after all. It was not to be granted her to play the providence, here, where she had so long played the petty tyrant. Well, so much the better. That was the lesson of those bitter hours of self-revelation. She must abdicate, once for all, her rôle of special providence; she must learn, though at this late day, to live and let live.

And lo, at this very characteristic stirring of practical good sense, the nightmare of remorse lifted a bit, and, in the turn of a hand, Georgiana was herself again, mistress once more of the situation, and of her own initiative.

With reviving courage, if in a profoundly chastened spirit, she watched the dawning of a new day, of a day in which she was to have another chance. Ah, but she would make David happy, yet; she would win him over to peace and content, in his own lot, at least. Whether he would ever again be content with her, was something she did not dare speculate about. But, for him at any rate, there should be comfort,—his own kind of comfort, not hers. What did it matter how she fared?

Verily, David Rice had spoken sober truth, even in his delirium, when he called Georgiana a good woman.

Just at sunrise, David opened his eyes, and lay there gazing at her with full intelligence.

"Why, '*t is* you," he said, in a perfectly natural, matter-of-fact voice. "Do you know, I thought it was an angel."

She leaned forward, and took from his forehead a handkerchief which she had kept moistened with cologne. As she sprinkled it afresh, a pleasant smile crossed his face.

"The angel never would have thought of doing that," he said.

Ah, the ineffable balm of that little speech, so characteristic, too, of David. He did love cologne; he always had. And never once in all these years had she let the supply run out.

How many hundred, how many thousand, times had she seen him lift the slender green bottle from its lacquer stand, and sprinkle a few drops on his pocket-handkerchief,—always a fresh handkerchief, right under his hand. It had been the finishing touch to his toilet. He had never bought a bottle of cologne for himself, nor had he ever expressed any surprise at the inexhaustible supply. He had taken it for granted, as he had taken for granted other good things of his wife's providing, could she but have recalled them for her consolation. But now he said, with a pleased smile (and it crossed her mind that he had not once smiled upon the angel), "The angel never would have thought of doing that."

As she readjusted the handkerchief, very skilfully, that no stray drop should go trickling down his face, the smile of satisfaction broadened.

"Did I call you an angel, last night?" he asked.

"Yes," she replied; adding, with commendable modesty,—"Wasn't it a funny mistake?"

"I suppose it was the hair," he mused.

"It must have been," she agreed, meekly.

"And the white sack. You always look so pretty in white, and with your hair down."

"I suppose angels can dress that way all the time," she observed, conscious of an unreasoning pang of jealousy.

"Like as not; only,—you would n't care what they wore."

"And why not?" she queried, with quick solicitude; for she could not but regard that angel in the light of a dangerous rival.

"Why not? Why, I suppose,"—and he touched her hand, diffidently,—"I suppose because,—you would n't be in love with them."

Poor Georgiana! In all their courtship she had heard no word so sweet as that; in all her married life her heart had not so melted within her. With a sob that was little short of "emotional," she sank to her knees beside the bed, and as David lifted a deprecating hand, she drew it to her, and, hiding her face upon it, she burst into tears,— genuine, heartfelt, delicious, tears.

The sun had got clear of the morning vapors, and, finding the town still asleep, could hit upon nothing better to do than send one of his brightest rays straight across that quiet chamber, till it touched the tousled hair.

And David, lying perfectly still, and feeling those wonderful, warm tears upon his hand, began remembering the words he had said in his delirium. And a strange, new, masterfulness entered into him. He had owned the truth at last,—owned it to himself, owned it to Georgiana. And there she was on her knees beside him, like any weak, soft-hearted woman of them all, and hot tears were wetting his hand. Well, well! He should not stand in awe of Georgiana any more, but, ah, how he would love her!

After a while, as the sobs subsided, he extended his other hand, and, laying it on the charmingly dishevelled head, he said, musingly, yet with the faintest thrill of lingering self-gratulation on the words,— "No, you would n't be in love with an angel, Georgiana!"

And Georgiana lifted her head and turning upon him a look of radiant assurance she said, with just a trace of her old decision of accent,—"David, I want you to promise me one thing."

It was a severe test to put upon a sick man, but he recognized the importance of the crisis. If he was ever really to assert him-self, if he was ever to reap the advantage of a happy accident, now was the time to do it.

Summoning every shred of courage that a life of benevolent assimilation had left him, he replied, firmly:

"I don't know about that, Georgiana. I can make no promises if they are against my better judgment."

For an instant she was taken aback, but for an instant only. Then a wave of strong approval crossed her face, leaving it clarified, subdued if you like, but indescribably en-gaging, as she said,—

"I want you to promise me that, from now on, you will smoke just as many cigars a day *as you think best!*"

IV.

WILLIAM'S WILLIE.

YOUNG William Pratt was afflicted with an incubus; a hateful, hampering thing which he had been carrying about with him for the better part of his life. He had got quite used to it, to be sure, for it had been lying dormant for a long time now, and a person does adjust himself to a mere dead weight. But one day something happened which rendered it extremely desirable to turn the thing out, neck and crop; and such was the tenacity of its hold upon him, and so mistaken was his estimate of his own powers, that the possibility of a summary ejection never once entered his mind.

It was just three days after Isabel Allen's return from boarding-school, transformed from a nice little girl into a young goddess,—

a phenomenon which William was among the first to observe.

They had been picnicking, very gregariously, with a party of young people, on Joy's Hill, it being Saturday afternoon and holiday weather. Scarcely was the fire covered in however than the little company had split into groups, quite after the manner of a ball of quicksilver, that goes gleaming off in a dozen different directions at the lightest pin-point of a touch. William and Isabel, assiduously chaperoned by Brady, William's mongrel terrier, had found their way to a certain clump of ancient oaks, well-known to Brady and William, from the shadow of which they could look out upon all the world and the kingdoms thereof; for the eyes of the young see far.

Isabel, having seated herself on a hospitable rock, in a cleft of which last year's leaves and acorns still found lodgment, her taciturn escort had dropped, acorn fashion, at her feet. She had taken off her little butter-plate of a hat, which might as well have been worn as a locket for all the good it did. Whereupon the God of Day, being in genial mood, fell to pelting with shadow oak-leaves not only the dotted muslin

8

frock that she wore, but her already well-burnished tresses. In so doing, the God of Day showed commendable good taste, for one of the very nicest things about Isabel was the way she did her hair; not in the awkward style then in vogue, but in two shining braids worn coronet-wise above the brow. Not every girl could have ventured that departure from the prevailing mode; but there was something in the way Isabel's head was set on her shoulders which seemed to invite classic treatment. People who knew the family—and everybody in Dunbridge who was anybody did know the Allens—declared that she got that queenly pose, and the level outlook of the eyes too, from her Aunt Isabel,—the aunt, by the way, who had been the first wife of William's father. Though, since Aunt Isabel had died many years before her little niece was born, the testamentary transaction must have been of a highly prophetic character.

As she sat looking down upon her companion, his long length spread out carelessly at her feet, his fingers toying absently with Brady's ear,—Isabel indulged in sundry observations of her own, the drift of which was hardly to be inferred from the remark wherewith she elected to break the silence. For all she said was: "Brady is a dear."

"He's only a cur," William felt constrained to own. He loved his dog, but he would not take unfair advantage of girlish ignorance.

"I always did like curs," was Isabel's rash rejoinder. For she did not in the least know the difference, and was merely generalizing from one particular instance. She might of course have argued that if Brady was a cur, that settled it, because he was just the kind of dog she did like. Perhaps Brady himself took that view; for he was no stern moralist. At any rate, he promptly wagged a self-satisfied tail.

"Looks as if you had a fancy for no-account folks," the young man hazarded, still thoughtfully playing with Brady's apology for an ear. "That must have been why you came along with me, just now, and left the other fellows in the lurch."

"The other fellows never asked me," she protested, with a little toss.

Then William sat up straight and declared, quite ferociously,—"They didn't get a chance!"

Whereupon Brady, conscious of a desolate

feeling in the abandoned ear, proceeded to crawl up his master's person, whimpering for more.

"He's a regular Oliver Twist," Isabel remarked, demurely.

"He *is* rather greedy," William admitted, as he relapsed again on his elbow. "I guess he had been kept on short rations before he came to me."

She could see William's face now, for he had turned his head a bit, and she found herself tracing a resemblance to the daguerreotype of his father, taken just before her Aunt Isabel died. It was not very marked, that resemblance; in fact the face was of a quite different type, though the brooding eyes were the same, and the hair grew like his father's. But, while the chin was strongly modelled, there was a sensitiveness of line in mouth and nose, that lent the countenance a look of ultra-refinement, unlike as possible to that of the elder William. These however were subtleties to escape the youthful observer and Isabel, as was to have been expected, found what she was looking for; namely, a resemblance to the soldier uncle, whose second wife, William's mother, had filched him from out the family

circle, away back in the dark ages, before
time began for Isabel. The likeness, such
as it was, touched the deepest sentiment
the girl had yet known. For Isabel could
recall the war, in its later phases, especially
the battered blue-coats that came straggling
home when it was over. The sight of those
scarred and crippled veterans had stirred
her heart, child though she was.

"How much can you remember of the
war?" she asked, abruptly.

A swift pang took him, a treacherous
thrust of that incubus that had been lying low,
watching its chance. But he gave no sign
of discomfiture, as he replied,—"Oh, I remember it from the beginning."

"Tell me about your father," she begged.

William hesitated a moment, while Brady's
ear profited by his preoccupation. Such
kind fingers as William had,—though in
this instance it was the incubus, rather than
Brady, that he was trying to pacify.

At last,—"There is n't much to tell," he
answered. "He had n't half believed in it,
thought there was no need of war, and so
on; but when they fired on the flag, he just
went down there and got shot."

"It was at Bull Run, was n't it?"

"Yes; but he must have fallen before the rout began, for he was shot through the breast."

"So it was victory for him, after all." The words were very low, but all the more penetrating for that.

And then William knew that his hour had struck. He glanced up at her, while a hot wave of gratitude surged to his heart.

"Yes, it was victory," he answered, in his deep bass that had never learned to vibrate until that instant.

That was four months ago, and all this time William had kept his own counsel so well, that he was justified in believing that no one surmised the case he was in; unless of course it were Brady. He had no secrets from Brady. And it never once occurred to him to mistrust Brady's growing intimacy with Isabel, though he often saw him telling her things on the sly; things which seemed to give her pleasure too, to judge by the quite intoxicating caresses she bestowed upon the good brute in return. But unless Brady had been indiscreet enough to mention the incubus, which seems unlikely, Isabel had no means of knowing

William

He had no secrets from Brady.

how it hurt when she talked to William of his father, as she often did, just because his presence set her thinking of that modest hero.

For William's father was his pride and his despair.

He was a very little chap when the elder William went to the war, not quite ten in fact, and his one distinct memory of his father dated from the hour of his going. He could still see quite plainly the tall, rugged form in its private's uniform,—for William Pratt fought in the ranks and asked no favors,—and the stern, set face, no longer young; he could still hear the deep, curiously unemotional voice in which he had said his soldierly good-byes.

Willie's mother had wept copiously at the time, and the child had got the impression that she was angry about something. It seemed likely enough, for when boys cried it was almost always from temper. Not until he came upon his sister Mary, after the parting was over, crying her heart out in a corner of the parlor sofa, did he perceive that there was a difference in tears. And it was still later, the day the brief word came over the wires: "Dead; shot in

the breast," that he himself felt the first
stab of grief.

The boy had loved his father in a remote,
unrealized way,—William had never understood making friends with his children,—
but, now, that latent, groping sort of love
was merged in an idealizing passion. And
always in the dark hours of the night, when
he chanced to wake, which he often did
(for Willie was a highstrung, sensitive little
lad), he thought of the man who had shot
the brave soldier, and thought of him with
pity. What a terrible fate, to go to war
and be made to shoot a good man dead!

After a while the call for men grew louder
and more urgent, and about that time rumors
reached the North of the extreme youth of
the Southern recruits. He heard of boys
of seventeen, of sixteen, finally of fifteen,
enlisting in the ranks, and his little soul
was sick with fear. The war had lasted
so long,—two years it was, now,—he never
thought of its stopping; and here he was
going on for twelve, and the age-limit
lowering season by season. He never could
do it, never. Supposing he were to be
drafted, and should have to go, and there
should be a bayonet charge,—he used to

read about them in the newspapers,—and
he should be driven to sticking a bayonet
into an enemy's breast!—the breast of a
good man whom somebody loved, so close
to him, too, that he could hear the tearing
wound and feel the spouting blood. He
should run away before he did that, he knew
he should run away, and his father's very
own name would be disgraced. For did
they not call him William's Willie?

At last he went to his mother about it.
He had never found much satisfaction in going to his mother, but then, one can't help
hoping, when it's all the mother one has.

He found her standing before the looking-
glass, putting the last touches to an elaborate
toilet in which crape largely predominated.
There was something curiously incongruous
in the spread and buoyancy of an enormous
crinoline under the sombre mourning raiment.

"Mother," the child ventured, timidly.

"Well," was the brisk response. "Been
getting into mischief again?" Willie was
not a particularly mischievous child, though
he had his lapses, but he was a boy, and
therefore he must be driven on the curb.

"I wanted to ask you a question," he
faltered.

"Then why don't you ask it, and not stand there, staring like a nincompoop?" She was in the act of affixing a large crape bow to her crape collar; for this was the 21st of July, and crape was the ultimate expression of Edna's mourning.

"What's the youngest boy you ever heard of being drafted?"

The crape bow fell to the floor in sheer amazement.

"Gracious, what a turn you gave me!" she burst out. "Did n't you know this was the anniversary of Bull Run?"

"Yes; I 've heard you say so several times. So—I thought I would ask."

"And I suppose you 'd like to go down there and get shot, like your father," she cried, irritably, as she stooped to pick up the bow and, rising with a flushed face, began twitching the offending ornament into shape. She could never think with equanimity of her husband's lack of consideration in leaving them all as poor as church mice, when he might have been a rich man in a few years more.

"No," said Willie, in a very small voice. "I don't want to go. That 's why I asked."

"So! You 're a coward, are you?" she

scoffed, as she fastened the bow in place. "To think of a son of mine being a coward!"

Willie's heart contracted at the cruel taunt; yet, as she stepped across to the closet and took down her silk basquine,— "But you have n't told me," he persisted.

"Told you what?"

"How old he was."

She turned and confronted the shrinking child, his supplicating eyes, his white, drawn face, and she felt honestly ashamed of him. For it was not brute courage that Edna lacked. If it had been, she would never have dared be as disagreeable as she often was.

"Old enough not to be a coward!" she answered, sharply; and upon that she left the boy standing there, to deal as best he might with this dreadful accusation.

So, he was a coward. He had n't thought of that; but of course that was it. His own mother had said it. He was a coward; his father's son, William's Willie, a coward. And henceforth the name, once so sweet to hear, sounded to him like a wanton gibe.

That was the last time Willie ever went to his mother about anything, unless it were to get a button sewed on, or some such matter; and he always preferred going to his sister Mary, even for that. This was not because he resented what his mother had said,—he supposed she had to tell him; but because he feared her, really feared her, as the burnt child dreads the fire. She seemed to know him so much better than he knew himself; and who could say what hideous thing she might point out to him, next time?

And so the boy withdrew more and more into himself, until he had grown his own little husk of reticence, and was quite secure against any further self-betrayal. And by-and-by, when he was thirteen, the war ceased, and the poor, shattered country set herself to dress her wounds, though with bungling hands, and many a delusive nostrum. But no hands were there to dress the wound festering in the deepest consciousness of a child. And although William's Willie, relieved of the immediate nightmare of war, did come to be a good deal like other boys, inside his husk as well as out, still, deep in the very centre of him was the one hard kernel that would not resolve itself into good, normal fibre,—the ugly, immovable conviction that he was a coward.

When William was sixteen, a few weeks before he graduated at the high-school, his cousin James Spencer, who was in the iron business, sent for him to come and see him. The summons was authoritative, for James was nearly thirty years older than William, besides being a man of standing in the community. Not a rich man, like his brother Stephen, who was a banker, and scooped the plunder right in, without sweating for it, but a man of ability and means. James had always mistrusted short-cuts, and with good reason, too; for he had just three times as many children as Stephen, nine in fact, and an invalidish sort of wife into the bargain, sweet and clinging, the kind that never takes any responsibility,— could n't dismiss a house-maid, or have the boys' hair cut unless he backed her up. But despite these hindrances,—or was it because of them?—he had more than held his own in the business world, where the old firm of Spencer & Co. was as prominent now as in his father's day.

"So you 're graduating, with honors?" he remarked, as soon as William took his seat.

"Not yet. There 's no list out, yet."

"Looking for a chance to contradict; eh?"

At which William got inside of himself and said nothing, thereby pleasing his cousin James quite particularly.

"Suppose you 're college-mad like the rest of the youngsters?" James went on. Every blessèd one of his own sons—their ages at the moment ranged from six to sixteen—had already requisitioned his father for a college course, with an eye undoubtedly to athletic glories. The thing was getting a bit on his nerves. And the girls too! Why that little snip of a Susie was talking Vassar, only yesterday. He himself had never been to college, he would have you know. A man could pull through without it; eh?

William was long enough in answering for James to get somewhat worked up over his own problems. It did n't take much to work James up. But the boy did answer at last, quite explicitly.

"I 'd rather go to college than anything," he said. "But of course I know I can't."

"Hmph! Glad you have the wit to see that. Now, what do you say to coming over to my place for a starter?"

Again William fell silent. He did not

feel particularly drawn to pig-tin or Russian
sheet-iron; but perhaps they might prove
more attractive on nearer acquaintance.
Anyhow he had got his living to earn, and
that was about the best thing he knew about
himself.

James had settled back in his chair, and
was weighing the chances of horse-sense
being discoverable in the boy's constitution.

"I think I should like to," William
answered, at last. "It 's a first rate chance."

"Good! And when shall we look for you?"

"The day after graduation, if you say so."

And on the day after graduation, now
five years ago, William's Willie, who had
taken honors and delivered the valedictory
to boot, might have been seen standing at the
sink in the closet of the private office,
earnestly cleaning out his employer's inkstand. In fact he *was* so seen; for James
came in at the moment, and stood eyeing
him with interest. It was a test which he
invariably applied to a new boy; he considered it important. In this instance he
observed that the boy was doing the rather
nasty job quite unostentatiously, without
any needless smearing of his own person,
but he was doing it right. Well, that was

very good as far as it went, though it did n't of course settle anything.

Now James Spencer, like many another blusterer, was a kind-hearted man, and he was glad to be doing his Uncle William's boy a good turn. If he had his doubts about William's Willie being quite worthy of the title, it may have been because of a reputation the lad had incurred of fighting shy of a scrimmage. For while James had been known to flog a boy of his own for a too frequent indulgence in black eyes, he would hardly have thought a youngster worth flogging who could n't glory in a fight.

"Well, James," Old Lady Pratt inquired, a week or two later, "how's William's Willie holding out to burn?"

James made it a rule to call upon his grandmother of a Sunday. He said it was because she was the most agreeable woman he knew. If Nannie, his wife, did not take this literally, why, all the better for Nannie!

"He's doing well, so far," he admitted. "He can clean out an inkstand, and he can get an errand straight."

"I told you he'd come up to the scratch."

Old Lady Pratt had as keen a relish for

the vernacular as James himself. That was
a great bond between them; a bond that was
cemented every Sunday over the cherry-
bounce and seed-cakes, a relay of which
Aunt Betsy had just brought in. This
particular form of indulgence had been
James's prerogative since about the time
he left off snapping spit-balls at the cat.
As he glanced at his grandmother over
the rim of his glass, he could not see that she
had changed much in the interval. How
straight she sat in that uncompromising
chair of hers! Steve, the old money-bags,
had once made her a present of a fifty-dollar
easy-chair. She was pleased with the attention, oh, very much pleased; for truth to
tell, Stephen was not often so lavish as that.
But to James's secret glee she could never
be induced to sit in it herself.

"Wait till I'm an old woman," she would
say. She was only eighty-seven, now!

"Well," the grandson threw in, as he
sipped his glass, to make it hold out longer.
"A new broom, you know."

"Now don't you be fooled by any old
saws," she admonished. "Most things are
jest as true, 't other way about."

"Then it's your opinion that there's

9

real stuff in the boy?" And James set down his empty glass. He would have been glad of another, but he knew better than to ask for it. Old Lady Pratt disliked excess.

"Stuff in him?" she repeated, sharply. "You appear to be forgettin' that he's William's Willie. I tell ye, James Spencer, that boy's a chip o' the old block, ef he *is* a leetle mite finical."

And just there Old Lady Pratt had put her finger on a defect in William, the recognition of which had gone far to confirm him in his morbid fancies. He *was* finical, and he knew it. He had done what he could to toughen himself, — gymnastics, cheap lunch-counters, and what not; but he was always conscious of a womanish streak which he had never been able to eradicate, although he had frequent resort to heroic measures, such as calling himself "Miss Nancy," and vindictively taking the young lady to lunch on leather-stew and kerosene pudding, and asking her how she liked it.

Things might have gone even worse with him if it hadn't been for Brady. But since the day Brady picked him up on the street a year ago, and deliberately took him in

training, William had got mixed up in so
many gory scrimmages, that he had learned
to face a ragged ear or an open shoulder
with only a passing shudder of repulsion;
even to bathe it and pull the hairs out of it.
Perhaps Brady knew he had a mission; or
perhaps he only fell in love with William.
At any rate, being a dog of parts, it is not
likely that he remained long in ignorance
of that miserable incubus that was leading
his master such a life,—why, he could smell
a woodchuck across a ten-acre lot!—nor that
he failed to take Isabel into his confidence
early in the proceedings. She certainly
gave him every facility for doing so, even
at the cost of extending like privileges to
Brady's master.

And although William persisted in regarding the way to Isabel's favor as "no-thorough-
fare,"—for he was only twenty-one, and
his judgment was fallible,—this did not
deter him from singeing his wings quite
recklessly; wings being independent of thoroughfares,—and it never having occurred to
him that Isabel's own might be inflammable
too.

"Just what is an ingot?" she asked, one
evening, after one of those pauses in the

talk which always made them feel such good friends. "I came across the word in a poem the other day, and I thought it was something a metal-merchant might know about."

So satisfactory of Isabel to put it that way! The ordinary run of girl seemed to imagine that a man passed his time hanging on the hat-tree in the intervals of philandering. But Isabel called him a metal-merchant. He was coming to know something about the metal-business by the way, inkstands and errand-running having proved but stepping-stones in a pretty steady advancement.

It had got to be November now, and they were sitting before the fire, Isabel in a low chair, where the waving flame seemed as much enamored of that coronet of braids as the great Source of Fire had shown himself to be on a certain day in June which William and Brady would never forget. Brady, being *persona grata* in the Allen household, was again acting as chaperon, and as the young hostess stooped to pat his head a moment ago, he had taken occasion to whisper something in her ear. Perhaps that was what had set her thinking about poetry.

But William, as beseemed a solid man of business, answered quite literally,—"Ingot is just a fancy name for pig."

"For what?" she cried.

"Why, a pig of iron, or a pig of tin, you know." And as she still looked rather pained,—William was not always as tactful as Brady,—he added: "A great chunk of metal, you understand, melted, and then solidified."

"Oh!"

"It 's mighty interesting when you know about it. You feel as if you had got hold of something real."

"I should think you might," she mocked, "when you had got hold of an iron pig!" But she looked receptive.

"I wish you could see those fellows of Cousin Jim's handle the stuff," he went on, warming to his subject. "There 's one chap we 've just taken on, that 's a regular Hercules."

"I don't think I care much for brute strength," Isabel announced, with light misprision. "A man need n't be so dreadfully strong, if only he 's got plenty of grit."

"Yes; if he 's only got plenty of grit," William echoed, thoughtfully. "That 's a big 'if,' is n't it?" He knew he was imperilling that husk of his, and it was not the first time either. But she had always shown herself so unsuspicious, that he had come to be rather off his guard.

They were both looking into the fire, and he did not catch the quick glance she gave him. Her reply was reassuringly impersonal.

"I don't believe our soldiers knew much about their grit, till the time came," she mused. "But look what they did."

"Do you suppose that was the way of it?"

"Papa says so. He says some of them were such unlikely soldiers. No great stamina, and had never had a taste of hardship. But when the time came, they just turned heroes."

And even then he never guessed that she knew about the incubus. He fancied it to be quite by accident that she had spoken that illuminating word.

She did n't believe our soldiers knew much about their grit, *till the time came?* Well, perhaps they did n't! And at that, it seemed to William as if the old incubus were shifting uneasily,—just enough to let the daylight in. Would he ever get his chance, and send it packing?

And the very next evening William's chance came, in guise of an event portentous enough to dislodge any incubus that ever crouched and clung.

It was the second Saturday in November, and by ten o'clock in the evening all Dunbridge was agog about the great fire that was burning the very marrow out of Boston, hardly two miles away. And those who had cupolas were crowding into them, watching the spread of the flames; and those who had valuables in jeopardy were calling vainly for horses; and those that had legs, but could n't lay hands on a horse, were footing it over the long bridge if the horse-cars were jammed full, as they mostly were; and those that had the gout were stumping about their piazzas, as James Spencer was doing, wondering why in thunder those boys of his did n't show up. The bigger ones had made a dash for the fire before anybody had guessed its magnitude, and that had been the last of them. It was clear moonlight, and he expected every minute to see Tom come sprinting up the path. What was the good of sending a boy to college, if he could n't sprint? But the young beggar was no doubt gawking at the fire, and his father tied by the leg with this confounded gout, and both horses laid up with the "idiotics" as Michael called it. He wondered if he should have to send Michael after all. No, that would never do. He'd as like as not get the "idiotics" himself, without his horses to steady him. And James sat precipitately down on a porch-chair and, grabbing an indignant toe, said "damn."

That really did seem to work; for in another minute there was the click of the gate, and a slim figure tearing up the path. Well, Tom had come to his senses at last. Good lad, good lad! But no, not Tom. Why, William's Willie, by the living Jingo! Of course! Might have known it. He'd be sure to be on hand.

"Cousin Jim," he panted. "I've just come from the fire. It hasn't got anywhere near us yet, but it's something big, and I think perhaps you'd better let me have your keys in case——"

"Don't stand there jabbering!" James cried, flinging the keys at him. "*Save those books*,—and look out for that small parcel in the right-hand drawer. The brass key fits it."

"But I can't lug those books far; they

weigh tons. And they are charging all creation for a cab."

"Then tell 'em *I 'll pay* all creation! But bring 'em here. And don't wait till they 're afire, either! Now, go it!" And in his excitement, James brought his stick down on his favorite toe, and, with a roar of pain, sank back in his chair.

But as he watched the agile figure, speeding down the path,—"Gad, but I 'd like to own that boy," he muttered. "Only 't would make ten, and what in all conscience would Nannie say to that?"

William meanwhile was easily outstripping the closely packed horse-cars, crawling in over the bridge; for he had got his first draught of a fiery brew, and the thirst for more spurred him on.

As he struck into the city streets, where weird flashes of heat and light beckoned from afar, his blood bounded to the call. Breaking into a run, he kept the gait till he was caught again in the turmoil. Then, pushing his way on and in, as close as the guards allowed, he stood for a space drinking his fill of that tremendous potion.

Yet it was not altogether the mighty spectacle that fired his brain, not the pande-

monium of crashing walls, of roaring, jubilant
flames, of throbbing engines, their whistles
shrieking for coal. It was the men, straining, sweltering, smoke-begrimed, *turning into
heroes!* He longed, with a fierce longing,
to plunge in among them,—any way, any
how, to have his part. God! But they
were men, to stick there in that rain of fire,
battling against such fearful odds! And
those other fellows, hauling their lumbering
"steamer" straight into the blazing furnace!
How slowly the unwieldy mass advanced,
how the men were tugging, and how thick
the burning fragments fell about them!
If there had only been horses! Anything
but this dragging pace among the firebrands!
Not a horse anywhere, except the rickety
nags hitched to that coal-cart over there,
and one of those was keeling over, got the
distemper no doubt, and the coal stuck fast,
out of reach of the gasping, famishing engines.
Yet there were cabs, he knew, prowling
about, reaping a fat harvest, just outside the
fire-zone. He had seen them an hour ago,
and he must find one now. That was his job,
worse luck!—to keep out of that splendid
fight and find a cab! If only he might
espy one in there in the very thick of it all!

In default of any such apparition, and hating himself for a quitter, he turned at last and, working his way back through the crowd, started off again on his own inglorious errand. And as he skirted the ever spreading fan of fire, winnowing the air with blasts of its own engendering, flying gusts of heat stung his cheek, and he chafed like a young horse at the bit which holds him to the ignominious beaten track.

He had left the fire far afield, and had turned into Oliver Street where his cousin's store stood a few rods further on. Thinking that he heard a cab approaching, he stayed his step. The street was only dimly lighted by its sparse gas-lamps, the moon being quite obliterated in the pall of smoke that hung over the city, shot through with the wild glare of the flames.

As William paused in that remote, deserted spot, trying to make out the direction of those hoof-beats, he saw a solitary bent figure hurrying toward him, clutching something close under its arm. An oldish man, William thought, as the sound of the horse's hoofs drew nearer.

Suddenly a bulky shadow loomed in a doorway, and fell upon the old man as he

passed, snatching at the booty. But the
clutch of avarice held fast, and before the
assailant, who appeared to be unarmed, had
time to deal a blow, William was upon him.
Not a word was spoken, and in the silent
scuffle, while the lad's breath labored, and
his young muscles knotted, the oldish man
sneaked off.

But William's blood was up. He had
fastened himself at the ruffian's throat and,
while the sound of hoofs came nearer, he
held on with a bull-dog grip, unmindful
of the savage mauling and pummelling he
got, as the fellow fought to get loose. He
was no champion, this great lumbering
brute that fell upon old men in the dark,
and his breath was rank with liquor. A
trained wrestler would have made short
work of him. All he wanted was to get
away, and all William wanted was to punish
him, to hold hard till those hoofs should
bring help, and Justice should get a lick
at him!

So there was William's Willie, the foregone coward, hanging on to a red-handed
ruffian, with a bull-dog grip! He never
once thought of his father, he never even
thought of Isabel, and least of all did he

think of himself, as he kept that vicious clutch at his enemy's throat, while the veins in his own neck were near to bursting. Indeed there was scant time to think of anything, before the struggling mass of liquor-soaked brawn had pulled itself loose, and dealt the boy a blow, the sheer weight of which knocked him senseless. None too soon either for the varlet's own welfare; for at that instant the cab pulled up at the curb, and the great bully went hulking round the corner, intent only on saving his hide.

As William recovered his senses, and tried hard to get his head off the sidewalk, where it appeared to be glued fast, the old man, still clutching his bundle of pelf, came slinking out of the shadow. And a husky voice was audible, offering $500.00 for a ride. The poor, scared creature did not say where to, as he glanced apprehensively over his shoulder, lest his enemy be lurking near.

But Pat, who was down off his roost by this, and bending all his efforts to pulling William's head loose from that glue, did not seem to be listening. So the old man came nearer and whispered, nervously:

"Come, come!   What 'll you take?   What 'll you take?"

"Yer blitherin' idjit!" cried Pat,—he had a wife and childer at home, no doubt, and none too much spare cash, but also he had a warm Irish heart in his breast, and he had seen enough, as he rounded the corner, to catch the gist of the situation,—"Yer blither- in' idjit!" he spat out.   "I would n't take a million dollars to carry you to hell!   Here 's *my* fare, a layin' on the bricks; can't yer *see* *un* there, yer snivellin' ould ballyrags?"

And the oldish man, who appeared to be anything but sensitive, hearing the rattle of wheels in the distance, went scuttling off in the direction of the sound.

"Here, me son," Pat wheedled.   "Git on yer fate, an' coom alang wid me.   Me ould race-harse 'll be knowin' the way to a dhrap o' whiskey!   Coom, pick yersilf oop, like a little man!"

Then William, staggering to his feet, felt the life come back into him, and with it that lust of battle, the fighting courage of his father that had been his pride and his despair. And clutching Pat's shoulder, more for compulsion than for support, "Could n't we overhaul *that coward*, yet?" he cried.

As the young fire-eater crossed the bridge an hour later, lolling somewhat limply in Pat's cab, the books piled at his feet, the cash-box on the seat beside him, that small parcel from the right-hand drawer buttoned tight in under his coat, he found himself idly wondering whether he did n't have a headache. There was a queer rumpus up there, which produced a dazed feeling, and caused him to yearn for slumber. But out of the blur and the rumble, two very clear resolutions stood forth, which he kept repeating to himself in order to stay awake.

First then, he must see to it that Pat got his $500.00,—always provided that the rascal kept his promise of not blabbing; and secondly, that that good man, Brady, should never have another thrashing for getting into a fight!

They found James still on the piazza, his hard-used leg propped up on a second chair. It was nearly one o'clock, and the rest of the family, except the youngsters at the fire, who seemed to be making a night of it, had gone to bed. But the evening was mild, and the feather-bed arrangement about the game-toe, weather-proof.

"We 've got 'em, Cousin Jim," William shouted, as he stumbled up the path,—he was still a trifle shaky on his legs,—while Pat puffed after him with the main bulk of the spoils. And then, dropping his voice,—"And you 'll have to pay the man $500.00!"

"Are you off your head?" James cried, going promptly off his, while he hauled his leg down, and got on his feet.

"But, Cousin Jim, you said you 'd pay all creation!"

"What if I did? That 's not saying I 'd pay $500.00!" Then, as Pat's arrival within earshot forced a change of tack, "Here, you!" he blustered. "What are you leaving your horse for? How do you know he 'll stand?"

"Wal, sorr, I would n't go bail for un mesilf," was the thoughtful rejoinder. "I 'm thinkin' he 'd *ruther* lay down!" And William, chuckling inwardly, knew that Pat's cause was won.

As he started to carry his own load into the house, "Shall I get it out of the cash-box?" he inquired, quite as if a fresh pocket-handkerchief had been in question.

"Out of the cash-box!" James spluttered.

"Never carry that amount in the cash-box. Don't sell goods over the counter."

"But you 've got it to-night, because I heard you carrying on about that crank from somewhere down-east that made you take cash this noon, too late to get it under cover."

"Well, then, why do you ask, since you appear to have taken charge of my affairs? Why not go ahead, while you 're about it, and clean me out? And—hold on, Willie! You 'll find some hard cider and doughnuts on the sideboard. Fetch 'em along."

The instant William was out of hearing, a change came over James. Laying hold of Pat's coat-front, and jerking him almost off his feet, "How did that boy get a black eye?" he demanded, in a stage-aside that might have been heard in Oliver Street.

"Wal, sorr, I dunno 's I could say," Pat replied, with great deliberation, "unless somethin' might ha' *hit un!*" And William, returning in time to catch that cryptic utterance, was so moved to gratitude that he tried his best to make Pat's glass of cider foam and look at least like beer!

"$500.00!" James fumed, while Pat and his racer went ambling off in quest of more

10

adventure. "Supposing we don't get burnt
out after all? Where 'll I be, then?"

"I should say you 'd be in luck," William
hooted, making good his retreat down the
path.

"And I never said thankee," Cousin Jim
told himself, as he went hobbling into the
house. "Well, there 's time yet."

And to James's credit be it said, that
although his worst forebodings were realized,
and the fire never got into Oliver Street at
all, it was not long before things were hap-
pening at Spencer & Co.'s which seemed to
indicate that a black eye, even when discreetly ignored by all concerned, may prove
quite as good a stepping-stone in a young
man's career as the inkiest of inkstands.

And when, a few days after the Great
Fire, William's Willie—no longer afraid of
that harmless little name, nor of anything
else, as far as that goes—concluded that
he was fit to be seen, he went to call upon
Isabel; and before he knew what he was
about, he had told her that he loved her.
It was rather abrupt of him, and Isabel's
very natural impulse was to temporize,
as was plainly to be seen in the quick lift
of the head, and the defensive flash of those

level eyes. They fell however as they met his, where the brooding look had given place to something altogether different, and as luck would have it, they fell on Brady, drinking in his master's words with such complacent relish that Isabel instantly knew that he had peached. So what could she do but surrender?

It was some little time after that before a lucid interval occurred, and when it did, Brady was discovered over on the hearth-rug, pretending to be asleep. Somewhat abashed by the implication, Isabel cast about for a diversion. Nor was it far to seek, in that damaged forehead which, by the way, was not nearly as fit to be seen as William in his impatience had made himself believe.

"When are you going to tell me about that?" she asked in the most casual manner; as if she had not been lying awake nights, thinking about it, ever since the first rumor of it set folks guessing.

"Never!" the battered veteran replied, with great firmness, while Brady, playing 'possum on the rug, dreamily thumped approval.

"Why,—never?" she demanded, bridling, lightly.

"Isabel," said William's Willie, the firmness melting into entreaty which, if Brady had but known, no Isabel alive could have withstood, "that horrid bump is somehow just my own. Will you let me off?"

"I suppose I must," she answered, with a little air of resignation. But she had read his face, and her eyes were glistening.

And so it came to pass that there was no real secret between those two, after all; because, since she had caught the essence of it, the substance did n't matter. And that is what comes of being on confidential terms with a dog of parts. One knows things without being told.

V.

A BRILLIANT MATCH.

EDNA PRATT was on the top of the
wave, and she found the situation
highly exhilarating. Justly too, for
under Providence she, and she alone, was
to be credited with the happy stroke which
had placed her there. In a word, her daughter Elsie, the beauty of the family,—not
merely of her own immediate family, be it
understood, but of the whole connection,—
was making a brilliant match, an achievement
the like of which had not heretofore been
recorded in the Pratt family annals; and
Edna, in her swelling self-gratulation, would
hardly allow Marcus Wilby himself any
determining part in the affair.

Happily, however, the young man was
quite unconscious of the extent of his obligations to his future mother-in-law, and if
he could not flatter himself that Elsie was

as yet very deeply in love with him, he never doubted that she had accepted him of her own motion. For, was she not an American girl? And were not American girls proverbially independent of parental dictation in such matters? This at least was an article of faith with the bridegroom elect, fresh from that sharply contrasting civilization which centres in the Paris studios.

But the excellent Marcus,—and that the heir-apparent to the Wilby shekels was the kind of young man that gets called "excellent" was the worst that could be urged against him—was reckoning without a certain crude force of character, by virtue of which Edna had established a dominant, not to say disastrous, influence over this favorite child of hers.

Not that Edna was of a kidney to cut any figure at all in a tale of crime or intrigue. She was merely a coarse-grained egotist, endowed with but a minimum of natural good feeling as against a maximum of worldly ambition. And, for a round dozen of years now, both maximum and minimum aforesaid had been concentrated upon her beautiful daughter. If Edna loved anything in the world, or out of it, which is matter of conjecture, (a rebel bullet by the way had made a widow of her,) it was this child, to whom had been transmitted, and with compound interest, that modicum of beauty which had rendered Edna Brown, the girl, so very much more attractive than the woman Edna Pratt had come to be.

Elsie (or Bessie, as she was called in the day of small things) had but just crossed the Rubicon of her teens, when she chanced to overhear from the lips of her own mother the unctuous statement that that lady's daughter Bessie had "the fatal gift of beauty." This was rather solemnizing to a girl of thirteen, and duly solemnized she was. Quietly, lest her involuntary eaves-dropping be discovered, the child stole to her own room, to see what her looking-glass might have to say about it. If the upshot of the interview proved disappointing, this was due less to any deficiency in the subject under consideration, than to the circum-stance that Miss Bessie's private ideal of beauty at that period was modelled upon the wax-doll type, no suggestion of which was discernible in the charming little phiz scowling at itself in the mirror. Evidently, then, the "fatal" kind of beauty was not as pretty as the other, the kind she had long admired in her little cousin Amy Spencer, for instance, who had flaxen hair, and dimples, and a pink and white complexion of the most orthodox hue.

As Bessie grew older, in other words, as she developed into Elsie, she also grew wiser. She perceived that, whether fatal or not, this beauty which had come her way was something that even a wax-doll might envy. Being, however, possessed of a fair share of the Pratt common-sense, she kept her head, thereby avoiding the twin pitfalls of vanity and self-consciousness. But if she did not spend an inordinate amount of time before her looking-glass, if she did not study anxiously the impression she was making upon others, it can not be denied that she did come to consider herself entitled to peculiar favors at the hands of Fortune. We are all like that. Once let us get it into our heads that the orchestra stalls are our just due, we are unable to conceive of the second gallery as having any possible bearing upon our case. Yet, ten to one, the gallery god—most complacent of deities—is having a far better time of it than we are, and thinks himself a lucky chap into the bargain to be at the play at all.

Now it will not be supposed that Edna's deliberate training of her daughter to worldly ends was lost upon so shrewd a body of commentators as the Pratt family connection. Harriet Spencer especially, the wax-doll's grandmother,—anything but a wax-doll herself, though as handsome an old woman as great decision of character would permit,—was in a chronic state of disapproval regarding her sister-in-law's "goings on." Being, however, no scandal-monger, she was apt to reserve her animadversions for the ear of her mother, Old Lady Pratt, whose relish of the humors of her kind never spelled indiscretion.

"Well, mother," Harriet once remarked, at the close of a stimulating interchange of views on the burning question, "there's one comfort about Edna. She's not a Pratt."

"No," was the old lady's devout rejoinder. "But thank the Lord her children are,—every one on 'em!"

"You don't mean to say that you call Elsie a Pratt?"

"Yes, I do; though she did get her good looks from her mother." This, with one of

those chuckles which betrayed the fact that
Old Lady Pratt in her tenth decade was
still lamentably unregenerate. But she
added, more seriously, "Did you ever see
her try to lie?"

"Yes, I have," Harriet testified, brighten-
ing perceptibly.

"Well, so hev I. Now that's her mother,
plain's the nose on her face. But—*she can't
do it!*—'n' that's her father. I tell ye,
Harriet, say what you please, that girl's a
Pratt."

But, Pratt or no Pratt, Elsie was too
deeply implicated in her mother's mis-
doings to go scot-free at the family judgment
seat. And, as time went on, everybody,
down to the wax-doll cousin, became aware,
and saw to it that her men-folks should
become aware, that Edna was scheming,
night and day, and not without the young
lady's tacit connivance, to make a brilliant
match for Elsie. Which, on the wax-doll's
part at least, was hardly fair play. For
had she not caught her John's heart on
the rebound? And if Elsie had known
how to value such a prize a few years ago,
where would Amy have been to-day?

And Elsie who, truth to tell, had had

rather a leaning to John, often thought the
same thing of herself. Where would she
have been to-day, if her mother had been
less scornful of Johnny Wenham's pre-
tensions? Johnny Wenham indeed, whose
grandfather had handled iron in Uncle Spencer's store, whose own mother had been
reduced to letting rooms to lodgers when
her husband went to the war and left her
with a brood of young cormorants on her
hands! Johnny Wenham who, when all
was said, was nothing but a bank-teller
himself, at eighteen hundred a year!

Early in the proceedings,—for John was
first in the field, and his devotion was of the
headlong kind that too often sweeps a girl
off her feet,—Elsie used to brace her resolution on the above oft-reiterated facts.
There 's nothing like a fact, persistently
driven home, for taking the starch out of a
fancy. But now that John had forgotten
his vows of eternal heart-break, now that he
had married Amy and was quite unblushingly content with his lot, Elsie perceived
how right had been her mother's estimate
of such things.

They lived the life of a pair of turtle-doves,
John and Amy, and were already possessed

of a brace of fledglings, but meagrely provided with pin-feathers. If any lingering pique attached to John's defection, it could not long survive the sight of Amy, opening the door of their little flat through which a smell of cooking issued, one baby tucked under her arm, another dragging at her skirts.

Well, it took all kinds to make a world, Elsie reflected; and not without a subconsciousness of the literal truth implied in a familiar figure of speech. There was her sister Mary too, now seven years married, cheerfully roughing it on Fred's great cattle-ranch, while doing her part, as she herself frankly boasted, to make the wilderness blossom like a kindergarten. Drudgery! Drudgery! How Elsie hated the word! Hated it by the way far more than she would have hated the thing itself when once at close quarters with it. For the young beauty, of whom her mother vaunted that she had never been allowed to "lift a finger," was a girl of much capacity run to waste, in missing the exercise of which she was missing one of the very best things life affords.

Nor was there any visible prospect of

her making good. For here she was, at twenty-five, engaged to Marcus Wilby, an excellent young man, of abundant means, to whom her lightest wish was law. What wonder that Edna was at the top of the wave,—so ostentatiously so indeed, that the rest of the clan found it quite impossible properly to rejoice in that most propitious of happenings, a family love-affair.

The Pratts as a race thought well of marriage, and usually took an engagement at its face value. Old Lady Pratt especially, who was nearing her finish, had, in this instance, peculiar cause for satisfaction, since she had been apprehensive lest this most dilatory of her own immediate grand-daughters might not be happily launched on the high seas of matrimony before she herself should be called to adventure that other uncharted sea whither all are bound at last. Yet even she could have wished that her daughter-in-law had borne herself more modestly.

"Well, Edna," she remarked, with a distinct trace of asperity. "It's better late than never. But I must say I sh'd feel safer about Bessie ef she'd got *broke in* a mite earlier."

"I guess there won't be any breaking in," Edna retorted, with commendable spirit. "Marcus Wilby worships the ground she treads on."

"More 'n like," was the pregnant comment. "But, as I said before, it's better late than never."

"I don't know what you mean by that," Edna declared, bridling, more on her own account than on Elsie's. "She's just the age I was when I married William."

"Mebbe so; but then—William was a widower."

If the old lady's line of reasoning was obscure, the sting of the reminder was no less telling, and, to her notion, richly deserved. For this was not Edna's first offending. Only the previous autumn, when William's only son and namesake had become engaged to that charming Isabel Allen, flower of one of the very best Dunbridge families, Edna had made a personal grievance of it because, forsooth, the girl chanced to be a niece of his father's first wife.

"Very bad taste, *I* call it," she had declared, for the benefit of all whom it might or might not concern,—"to go and marry into that family. An Isabel Allen too, exactly the same name. Why, I call it positively indelicate!"

"But he's so happy, mother," Elsie once ventured to urge; for she had a soft spot in her heart for this young brother,— one of the spots that Edna had neglected to sterilize.

"Happy! How long do you suppose that sort of thing lasts?"

Such heresies and worse had reached Old Lady Pratt's ears, confirming her distrust of Edna's principles. Hence, although she came perilously near being an advocate of "matrimony at any price," she could not forbear a thrust where, as in this instance, that admirable instrument of destiny appeared to be serving as cat's paw for the acquisition of chestnuts.

No mere verbal thrusts, however, could dislodge Edna from her precarious eminence. Elsie was engaged, engaged to the sole heir of a very rich man, as riches were then measured, and Edna was on the top of the wave.

That, alas, was more than could be said of Elsie herself, or of the excellent Marcus either. And really it is high time that the latter should be formally introduced; though, as a matter of fact, he was holding himself so much in the background at this juncture that he was in danger of being overlooked altogether. This would have been a gross injustice, since Marcus was by no means a nonentity. On the contrary, he was a young man of much character and a good deal of ability, handicapped, but in no sense perverted, by an overplus of worldly goods. The handicap consisted primarily in a liberty to spend the best years of his life in foreign studios, vainly striving to become a portrait-painter, when Nature intended him to do extremely clever character sketches in pen and ink. And by the same fortuitous handicap he had latterly been betrayed into winning the hand of a girl who made no real pretence of loving him.

He had first met Elsie, now some six months ago, at her cousin, Dick Spencer's house at Wilbyville, seat of the great Wilby cotton-mills, as also of the Dunlap Manufacturing Company with which Dick was connected. The young artist—he was at this time barely turned thirty—was, as Elsie knew, on the point of returning to Paris after his annual visit to America.

Consequently when, at that first meeting, she casually inquired as to his date of sailing, and he replied that his plans were unsettled, both knew exactly what had happened to him.

The discovery gave Elsie something of a turn. Not because of anything unusual in the occurrence itself, certainly not because of any hastily conceived bias, favorable or otherwise, toward the excellent Marcus. But because of her instant recognition of him as the "logical candidate" so to speak, of her mother's long and arduous campaign. She could almost hear that good lady's purr of satisfaction at this benignant overture of Fortune.

"Do you find it so hard to tear yourself away from Wilbyville?" she inquired, with light sarcasm. That purr of satisfaction was setting her nerves on edge.

"Oh, no; it 's not that," was the best poor Marcus could muster from the débris of his wits. At which Elsie smiled, a smile of indulgent comprehension, in itself so enchanting that no one could take it amiss.

It was Sunday evening, and "high tea"; as great an altitude as Dick and Julie in their young *ménage* had yet risen to. The "logical candidate," all unconscious of such factitious advantage as the term implies, was seated between Elsie and his hostess who, as the modest function progressed, beamed with pleasure at finding herself egregiously neglected. For with Julie, herself little better than a bride, that match-making instinct which springs from a fellow-feeling was already in full flower.

"Did you ever see anything so sudden?" she triumphed, the moment she could get private speech of Dick. "He only spoke to me twice, the whole time, and he never so much as *looked* at Hannah's delicious waffles!"

"That's just the plague of it," Dick demurred; for he too was experiencing stirrings of a fellow-feeling. "The poor chap was so flattened out that he did n't do himself justice. I don't think Elsie cottoned to him; do you?"

"Perhaps not," was the reluctant admission. "I'm afraid she's rather spoiled."

"Oh, well; it'll all come out right in the end," Dick opined, cheerfully; for he delighted in Julie's artless manœuvring. "Aunt Edna 'll see to that."

"Is your Aunt Edna such a matchmaker?"

she innocently inquired, recognizing for the first time a bond of sympathy with that rather unprepossessing relative-in-law.

"Maker or breaker, according to circumstances," was the oracular response. Whence we may conclude that although Harriet was herself no scandal-monger, she had been unable to prevent her grandson getting wind of those "goings on" which she so sincerely deplored.

Nor was Dick far afield in his rough and ready summing up of his friend's case. Marcus Wilby *was* badly flattened out, and his conversation likewise. Incredible as it may seem, what this young man of the world was undergoing was nothing more nor less than the discomfiture of the novice. Fancies he had had in plenty, will-o'-the-wisps which he had chased a little way, but never far enough to get caught in the bog. But here was something totally different, something which at first sight he recognized as a lodestar. And so immediate and so irresistible was its fascination that, like the tyro at golf (of a later period), he failed to keep his eye on the ball.

One effective stroke, however, he did manage to get in; for, before the party broke up, he had secured from Elsie the promise of a few sittings.

The fact that she agreed to these with a full consciousness of the inevitable outcome must, it is to be feared, implicate her beyond recall in her mother's machinations. She did know what she was about, and she did intend to play the game to the end,— keeping her eye, too, had she but known it, unflinchingly upon the ball. But if no nice girl ever did such a thing before, there are nevertheless quite a number of wise old saws, touching the bending of juvenile twigs and so on, which might be adduced in extenuation. Besides which, as any unprejudiced critic will allow, if you are under the obsession of a fatal gift, you may as well wash your hands of the consequences.

At any rate, Elsie did promise the sittings, thereby causing Marcus to walk away from the tea-party on air—than which, to be sure, no procedure would seem to be more natural in a person under the immediate sway of a lodestar. The only wonder is, when you come to think of it, that so many good people who profess subjection to sidereal influence are able to keep in touch with solid earth at all.

The sittings went off better than that

first encounter. Partly because Marcus forgot himself and his agitations in his eagerness to do justice to his subject, and partly because Elsie forgot everything else, even the maternal purr, in talk of Europe, of which she was, for the first time in her life, getting her fill. And Marcus, finding that no topic brought so delectable a glow into her face, was quick to take the cue.

"I wonder you can stay away so long," she said, one day. "It must be a wonderful life over there."

He did not answer at once. He was wondering whether any other fellow—Boudigne for instance, with his *Prix de Rome*, or Nick Belton, the little chap from Iowa who made the *Salon* last year—would have known how to catch that look, which seemed less a matter of line and color than of indwelling light. And, in truth, Elsie's grace of countenance, being in its essence mobile, was as difficult to capture and fix on canvas as if it had really been the emanation of a lovely soul, a possession which no one but Marcus Wilby would have felt quite safe in ascribing to her.

At last, having satisfied himself that neither Boudigne, that blatant materialist,

nor little Nick himself, could paint a soul,
he answered: "It *is*—a wonderful life.
But"— with a tentative glance, lest that
look should elude his brush altogether—
"may not life be wonderful anywhere?"

Marcus never hesitated to say the obvious
thing, provided it was also true. He did
not always realize that a remark fresh from
the mint of his own experience might prove
a platitude scarce worth the coining. But
Elsie, whose sense of values was very keen,
coolly rejected the humble offering.

"I've never found it so," she returned,
ungraciously enough.

He had seen the light go out, and a quick
compunction seized him.

"That does n't seem fair," he ventured.

"Why not?"

"One who makes life beautiful for others
should find it so herself."

All his heart was in the words, but not
in his tone as he spoke them. He might
have been enunciating an axiom of the
studios. She half guessed, but only half,
the feeling he was so rigorously repressing,
and, impatient of his halting speech, she
inquired, flippantly, "Are n't you mixing
me up with Julie?"

Elsie

But Elsie, whose sense of values was very keen,
coolly rejected the humble offering.

The sittings were held in Julie's parlor. It was morning, and the young chatelaine could be heard stepping lightly about the house, intent, as Elsie knew, upon "making life beautiful" for Dick.

"No; I was not thinking of Mrs. Spencer," Marcus replied, gravely.

He felt rebuked for excess of feeling. It seemed to him that he had shouted his secret from the house-tops; while Elsie was wishing, irritably, that he would give over whispering behind his hand.

"That 's why you can't paint," his fellow-countrymen at the *Atelier* used to say, with the brutal frankness of their guild. "You 're a hidebound Yankee. You 'd rather bust your biler than let yourself go."

And here, in this still more critical emprise, not for a moment did he let himself go. Not a sign did he display of that ardor, by force of which John Wenham, for instance, the hopelessly ineligible Johnny, had so nearly swept his first love off her feet. Bent on consuming his own smoke, lest perchance it incommode the goddess, poor Marcus consumed his own fires as well; so well indeed, that Elsie, lacking the insight of a *bonâ-fide* goddess, came to regard him as

rather lukewarm. And when, a few weeks
later, there in her mother's house, where
she had been so assiduously taught the true
values of life, she promised to marry him,
there was no better guarantee of happiness
in the pledge, than guarantee of a successful
portrait in the sittings she had accorded
him. That the portrait was a brilliant
success Marcus would have been the last
to claim. Then how about the girl herself,
he might well have questioned, now that
she had engaged for what it is perhaps not
too fanciful to designate as a lifelong sitting?

These were speculations with which Elsie
did not propose to concern herself. That
she should accept him had been a foregone
conclusion. Indeed Edna, in the zeal with
which she espoused the cause of this unexceptionable suitor, was doing but scant justice to her own educational methods.   For
so carefully had the twig been bent that the
tree might safely have been trusted to
incline accordingly. And if Elsie not only
suffered, but positively invited, those prod-
dings and preachments which were so freely
administered, who can say that it was not
with a sneaking desire to clinch the responsibility, there where it properly belonged?

The first time Marcus Wilby kissed her, he knew that she did not love him; but also he knew, as he had not known before, how desperately he loved her. And promptly the hidebound Yankee took command, the Yankee who could not let himself go, and who, by the same token, would not let go anything else, whether semblance or substance, on which he had fairly set his grip. Heedful, therefore, lest he forfeit the semblance he had won, and which he was resolved that nothing short of grim Fate should wrest from him, he refrained from pressing the advantage of his position. In so much that from that hour it was but a seemingly perfunctory salute that he bestowed upon her, and the girl began to feel as if being engaged, as far as that went, were a negligible condition.

If a teazing sense of something missed, or something hovering, did beset her from time to time, that might be fairly charged to the account of her brother William. What business had he to be so absurdly happy in his long-drawn-out engagement? Why must he, who had n't yet scraped together pennies enough to get married on, go about looking as if he had struck a gold-mine?

William had been a quiet, reserved boy, whom nobody seemed to know very well, plodding to his daily work in the city, plodding back again, consorting chiefly with Brady, the cur-terrier that he had picked up on the street. And all of a sudden this thing had happened to him. What was there so wonderful about Isabel Allen, Elsie would like to know? What was there so wonderful about William himself, for the matter of that? And why, of all things, should she puzzle her head over a boy-and-girl affair like theirs? She was only thankful that her little brother was getting his innings at last, for somehow he never seemed to have had much fun before. She hoped he might be a long time finding out that that sort of thing did n't last.

Whence it may be justly inferred that Elsie still regarded her mother as the ultimate authority in matters relating to "that sort of thing."

Meanwhile there was the *trousseau* to distract one's thoughts, and what with the ambitions that visit the top of the wave, and the steady undertow of a too rapidly draining exchequer, the effort of living up to the situation was proving to Edna at least

anything but a negligible proposition. Valiantly this devoted parent laid siege to
dry-goods and linen-drapers' shops, achieving
unheard-of bargains; early and late she
toiled with dressmaker and seamstress.
Even Elsie, usually exempt, was pressed
into the service, and found to her surprise
that that hitherto unlifted finger of hers
took very kindly to homely activities. Once,
to be sure, she caught herself wondering
whether Marcus would ever guess who had
fashioned a certain muslin fichu designed
to be worn crossed on the bosom, *à la* Martha
Washington. And swiftly a nervous color
flushed her cheek, and throwing down the
filmy substance, she remarked, crossly, that
she was tired of the thing and Miss Simpkins
would have to finish making it.

Her mother glanced up, anxiously alert.
It was not the first sign of unrest that she
had observed.

"Go and take a walk, Elsie," she commanded. "You look cross and tired."

"I *am* cross and tired."

"Well, I can't have that. What would
poor Marcus say?" Miss Simpkins had
opportunely slipped down-stairs to press a
seam.

"I don't care what poor Marcus would say. You know I don't. What 's the good of pretending?"

"Now, Elsie," her mother admonished. "This will never do. You 've got to care what he says, and what he thinks too,—at least until you 're married."

"And then be as cross and tired as I like?"

"There won't be anything to make you cross and tired when you have twelve thousand a year. That 's what his father is going to allow him, is n't it?"

"I don't know, and I don't care, what Mr. Wilby is going to allow his son."

"That 's sheer affectation, Elsie," her mother declared, severely. She had always allowed her daughter considerable latitude of speech, but this bordered upon profanity. "You do know, because he told me himself, and I told you. And if you don't care, you 're a very foolish and ungrateful girl, after all I 've done for you."

This rather involved reasoning was perfectly intelligible to Elsie. It *had* been her mother's doing; she had no mind to deny that.

"Well then," she conceded. "Supposing

I get cross and tired on twelve thousand a year. What then?"

"Oh, that will be his look-out," Edna returned, complacently. "But now, while I am responsible for you, I can't have you fretting and fussing. You won't have any looks left."

Elsie regarded her mother moodily. Was it possible that she used to be a beauty? And her father? Had he just let her fret and fuss, and spoil her looks? Did n't they care, when once they had married a girl and made sure of her? Did n't they care any more? Well,—all the better. It would certainly be very awkward to have Marcus persist in caring, when she did n't care herself.

By this, she was walking rapidly along the sidewalk, headed for she knew not where. It was late afternoon of a September day. As she turned a corner, she espied William, striding toward her on his way out from town, a tell-tale bunch of pinks in his hand, that he had bought for a few pennies at a street corner.

At sight of his sister he waved his hat, but the pinks he kept discreetly in the background.

"Out for a walk?" he called.

"Yes; don't you want to take me along, as far as Isabel's? I see you 're going there."

"Are *you?*" he asked, while his face fell.

"Only to the gate, you silly boy!"

William laughed.

"How you girls do see through a fellow!" he exclaimed. "Now Isabel 's the most perfectly—" and as brother and sister walked briskly along under the maple-trees, which were still pretending that they had no idea of ever changing color, he launched forth upon a panegyric touching Isabel's astounding penetration which threatened to last to the Allen gate.

"William," Elsie asked, abruptly, though with the most curious feeling that she had better leave touchstones alone. "How did you ever,—well, how did you—know?"

"Know? Know what?"

"That she was so—wonderful?"

"How did I know, Elsie? How did I know? Why, the first time I saw her,— really saw her, you understand, not just looked at her the way you look at a mere person,—I knew she was all there was,— just all there was."

"Oh," she returned, with difficulty keeping pace with him; for his long legs were making record time as they neared the goal. "And— Isabel? Do you suppose she thinks *you* are all there is?"

"Thinks it, Elsie?" And the long legs came to a full stop. "But I *am*—I am all there is, for her. Do you suppose I'd *have her*, on any other terms?"

How sure of himself he was, how sure of being all there was, to Isabel! Yet, as they started off again, a sudden shyness took him, and, glancing sidewise at his sister, he said, rather shamefacedly: "You shouldn't make me explain things that you must understand, you and Marcus, as well as I do. As if you didn't know that he was just all there is, for you!"

The brilliant match was to be consummated in a month now; the time had almost come for putting her mother's precepts to the test. And William's? Would that test be as easy to meet? As Elsie turned again toward home, the spring had quite gone out of her step—that spring that she had caught of William. A dull resentment had laid hold upon her, resentment against Marcus for holding himself so cheap.

"Do you think I'd *have her*, on any other terms?" William had cried, in hot repudiation.

If Marcus were like that—if he were like that! Well, and what then? She simply would n't be going to marry him; that was all. There would n't be any Europe, any big income for her mother to fling up at her. There would n't be any fichu *à la* Martha Washington either, which Marcus must not be tempted to study too closely. Would she be glad, or sorry? Which?

No; Elsie was not on the top of the wave. She was not there when its crest was gleaming in the sun; she was not there when it toppled over and came crashing and thundering down. Edna it was who got the tumble and the drenching, and had to make her way as best she could to dry land. And Elsie merely stood on the shore and looked on, wondering stupidly what would happen next.

The first thing that happened, after the papers had printed themselves black with news of Edna's discomfiture,—for that was all the poor woman was capable of seeing in the great financial disaster,—was a letter from Marcus. It was very brief and very friendly,—a model of self-restraint.

Elsie must not worry about them. Things were not quite so bad as they looked. Everybody knew that his father had merely got caught in the great panic which was sweeping over the country, and that he would eventually meet his obligations, dollar for dollar. Meanwhile, his mother had a competence of her own, so that she was provided for. She sent her love to Elsie, and the dear old pater sent his too.

It was only in a postscript that Marcus added: "I shall be over in a few days, as soon as they can spare me. And then everything shall be exactly as you wish." There was nothing in that carefully restrained statement to indicate that he was signing his surrender to grim Fate. And yet, everything was to be exactly as Elsie wished.

Well, there was only one thing to wish, of course. Her mother was quite right. She must ask to be released. That was perfectly clear; was due, indeed, to Marcus himself. Even if she had—well—felt differently about him, she would not have been justified in holding him to his engagement now, when she could be nothing but a drag upon him. Oh, yes; that was perfectly clear.

12

She wondered why she did not find herself thinking more about Europe, more about her own future. She felt quite as if she did n't have any future. It was Marcus she was thinking of, Marcus, who could n't be spared just yet. How they must be leaning upon him—the old people! Yes, he was the kind of man one would depend upon in time of trouble; she could readily understand that. She could picture him to herself, sharing their burdens, feeling it all with them, feeling it with them so much that he found it natural to suppose that they must be her first thought too. She must n't worry about them. Of course not; she had no idea of such a thing. Well, then, what was it that she was worrying about? Not about herself; somehow she felt mortally tired of herself. And yet, she was worrying, worrying. Could it be about Marcus? Could it be a dread lest he should misconstrue her action? That was really all there was to consider as far as he was concerned. For she could not really believe that he would so much mind letting her go, when it came to the point. She could not have meant very much to him, these many weeks, since she had been wearing his ring.

A single diamond it was, not over large, as her mother would have preferred, but of the very first water. Merely the whitest and most perfect stone the jeweller could find in the country. So Marcus had told her, and then had apologized for making so much of it. And she had not let him see that she understood how he meant its perfectness as a tribute to her, only that he was too reticent to say so. No, she had never met him half way. He had never possessed anything at all in her, beyond something to be looked at, something to be considered and deferred to, something willing to suffer a gingerly caress, only it must be very gingerly indeed. It was no doubt all a surface matter with him, as with her. His real heart was with his father and mother, and most of all, with the "dear old pater," so cruelly caught in the great panic.

And Elsie let her mother talk and expound, as she made her way, floundering and sputtering to shore, and it is to be feared that she paid very little heed.

It was nearly a week later that she came in from a morning walk,—it was early October now, and the maples had been caught changing color at last,—to find her mother in a high state of excitement. Marcus Wilby had been there, and had behaved extremely well. She would say that much for him, if he *had* put her to very serious inconvenience and expense, through his imprudent behavior a few months ago.

"I was of course very sympathetic," Edna announced, "and I was at pains to show him what an interest I took in his unfortunate affairs. I said I understood that his mother was well off, and no doubt she would do something for him. But he seemed rather offish about that,—should n't wonder if she was close,—and said he proposed to get on his own legs. Not a very refined expression, I must say. He said a little roughing it never hurt a man, and I put in, 'No, that sort of thing did n't hurt *a man*.' He took the hint at once, and said that he had no right to expect you to accept such a change of prospects. I don't know that he put it just that way, but that was what he meant. I said, 'Of course not'; that you would not consider yourself at all the wife for a poor man. I was glad he had so much right feeling, and that I would tell you what he had said. He said he preferred telling you himself, and that he would look

in again at twelve o'clock. But really,
Elsie, I should think it might be quite as well
if you did n't see him. You could have an
engagement you know, at the dentist's or
somewhere. I would make it all right, and
when——"

"I shall see him," said Elsie, in a hard,
expressionless voice. She had not taken
off her coat and hat, nor had she seated
herself.

"Very well," her mother answered, from
her comfortable easy-chair. "You 'll do as
you please. And I suppose after all you 've
got to give him back his ring. But you
need n't look so sober about it. I 'm sure
you never pretended to care anything about
the man himself, and as for all the rest of
it, there 's no use in crying over spilt milk.
I 'm sure if *I* can bear it, after all I 've——"

"Did he say what he was going to do?"

"I believe he 's been offered a job on a new
picture paper some college friends of his
are starting. They 've been after him before; they think him 'quite a dab as a
cartoonist,' whatever that may mean. He
says he has known for some time that he 'd
never make anything of a painter, only he
would n't give in. And really, Elsie, I do

think it was most inartistic of him to paint
you in that plain white muslin, when I
wanted you to wear your rose-colored silk
over-skirt with the velvet shoulder-straps.
I guess he's right when he says he's better
at pen-and-ink work. Most anybody can
do that. I'm sure I was very clever at
it myself, when I was at the Miss Etchems's
finishing school. There was a weeping willow
beside a brook that I did that took second
prize."

"Where are they going to start the paper?
Here, in the city?"

"No; in New York. And I think it's
just as well, all things considered. They
guarantee him eighteen hundred a year to
start with. I asked him, just to show my
interest. It's only what Johnny Wenham
gets, you know, but it does seem a good
deal for that cheap sort of work. However,
his cousin, Hugh Wilby, is backing them up,
and I suppose they're ready to stretch a
point for him. That branch of the family's
been out of the mills since before the war,
you know, so they're not hurt a mite.
And—why, Elsie! Didn't Julie Spencer
tell me that Hugh Wilby was rather smitten
with you?"

"Mother! Don't make me hate you!"

The girl had not stirred from her post over by the centre-table. She had been listening, with what seemed but a listless attention, asking a question now and then, in a monotonous tone of voice. But at her mother's last words something broke loose.

"Don't make me hate you!" she cried; and, with revolt in every line of her figure, she left the room.

Edna did not know what to make of it. She had never seen Elsie like that. Why, it was as if she really did hate her mother! Though of course that was impossible. It would be against nature!

Poor Edna! As if she had ever, in all the course of her life, concerned herself with nature! And even now, it was only a passing recognition she paid that redoubtable dame. She was chiefly conscious of a blind resentment against Elsie, for planting a thorn somewhere in her anatomy—she did not quite know where (for her heart was the last thing Edna ever took into consideration),—but it rankled. And when, at twelve o'clock precisely, the door-bell rang, and Elsie came down-stairs again, to meet Marcus Wilby, Edna found herself giving very little thought to what might be passing between the two young people whose affair she herself had so satisfactorily wound up. She was too busy applying liniments and lotions of her own devising to that rankling hurt, which had gone deeper than she knew.

The interview was very short; disgracefully short, Elsie pronounced it afterward, when she came to review it in the light of her own behavior. But really, from the moment she took Marcus Wilby's cold hand, and looked up into his tense, drawn countenance, she had so completely forgotten herself that she was hardly to be held accountable for the sequel.

He looked somehow taller, older, than he had looked ten days ago. There were lines too at mouth and eyes that she had never seen till now. But—had she really ever looked at him before?

"I had meant to tell you everything myself," he said, with a quiet dignity that was infinitely appealing. "But your mother has got the start of me."

"That's not the same thing," she heard herself say.

"No—but I thought she had the right. A girl's mother, you know."

"The right?" she repeated mechanically. But she no longer heard her own words, nor was she paying heed to what he was saying. Curiously enough, it was William's voice that she was listening to, as she looked into that face that she had never seen before. No, she had never seen it before, not once, in all these months. That was why she had been so stupid. She had not thought to look. He had been her mother's choice, not hers. But, now! Why! now she was choosing, herself, and William had furnished the touchstone. "As if you did n't know that he was just all there is—for you!" That was the touchstone.

But Marcus was speaking too, and presently her attention was arrested.

"So there seems really nothing left to say, but—good-bye," he was saying.

Neither of them had thought to be seated. They were standing, face to face, as one does stand at some solemn ceremony.

"Good-bye?" she echoed, vaguely.

She could not bear to see his face like that. He must be comforted at once, at once.

But there was no break in his self-control, as he answered:

"Yes. For I am going away. And you—"

"And I?"

"I wrote you that it should be exactly as you wished."

"And how do you know what I wish?" she murmured; and it never once occurred to her to tax herself with forwardness. But then, that was because she was thinking only of Marcus, and of how he loved her.

"Your mother told me. She said you would not consider yourself fitted to be the wife of a poor man, and that——"

Do what he would, he could not keep his voice quite steady, and those clean-cut lips of his, that had been so firmly set, were getting quite out of drawing. No, she could not bear it; she could not bear it another minute.

Moving a step nearer, she lifted to him a face that he, too, for all his study of it, had never seen before, and said, with the drollest little twist of feeling:

"You might give me a trial!"

"Elsie!"

At that cry of joy, the hidebound Yankee beat a hasty retreat, leaving Marcus himself in full possession of the field. And lo,

Elsie, the incomparable Elsie, found herself swept off her feet at last, quite as if she had been the merest wax-doll that ever melted in the sun.

"For you see, mother, we think it's going to be the greatest fun in the world to be poor—together!"

Thus did Elsie slip the domination of a lifetime. But as she did so, she stooped and kissed her mother, so naturally, and so sweetly, too, that that unpractised heart gave a throb of relief, more easily to be located than the rankling thorn had been. It was almost as if she really did love the girl, in that every-day, commonplace way that most mothers have. And if she loved her now, the inference must be that she had always loved her. For certainly, as her very first words demonstrated, Edna had by no means changed her nature.

"Well, Elsie," she declared. "I'm glad you're so happy, and I hope you'll never forget who it was that insisted upon your getting engaged to him, when you didn't know your own mind. Perhaps you'll believe now, that your own mother knows what's best for you."

And once having taken her stand on this indisputable fact, Edna rose to her full height; a height far more secure than any wave, however topping. She rose to the height of her own moral stature, whence she adroitly snatched a laurel from defeat.

"Yes, he 's a very gifted young man," she was at pains to assure her intimates. "So much the gentleman, too, and so very well connected; and that counts for so much in these days, when everybody is chasing after money. I consider it myself quite a brilliant match, even for Elsie. Besides," she would add, blissfully unconscious of an anti-climax, "this opening in New York is more than promising, especially when you think of the backing they 've got in his rich relations,—and those picture-papers all the rage too. I should n't be surprised if, in a year or two, what with his Art, and that paper and all, he should be making a handsome income."

"All the same," Harriet observed, dryly, to her mother, "they 're only sure of eighteen hundred to begin with; just what John Wenham is getting."

The old lady's eyes snapped, as only

those eyes could, (for had they not had ninety years' practice?) as she answered:

"Did n't I tell ye, Harriet? Say what you please, that girl's a Pratt,—and if she had forty mothers!"

VI.

JANE.

THE skeleton in the Pratt closet was
Jane, and she looked the part. She
was spare and wiry, sharp-featured
and sharp-tongued. Poor she was, too, and
old, and she would n't take a penny from
her rich relations.

Jane was, of course, a widow, as her particular type of skeleton is pretty sure to be.
The family were divided on the question
of cause and effect: her eldest nephew,
James Spencer, declaring that such a disposition as hers was enough to make a widow
of any woman; while Martha, her brother
Ben's wife, testified that she had always
found a great deal to like in Jane, even if her
bereavement *had* made her a bit "difficult."

Happily for the family peace of mind,
Jane was not a resident of Dunbridge.
When, at the age (or youth) of seventeen,

now more than fifty years ago, she had
freakishly married Henry Bennett, a blame-
less but impecunious young man, boasting
neither antecedents nor prospects, she had
migrated with him to Westville, a fourth-
rate manufacturing town some ten miles
removed from Dunbridge topographically,
while socially it was looked upon as quite
the antipodes of that genteel suburb.

Jane's mother, destined later to be known
as Old Lady Pratt, had strenuously opposed
the match, whereby she had made one of the
few blunders of her career; for no one knew
better than she that Jane was not to be
"druv." The wisest have their lapses,
however, and when once the keen-witted
little monitor had been betrayed into speaking her whole mind, the die was cast.

"No, Jane," she had declared, " 't ain't
because this new beau o' yourn is a poor
man, 'n' ain't got any folks to speak of,—
that ain't why I 'm so sot ag'in him. It 's
because you 'd think you was doin' him
a kindness in marryin' him; 'n' wuss still,
he 'd think so too—'n' that would be the
plain ruination o' you."

"I 'd like to know why," Jane flouted,
setting her neck at an ominous angle.

"You 'd like to know why? Well, I 'll tell ye why. Ef you was to marry a man foolish enough to look up to you, you 'd git to be so self-satisfied, that instid o' broadenin' out, you 'd jest narrer down; 'n' you 'd stay narrered down till doomsday."

Many persons affirmed that Jane was the "livin' image" of her mother, and never was the resemblance more pronounced than when the two were most at odds. To-day, as Jane straightened her back, while her black eyes flashed defiance, the very look and attitude of her seemed a usurpation, and as such it was regarded.

"You 're a smart, likely enough girl," the mother persisted, with stinging emphasis, "but what you 're in cryin' need of is a master!"

At that moment, had he but known it, Henry Bennett's suit was won.

"A master!" cried Jane, now in open and jubilant revolt. "I 'd like to see myself knucklin' down to a master."

"So should I!" The retort came back like a whip-lash. "I 'm glad we kin agree on that."

All this was ancient history now. Both Old Lady Pratt and Henry Bennett, aggressor and *casus belli* in that memorable engagement, had passed beyond the clash of arms, and only Jane, duly "narrered down," and sharply acidulated in the process, remained, a living witness to its enduring consequences. Thanks to a liberal endowment of "spunk," she had kept a "stiff upper lip" through many a depressing experience in the dingy little town where her husband plied his trade of optician, and where, after his death, she and her son, Anson, continued to dwell in obscurity, not to say indigence. Yet, if her relatives had thus been spared the mortification of seeing one of their number grow shabbier and thinner under their very eyes, they had been nevertheless poignantly aware of the circumstance.

Not that the Pratts were peculiarly sensitive to the sufferings of other folks. They were doubtless quite as philosophical as the rest of us when it came to resigning themselves to their neighbors' misfortunes. Only where the family credit was involved were they disposed to take things hard. And that an own daughter of Old Lady Pratt should "want for anything," that a near relative, an aunt in fact, of the wealthy

13

banker, Stephen Spencer, should be reduced to doing her own work in her declining years,—it was even whispered that she bought her coal in small quantities!—that did touch them sorely.

Various overtures made from time to time, looking to the amelioration of Jane's condition, had formed a chronicle of failure, in the grim humor of which the intended beneficiary had found such satisfaction as a well-seasoned family skeleton may be supposed to derive from the embarrassment it causes. And when at last Anson too had passed away (a characteristically spiritless procedure), leaving his mother in still more straitened circumstances, with neither chick nor child to look after her, the situation was felt to reflect grave discredit upon the whole connection.

Perhaps humor is too genial a word to apply to Jane's relish of the general discomfiture. The quality of her perceptions, which were as keen as they were limited, had a tendency to turn things sour; while humor, as we know, is the prime sweetener. Whether or not her grocer was correct in his surmise that "the Widder Bennett" lived mainly on pickles,—the cheap brand,—

morally at least such had been the case now these many years. She lived on pickles,— the cheap brand. What wonder that her sharp little teeth were set on edge?

But Jane was not the only one of Old Lady Pratt's descendants who had a mind of her own, and when, a few months after Anson's death, her sister Harriet went the way of many a less dignified mortal, the heirs, as they were quite justified in styling themselves, determined upon heroic measures.

"It's agreed, then," said James the executor, in family conclave, "that we make Aunt Jane a regular allowance."

"In mother's name," Lucy threw in. "She wouldn't touch it otherwise."

"Of course, in mother's name," Arabella declared authoritatively. "We all know she'd rather starve than be beholden to live folks."

"She's grown more peakèd every year since Henry Bennett died," James remarked testily.

"Yes," was his brother Pratt's sardonic comment. "That's just the plague of it,— her *looking* starved. We could make out to put up with it if she only had the sense to look as if she had enough to eat and wear."

"Who's going to see her about it?" asked Lucy, the peacemaker

"Why not you?" her husband suggested. "You're a great hand at getting round folks."

"Nonsense, Frank!" But although she scouted the notion, she did so with her brightest smile; and Lucy's smiles were jewels of the first water.

"The proper person to interview Aunt Jane is undoubtedly the executor," Arabella adjudicated unhesitatingly.

"What are you thinking of?" cried Susan. "James couldn't keep his temper two minutes."

"Couldn't keep my temper?" James thundered.

"Pratt's the man," Stephen interposed. "He understands Aunt Jane better than anybody. He never riles her."

"Nor he don't try to bamboozle her," James growled vindictively, and with considerable acumen too. For, in view of the skeleton's eccentricities,—and they were anatomically well-defined,—the astute Stephen was scarcely less disqualified for this particular mission than the explosive James himself.

Pratt, on the other hand, being an avowed misanthrope, might be considered more akin to his aunt than any of the others. His tongue was caustic but never hasty, his temperament bleak but equable. Furthermore, although he was a lawyer, and a clever one too, he had never made money enough to incur an imputation of that smug self-complacency which Jane was so quick at ferreting out. People said he was too clever to take his clients seriously; they felt that he saw through them, and that made them restive. What they were paying him for was to see through the other fellow. It may also be mentioned, though he himself would never have owned it, that he was not infrequently handicapped by a sneaking sympathy for the under-dog.

When, a day or two later, the chosen emissary presented himself before his aunt in her dreary little sitting-room, where the winter's chill still lingered, though April was setting things sprouting and simmering outside, she struck him as looking more than ever like a small, elderly kobold on short rations. The hue and texture of her skin, the cut of her wizened features all bore out the impression, which was still further accentuated by a certain elfish alertness of glance and gesture, as of a creature not quite domesticated. Jane's hair, which she wore pulled straight back, and fastened in a tight little knob at the nape of her neck, was, like her widow's weeds, of a rusty black. But neither years nor reverses had availed to tarnish the sparkling jet of her eyes, nor to modify the acrid tang of her speech. Touching the latter, indeed, Pratt Spencer used to declare that her waspishness was so purely automatic that no one had any business to take it amiss.

"Well, Pratt," was her tart greeting. "This is the second time since Christmas. Ain't you gettin' to be quite a society man?"

"Oh, this is not a duty call," he returned cheerfully. "I 've come for pleasure."

"You hev, hev you?"

"Yes; I 've come to make myself disagreeable."

"Hm! Could n't you do that nearer home?"

"Not this time. I 'm depending on your coöperation."

"Hopin' to raise a loan, perhaps?"

The masterly sarcasm of this sally was

enough to put even Jane into a good humor. Perceiving which, he made haste to follow it up.

"How did you guess?" he inquired, in simulated wonderment.

"Well, I thought you was lookin' kind o' sheepish."

"You 'll not make it too hard for me, will you, Aunt Jane?" he wheedled, unreeling his line, as it were, to give free play to her caprice.

"Dunno 'bout that," she returned, with a quite piscatorial whisk of fancy. "Never did approve o' young folks runnin' in debt."

Young folks, indeed! As if she did n't know her nephew's age to a day!

"We might call it a gift," he grinned, with a crafty turn on the reel.

"A gift!" It was a very polysyllable of misprision,—the sinuous protest of the trout as the line tightened.

"Why not?" And he turned upon her a pair of inquisitorial glasses. Goggle-eyed as he called himself, Pratt managed to make those glasses of his do a power of execution.

"Well, I never seen a Pratt yet that *I 'd* offer money to; did you?"

This was by good rights a poser.

"Not my own, perhaps," he admitted, "but, look here, Aunt Jane,"—unblushingly sacrificing syntax to rhetoric,—"how about when they 're gone where they 've no more use for their money?"

But she had him there.

"Then of course you could n't offer it to 'em," she retorted, with the ready logic of perversity.

Whereupon, conceiving that he had given her line enough, he dropped his angling, and came straight to the point. Yet, although he put the matter clearly and persuasively, and with entire sincerity, such was the force of skepticism bristling in every line of that gritty little face and figure, that he could n't for the life of him keep from feeling the hypocrite; especially when it came to the peroration.

"You must know better than any one," he urged, beshrewing the inevitable platitude, "how glad mother would always have been to see you enjoying the comforts you were born to."

It is painful to record that at this point Jane sniffed.

"Oh, yes," was the derisive comment. "You can't expect folks to be exactly proud o' their poor relations."

"Have it so, for all me," he acquiesced cordially. "I should be the last to deny that we're a parcel of egotists. But all the same," taking quick toll of his acquiescence, "mother did want to see her own sister comfortable. And now's the time for carrying out her wishes."

"No, 't ain't," Jane objected, shrewdly. "The time for kerryin' out her wishes was when she was makin' her will."

But this was overstepping, and he promptly called a halt.

"You're out, there," he said with decision. "Right or wrong, mother had her own ideas about the family property. She would not have felt justified in——"

"Well, then," she broke in, "that settles it. I should n't think of crossin' her, now she's dead 'n' gone." Then, with one of those quick movements with which she was wont to punctuate an ultimatum, "S'posin' we hev a taste o' raspberry vinegar,—seein' 's you've come so fur for nothin'," she added maliciously.

"Not for me," he gave back, in frank tit-for-tat. "That would be too much of a good thing."

"Well," she snapped, "if you don't relish

what 's offered, you 're free to refuse it.
We ain't any of us so poor but we kin do
that!''

Brisk as the retort was, she looked fagged,
not, as usual, stimulated, by the fray. He
marked the strain in the little pinched face,
and straightway the under-dog began pulling
at his sympathies.

"Come, come, Aunt Jane," he pleaded,
with gruff kindliness. "You 're out of sorts,
and no wonder,—living here all by yourself
without so much as a kitchen-maid to
plague you. I suppose your mind gets
running on Anson, and it wears on you."

Well though he knew her, he half expected to see her soften. But he was
reckoning without the innermost core of his
fierce little antagonist. A hard glitter in
those jet-black eyes warned him that he
had trespassed.

"Anson wa'n't ever much company,"
she averred harshly. "I ain't missin' him
particularly." And Anson, her own son,
scarce six months dead!

Pratt Spencer was sharply on the alert.
A new element had entered into the case.
Here was no thrust and parry of small-arms;
it was a cry of distress from a starving

garrison. Not temper, but heartache had
forced that cry,—plain, grinding heartache.
Hateful word that; hateful thing too. And
the man's mind jerked backward, twenty-
five years, to the day when Clara Dudley
threw him over for a light-weight fellow
who sang tenor.

How that tenor voice had rankled, all
these years! And he, the lean six-footer, encumbered with a portentous bass that flatted
from sheer force of gravity, had behaved
then exactly as Jane was behaving now.
He too had lied, doggedly, bitterly. He
had lied to his people, he had lied to Clara,
he had lied to himself. He too had sworn
that he did n't care. And in course of time,
when he considered himself cured of what
he was now pleased to characterize as an
acute cerebral dyspepsia, he had clinched
the argument by marrying another girl,—
a capital girl too, and one who had no ear
for music. Yet, on the day, two scant
years after Clara's untimely death, when
her husband had consoled himself with a
new wife, Pratt Spencer had carried flowers
to the grave of the girl who had jilted him.
And always after that, on the anniversary
of her husband's second marriage, he had

deliberately, punctiliously, carried flowers
to her grave. Another man in his case
might have kept her birthday, or the anniversary of her death. He chose to mark
the day on which her husband had consoled
himself. Thus he clearly demonstrated that
it was an affair, not of sentiment, but of
homely justice. She too merited consolation on that day, and he would see that she
got it. For he could be judicial, since he
did n't care.

And Jane did n't care. She was n't missing
Anson particularly; he was never much
company. Had she too been jilted, he
wondered,—jilted by her own son? And—
for whom?

"Aunt Jane," he asked, abruptly, "was
Anson ever great friends with anybody?"

"I dunno 's he was—unless 't was with
that old allopath, Dr. Morse, over to East
Burnham," she added grudgingly.

"Hm! That was where he practised
medicine, was n't it?"

"Yes; 'n' Dr. Morse took good care that
he did n't practise medicine long!"

Pratt had heard, years ago, and with cold
disapproval, of his cousin's fiasco. How,
beguiled by the apparent simplicity of

homœopathy, then just coming into vogue,—
pushed into the practice of it indeed by the
rash little martinet who was his mother,—
he had suddenly turned doctor, much as
he might have turned haberdasher, with
no professional training, no conception of
the need of it. How he had made a surprising success of the thing for a few months,
and then had suddenly turned his back on
fortune, and come home to sell spectacles
over his father's counter. A bitter pill that
must have been for Jane. And now, in
the stark impoverishment of her lonely life,
what more natural than that she should
ruminate upon it till it played the mischief
with her constitution? Plainly an antidote
must be found, and who more likely to
know the formula than that East Burnham
doctor whom Anson had been so thick with?
Indeed where was the good of being a
doctor at all, if you couldn't cure folks?
With which somewhat revolutionary dictum,
Pratt elected to pronounce the question closed.

Certainly it could do no harm to step over
to East Burnham and have a word with the
"old fogy." To-morrow was Sunday; the
weather seemed promising for a country
jaunt,—an important desideratum, by the

way. For as often as Pratt Spencer con-
templated any enterprise which could be
remotely construed into a good deed, he
was at pains to convince himself that he was
acting in obedience to a whim of his own.
Yes, a trip to East Burnham was the very
thing for an April Sunday, and if it turned
out that the old doctor really did have that
antidote up his sleeve, why, all the better.
That affair of the allowance, a confounded
bore at the best, could go over to a more
favorable moment. He'd have his country
jaunt at any rate.

"Well, Aunt Jane," he said, as he took
her hard little hand in parting,—how many
years of poverty and toil had gone to make
callous that little hand,—and that little soul
too as far as that went!—"Well, Aunt Jane,
I guess you and I are a good deal alike, and
fight shy of our feelings. But we all know
what a devoted son Anson was." And now
he was too much in earnest to bother about
platitudes. "He loved his mother, if he was
not much company."

Again she sniffed.

He had got to the door and his hand was
on the knob, when a sharp, strained voice
arrested him.

"Pratt Spencer, you come back!"

He turned, and stood, waiting for her to speak.

"You appear to think you know pretty much all there is to know 'bout other folks' affairs," she rasped. "I should like to hev you tell me when Anson ever poured out his heart to you."

"Can't say he ever did."

"Hm! Thought as much. To hear you talk, a body'd think he'd been in the habit of tellin' you *what store he set by his mother!*"

The words were scornful, but there was an eager light in the eyes, and a sharp catch in the breath, as she waited his reply. Pratt Spencer, for all his pride of misanthropy, would have given much to answer in the affirmative. Being, however, but an indifferent liar at best, he found himself constrained to say, lamely enough:

"I never knew Anson very well, Aunt Jane, but he had the name of being a devoted son."

The eager light went out like a candle,— not blown out by the wind, but guttering in the socket from lack of nourishment. There was no more catching of the breath as she rejoined, dully:

"Well, I dunno 's anybody 's ever denied it."

And now the door had closed upon her visitor, and Jane stood, a forlorn little wilted figure, in the middle of the room, wondering what on earth she had been thinking of. Why had she said that foolish thing that did n't deceive anybody, least of all herself? She did not miss Anson particularly?—did not miss him? No; because he was ever with her,—right there before her eyes,—*his face turned away!*

With a hard, dry sob, she dropped upon the nearest chair, and sat there, clutching the arms of it, and staring at the wall. There had been smirking shepherdesses on that wall six months ago. Here, in this room, the operation had taken place,—the operation which Anson had undergone at the hands of a rising young surgeon, James Ellery by name, whom Dr. Morse had summoned to the case. Here, right here, she had sat for hours afterward, watching for a look, a movement, any smallest token that the patient was thinking of his mother. But no, he had thoughts only for the doctors, only for the operation. When they told him that he could n't pull through, "That 's no account," he had pro-

Jane

With a hard, dry sob, she sank upon the nearest chair.

tested feebly. "The operation's the thing. That's all we care about."

Ah, but the irony of that had struck home, —the sheer irony of it after all these years. For a long, dragging quarter of a century he had quietly, stubbornly held out against her, —quietly, stubbornly, he had gone his ways, oblivious apparently to the profession he had wilfully renounced, the profession on which she had staked her all of motherly pride,— and now at last, when it could profit nothing, so alive to the appeal of it that he had never a word of good-bye for her. Not wounded pride, not thwarted ambition—the master-grievance of her life hitherto—was wringing her heart in that hour, but just the primitive, indomitable mother-instinct, clamoring for its own.

"Why, mother! You up so late? Why don't you go to bed?"

She might have been the merest stranger intruding upon the scene,—one of those smirking shepherdesses that seemed to come alive and mock at her. The mocking shepherdesses had since been pasted over with a cheap sprawling wall-paper which her own hands had applied, but in imagination she could still see their smirking faces, their silly frills and furbelows, through the sprawling pattern. And so, under the stiff crust of indifference she so jealously guarded, that hidden wound had festered, unacknowledged, and when the chance probe of her nephew's words pricked through, she could only cry out in a blind, senseless repudiation of that primitive instinct which had been mercilessly preying upon her for months past. Anson was never much company! She was n't missing him particularly! Poor little undisciplined soul, caught in the tangle of its own tragic waywardness!

There was a timid rap at the kitchen door. A neighbor's child stood outside. Jane's neighbors were very small-fry nowadays; those who could afford it had long since moved uptown.

"Please, Mis' Bennett," came a whining voice, "ma thought p'raps you 'd accommodate us with a few eggs. It 's Saturday night, and she 's all run out."

"It 's Saturday night over here too," Jane observed dryly.

The Dannings were arrant beggars, but Jane was never averse to playing the Lady Bountiful.

She stepped to the pantry. There were

just three eggs there. She put them in a
paper bag and handed them to the child.

"Tell your ma that's all I can spare
to-day," she said. "I'm kind o' short
myself."

And with a hasty "Thankee" the child
trotted off.

Jane returned to the sitting-room much
cheered. She understood that certain of her
well-to-do relatives had theories about en-
couraging mendicancy. She for her part
would like to know how you could expect
your inferiors to look up to you if you did n't
assert yourself.

She was crossing the room in quest of her
work-basket, when she noticed that Pratt
had left the evening paper behind him. She
glanced at it in quick suspicion. Did he
know she could n't afford a paper? She had
half a mind to mail it to him,—to put the
price of it into a stamp. But no. She liked
Pratt. She did n't mind accepting that much
from him.

She picked up the paper and, seating herself, began reading it, diligently, system-
atically, as a person does to whom the daily
paper is a luxury. Suddenly her heart
contracted sharply. What was this about

Dr. James Ellery and the amazing operation
he had performed? She glanced furtively
across the room to where the bed had stood.
There was no bed there, and the shepherdesses that might have witnessed to it were
pasted over.

With a sense of relief she returned to the
perusal of the paper. Hastily, eagerly now,
she ran her eye down the column,—a whole
column, more than a column, all about that
young man who had been Anson's doctor.
An odd movement of pride in the fact had
succeeded to that first twinge of pain. She
could not make out much about the operation
itself, the technical language puzzled her;
but there followed a sketch of the young
surgeon's career, and that was easily intelligible. He had been a poor boy, orphaned
son of an East Burnham mechanic, and had
owed his education to an unknown bene-
factor, one who had never, to this day,
revealed his identity, even to the beneficiary
himself.

She liked that about the unknown bene-
factor. It would have been her own way of
doing if she had had the means. Old Martin
Crapp had not guessed where that five-dollar
bill came from the time he broke his leg; and

little Miss Elson, dying of consumption, had eaten her oranges with never a suspicion. No, Jane had never been one to ask for thanks. Willing as she was that her inferiors should look up to her, upon really self-respecting folks she would not impose that sense of obligation which she herself refused to tolerate.

Suddenly, by an oblique association of ideas, her mind reverted to a certain paper which she had found in Anson's meagre collection. He had carefully destroyed everything which could give a clue to his interests and preoccupations. Not a letter had she found, not the smallest jotting of a personal nature. Only a few files of receipted bills, his old high-school diploma, and this life-insurance policy—this sop to conscience, as she resentfully termed it, with which he had sought to condone his lack of filial feeling. In a fierce revolt of spirit, she had thrust the paper out of sight, not so much as breaking the seal.

To-night, as she read the account of James Ellery's career, as her mind dwelt upon the excellence of unacknowledged benefactions, she perceived for the first time that this legacy of her son's was no after-thought, no perfunctory quit-claim. It came to her as a revelation, that such an offering as this represented foresight, sacrifice,—that it was in the nature of a secret benefaction. He had never hinted at what he was doing. That same reticence which had been the chief sting of his quiet, persistent insubordination, had governed him in his care for her welfare. She found herself wondering how far back the instrument dated. Perhaps some day she would break the seal; but not now, not yet. She would not even draw the paper from its hiding-place and examine the superscription. In truth, there was no need of that; it was as clearly engraved upon her memory as upon the long white envelope:

"Life-insurance policy, in favor of Mrs. Jane Bennett."

The very wording of it, in Anson's familiar hand, had been an offence. "In favor of Mrs. Jane Bennett." His last written message, like his last spoken word, had held her at arm's length. And yet, that policy stood for foresight, for sacrifice. What was that Pratt Spencer had said? Anson had the name of being a devoted son? She liked Pratt. If you could n't fool him, at least he never tried to fool you. That was why you trusted him.

The dusk was already gathering. She laid the paper down and, fetching her work-basket, lighted the drop-light. It was well past supper-time, but Jane did n't mind that. She would have a bite on her way to bed. She would n't have to bother with cooking an egg to-night,—nor to-morrow either, for that matter!

As she adjusted her glasses, she recalled, with a sore, teasing compunction, the pains Anson had been at to fit her eyes precisely, and his rather fussy solicitude lest she should strain them. He *had* been a dutiful son, in many ways. He had tried to spare her where he could. Nor had he ever doubted that he was contributing handsomely to the household expenses; for, noting how penurious he was grown, she had scorned to tell him that the cost of living had increased. And all that time, while denying himself the smallest luxury or diversion, he had been making careful provision for his mother. Queer that she had never thought of it in that way before. Well, now, at last, she would know how to value his gift.

And yet, strange as it may seem, she did not feel the slightest inclination to examine the document. For Jane's crabbed nature, within its own hard-and-fast limitations, was not devoid of a curious, twisted streak of ideality. It was really a fact that she cared not at all for things, for possessions, as compared with what they stood for. That was why she would have elected to scrimp and shiver and toil to the end of the chapter, rather than accept aid which could be accounted a charity. And that same idiosyncrasy of disposition, that same twisted streak of ideality, still determined her attitude toward the policy. As she had rejected the offering when it seemed to her but a perfunctory quit-claim, so now that she had an intimation of its essential meaning, she felt no immediate impulse to investigate further. It simply did not strike her—yet—as having any direct bearing upon her own degree of personal solvency. What she would have liked to do about it was to show it to Pratt Spencer, in confirmation of his estimate of Anson's devotion.

Yet when, the very next day, her nephew came again,—came, by the way, in a pouring rain that made ducks and drakes of his theories touching April Sundays and country jaunts,—she expressed neither surprise nor pleasure at seeing him.

"Did you come back for your paper?" was the cynical inquiry, as he laid his hat down on the table, cheek by jowl with the printed sheet.

"To be sure," he returned complacently. "I could n't sleep a wink all night, for worrying about it."

"Speakin' of that paper," Jane threw in, glancing keenly at him, as he took his seat beside the table, "I don't s'pose you happened to notice quite a piece about young Dr. Ellery, and the remarkable operation he 's been performin'."

"No; I had n't noticed it, but Dr. Morse was telling me about it."

"Dr. Morse? I did n't know's you knew Dr. Morse."

"Never did till this morning."

"Where 'd you make his acquaintance?"

"In his own office."

"You went 'way over to East Burnham in all this rain?"

"Yes," with a deprecatory shrug. Why the dickens must the weather man play him a trick like that?

"What for?" she queried peremptorily.

"I wanted to have a talk with him about Anson."

All unconsciously she was managing the case for him. He had but to follow her lead.

"About Anson?"

"Yes," and he settled back in his chair as if for prolonged deliberation. "The truth is, Aunt Jane, I've been feeling that there was something about Anson's later years that perhaps we did n't altogether understand. And it occurred to me that Dr. Morse might be in a position to clear things up for us."

Jane bridled.

"I guess there wa'n't much that Dr. Morse could tell me about my own son," she scoffed.

"I would n't be so sure of that. Anson was very reserved, but you never can tell where one of those close-mouthed fellows will break out."

The storm had suddenly gathered energy; a great gust of rain struck the window-panes. There was something petulant about it, something not unlike Jane's own nervous vehemence.

"Pratt Spencer, what are you drivin' at?" she demanded.

"The truth," he returned, quietly picking up the gauntlet. "Will you hear it?"

She sat, for a moment, rigid, yet shrinking.

"If that man over to East Burnham's been sayin' anything to Anson's discredit," she declared at last, "'tain't the truth, 'n' I won't hear it."

"I've a notion that the whole truth about any one of us would be partly to our discredit," he opined. "But I don't believe many men could strike a better balance than Anson, when all was told."

She had laid hold of the arms of her chair, bracing herself against them, while her eyes transfixed his face. In spite of herself she was solemnized, as he meant she should be. For it was a critical moment with Jane. That cheap defiance of hers must be held in check at any cost. He took off his glasses and fell to polishing them. She was not to feel herself under scrutiny.

"I wonder how much Anson himself ever divulged, of his reasons for giving up practice," he speculated thoughtfully.

Upon that, she let go her hold on the chair-arms; the spirit of contradiction might be trusted to sustain her.

"He said he did n't know enough," she

flung out, "but I'd like to know how he could hev made such a success of it if——"

She had caught Pratt's unspectacled gaze bent questioningly upon her, and she broke short off.

"Aunt Jane, he didn't know anything; and he *found it out.*"

"Through Dr. Morse?" But the gibe was pure bravado, and she knew it.

"Through being guilty of malpractice."

There was no use in mincing matters; it could only serve to confuse the issue.

"Who accused him of malpractice?"

"The facts in the case."

"Well?"

"He lost a patient."

"You ain't claimin' that he was the first doctor that ever lost a patient?"

"No;" for again she had given him his cue. "And he was not the first doctor to do so through malpractice. But he was the first doctor I ever happened to hear of who devoted his life to making good his—error."

He had resumed his glasses, which were now turned full upon her.

"Aunt Jane, Anson lost a patient because he was too ignorant,"—she winced visibly, but there was no help for it,—"he was too ignorant to recognize pneumonia when he saw it."

But once more she rallied her forces.

"That man has prejudiced you, Pratt Spencer. He was always jealous of Anson."

"You think so?"

"I know it. It was he that made him give up practice,—it was he that——"

"Would you like to hear what Dr. Morse had to say about Anson?" he interposed quietly.

"I ain't very particular."

"But I am. He is an old-fashioned man, the old doctor, and he expresses himself in an old-fashioned way. But I am convinced that he meant it with all his heart when he said that he had come to love Anson as a son, and to revere him as a saint."

She made a half-hearted attempt to sniff.

"Aunt Jane," he proceeded, gravely and firmly, "Anson gave his whole life to making good the wrong. Secretly, and with the connivance of Dr. Morse, he supported his patient's widow out of his slender means. He educated one of her boys, still in secret, mind you, to be a doctor. And that boy was —can't you guess?"

Her lips were parted, and now she was leaning forward, avid for the truth.

"The boy Anson educated was James Ellery, the young doctor who was in charge of his case at the end—the doctor whose name to-day is known to half the profession. And your Anson made all this possible for him. Whatever that young man achieves, the world owes it primarily to Anson."

On that, he paused, conscious of an awkward access of emotion. The rain had subsided to a gentle, conciliatory patter; there was already a streak of light in the west.

"Does n't this clear up some things that you had n't quite understood?" he asked presently. There was an indescribable gentleness and forbearance in his tone.

She sat for some seconds so still that it was impossible to conjecture her mood, her eyes fixed—though he could not know it—upon that corner of the room where she had chafed and hungered for the word that never came. At last she spoke, musingly, and with a curious tranquillity, foreign to her stormy spirit.

"I see now," she said, "why Anson did n't think to say good-bye. He had more important things on his mind."

So here was the key to that ghastly speech of hers! He had n't thought to say good-bye, poor chap, quite taken up, no doubt, with watching that substitute recruit of his under fire. Rather stupid of Anson, certainly. But, after all, who could have guessed that the incorrigible little outlaw would have been such a stickler for signs and tokens? And now she understood: Anson had had more important things on his mind. Well, well! There *was* a vein of nobility in the little aunt. And this concession to something bigger, more "important" than herself, —why, it was like the breaking of an evil spell. For the first time in her nephew's recollection she seemed a perfectly normal human being

"You 're not hurt, then," he ventured. "You 're not hurt because Anson made such a secret of it?"

"Hurt? Not a mite. It 's exactly the way I should have acted myself. Anson and I were more alike than you 'd think for." There spoke the old Jane, promptly self-assertive. And yet—the motherly pride of it was good to witness—"He was always more Pratt than Bennett."

"That 's certainly something for us Pratts

to be proud of," was the hearty response.
Upon which, with an adroit turn, and almost in the same breath, "And now, Aunt
Jane," he urged, "you 're going to let us
treat you *as one of us?*"

Her black eyes snapped enigmatically.
"Oh, yes, if you 're a mind to," she
answered with suspicious alacrity.

She was already on her feet and stepping
briskly across the room to the old mahogany
secretary where Anson had kept his papers.
"There!" she exclaimed, as she drew a long
white envelope from the top drawer and
handed it to her nephew, who had also risen,
and was standing, tall and watchful, beside
her. "You 're a lawyer, 'n' I dunno 's there 's
any need o' goin' out o' the family to hev
your business affairs attended to. You
might see to this for me"

"But it has n't been opened," he demurred,
turning the paper in his hand. "How did
that happen? Have you only just discovered it?"

"Well—rightly speakin' I discovered it
last evenin' after you 'd left. I 'd seen it
before, but I *had n't understood its value.*"

Pratt paused, his finger on the seal, looking
down upon the taut little figure in which

suppressed excitement was straining at the leash.

"No, Aunt Jane," he said, "I can't open this."

She hesitated an instant. Then, with a forced laugh, and observing, "Then you ain't so smart as you 're cracked up to be," she snatched the paper and, with nervous, trembling fingers, broke the seal. Inside was a further inclosure, unsealed, bearing also a superscription. Without a glance at the document itself she handed that to her nephew, retaining, however, the second envelope.

"I guess I 'll keep this," she said under her breath, while a slow color tinged the seared old cheek, and something dimmed the brightness of the eyes. "'T ain't exactly business."

Nor was it exactly business. For, written in Anson's own hand, and speaking to her in Anson's own quiet voice, were the words:

"For mother, with love and good-bye from Anson."

15

VII.

PEGGY'S FATHER.

M R. STEPHEN SPENCER was perplexed, and he did n't like it. Not
only did it hurt his self-esteem, in
that he prided himself upon a clear head and
a dispassionate judgment, but it worried him
too, on Peggy's account.

To make a long story short, young Harold
Burke appeared to be falling in love with
Peggy, while Peggy's father found it quite
impossible to fall in love with Harold Burke.
In truth, he distrusted the man, root, stock,
and branch, and he could n't tell why,—he,
who could usually give chapter and verse for
his opinions, let alone his prejudices.

In the first of it, Peggy's father had not
paid much heed to the question of Peggy's
own state of mind. There were so many
young fellows dangling about her, and to so
little purpose, that he had somehow lost
sight of the fact that girls do occasionally lose

their hearts and, worse still, their heads in such affairs. Several straws, however, had recently indicated, if not the direction of the wind, at least the fact that it was rising, and Stephen, in his study of the weather-vane which was Peggy's fancy, had become anxiously alert. At last he spoke out. This again was contrary to precedent, his custom being to let the other party do the speaking out.

He sat, reading his paper in his own den one winter's evening, wrapped in smoke and comfort, when Peggy appeared before him, all rigged out for a dance. She looked such a fluff of billowy white, with a touch of pink in cheeks and sash, that he felt as if something had blossomed there in the unlikely flower-bed of his "brown study." He often felt that way when Peggy came in; barring the maids, she was the only bit of femininity about the house. For Stephen was what his brother Pratt called an "unreconstructed widower."

Peggy, meanwhile, had stayed her slippered foot mid-way of the room, a small pucker of solicitude between her eyebrows, which was not more than half affectation either.

"Will I do?" she inquired, with a fine

disregard of the niceties of her mother-tongue. Her father was fastidious; she placed more trust in his judgment than in that of her looking-glass, which was apt to approve the latest fashions in an unthinking manner.

"Yes; you 'll do," was the reassuring reply. "Is it the German?"

"Yes."

"Who 's your partner?"

"Harold Burke."

"Sorry to hear it."

"Why?"

"Don't like him."

"Why not?" It was evident that father and daughter were on terms of easy familiarity.

"Well, Peggy, I may be wrong, but, in my opinion, the man 's damaged goods, and I don't relish having him palmed off on my girl for a whole evening."

Peggy tossed her head.

"I would n't give a penny for a Miss Nancy kind of man," she retorted; and the toss in her speech was as perceptible as that in the mutinous head itself.

"He might not be on sale," her father threw in; while it occurred to him that when he had so warmly desired girls to his portion, he had been reckoning without that propensity of the girlish head—and tongue.

Stephen Spencer, though anything but a mollycoddle, dearly loved peace and a quiet life. He had mistrusted the genus "boy," as being given to profanity, fisticuffs, and general insubordination; had a theory, so to say, that every male child was booked to turn out a handful. And here was Peggy, the longed-for girl, after letting her two brothers steal a march on her, turning out more of a handful than either of the boys had been. One of these, to be sure, had died in early youth, and the other was studying for the ministry; while Peggy!—it needed but a glance at that head of hers, which had kept the angle of defiance achieved in the initial toss, to perceive that here was an incipient rebel,—and not so very incipient either!

"Peggy," her father asked, abruptly,— "What is it that you like about the fellow?"

"What does anybody like about anybody?" she answered back. "I just like him." Peggy was certainly growing fearfully sophisticated.

"Hm! Think him straight,—honest,— above-board?"

"If he was n't, *I* should n't know it!"—this with a shrug that a girl of twenty had no business with.

"Your mother would have," Stephen opined, thoughtfully. Did n't nice girls have any intuitions at all now-a-days, he asked himself.

"Pooh! Just because she happened to fall in love with you, you think——"

"Just because she fell in love with me, Peggy, I know the kind of girl she was."

"Oh, well; we can't all be alike." Clearly there was something very much askew about Peggy to-night. But she had given him an opening.

"Then the other girls don't like him as well as you do?" he queried.

She had crossed the room, and was standing with her hand on the mantel, looking down into the glowing bed of cannel-coal. As the last big chunk broke apart, the wavering reflection of the leaping flame playing among her features gave them a shifty, uncertain expression, which teazed him. With a touch of impatience, he repeated his question.

"The other girls don't like him as well as you do?"

"I did n't say so," she gave back, coolly, and without looking up. Then, with another shrug, "At any rate, they 're all spoiling for the chance."

"And there 's not a girl in the bunch that sees through him?"

If she really liked the man, Stephen reflected, she would n't stand that. But she was not in the least ruffled. On the contrary, as the leaping flame played itself out, and the fire settled back into its steady glow, a complacent little smile revealed itself, sole residuum of those shifting changes which had teazed him.

"We all think him interesting," she observed, musingly.

"Fallen angel business, eh?"

"Something like that, perhaps. Hark!"— at sound of wheels on the driveway. "There's Aunt Lucy and the girls." And, with a hasty kiss, she vanished from the room, leaving Stephen under an impression as of lights having been turned down.

He did not follow her to the door; he should see her when she got back. A Dunbridge dance in those sensible days, a generation ago, was over soon after midnight. Stephen always sat up for his daughter. He

had old-fashioned ideas about girls. And
besides, he loved to see her come breezing
home from a dance. Only, latterly, the
quality of the breeze had been variable. And
once, last time in fact, she had returned in a
dead calm. That was what had set him
thinking.

At this point in his meditations, Stephen
became aware that he was not relishing his
cigar, one of a new brand which his dealer had
asked him to try, and, with an irritable
gesture, he tossed it, half-smoked, toward the
grate. It just missed fire and, rolling back
upon the bricks, lay there, emitting a vile
smell. That was the worst of things checked
untimely: they deteriorated. He wondered
how Peggy would stand checking. Would
she too sulk and smoulder and grow sour?
She was a little fool, of course, with her
babyish cynicism, her preposterous worldly
wisdom. But she was a stout-fibred little
fool. There was nothing weak-kneed about
Peggy. Only, if she were denied, thwarted,
treated like girls in story-books,—in the
good old story-books where the stern parent
stalks through the pages like a Nemesis in
trousers and top-hat,—would she be the
same Peggy? Handful though she was, the

thought of a different Peggy was not to be tolerated for a moment.

As Stephen sat there in his quiet den, darkened as it seemed, in spite of chandelier and drop-light, by the passing of Peggy, he fell into rather depressing cogitations. Perhaps his sister Susan, the family mentor, was in the right of it. Perhaps he ought to have provided Peggy with a step-mother,— some good, sensible woman, who would keep her in order, without that clumsy, mannish interference which he had a morbid horror of blundering into. Ought he to have done violence to his feelings, for Peggy's sake? She was only ten when her mother died. Certainly her need was plain. But he had balked the issue, as a man will, when nothing occurs to bring it to a head. Stephen had not perhaps loved his wife more sincerely than many another man, but he had been less able to break the habit. He did not over-sentimentalize the situation, but he never could rid himself of the impression that he was none the less a married man, because of the accident of Margaret's death.

Peggy's father, like the majority of Old Lady Pratt's grandsons, was a successful man though, being long-headed beyond the

average, he had taken his time about it. He
had even spent four years at college; not
from any strong bookish tendency, but because he believed in a college degree and
college affiliations, as a good asset in the
banking business. Such they had proved;
and, although he was banker and broker in a
very small way as measured by the standards
of to-day, he had made what Dunbridge
accounted a great deal of money. He loved
money, too, not so much for what it might
purchase, as for that vague, far-reaching
potentiality that spending dissipates. Which
is merely a euphuistic way of stating that he
was what Old Lady Pratt would have characterized as "a little near."

"Call it contiguous, and done with it!"
his cousin, Robert Pratt, had once burst out.
But that was shortly after Stephen had
declined to "accommodate" his cousin on
insufficient security, and the latter was feeling
rather sore about it.

To-night, as Peggy's father sat there in
the crude gaslight, his brows contracted in
thought, his newspaper lying forgotten on his
knees, the mere physique of the man, modelled as it was on lines of strict economy,
furnished a pretty fair index of his character.

One saw at a glance that there was nothing
large about Stephen, nothing in the least
degree expansive. His figure was close-
reefed, his expression in-drawn. He wore no
beard, and his hair, only lightly grizzled at
sixty, was so judiciously brushed as to conceal
any possible hiatus. Nature had done much
assiduous buttonholing about his features;
mouth, eyes, nostrils, all seemed fixed in a
permanent mould by the series of faint
convergent wrinkles that looked like stitches
of a painstaking seamstress. No thoughtful
observer would have adjudged the man capable of spontaneous action, and, by the same
token, none would have hesitated to trust
him with the half of his fortune. If Stephen
Spencer was a jealous guardian of his own
interests, he would prove no less vigilant in
his neighbor's behalf,—at so and so much per
centum, be it understood. And Stephen was
a shrewd investor,—a conservative, through
and through.

A shrewd observer of men he was too, and
little as he had yet seen of Burke, he had
already sized him up pretty accurately. A
plague on the fellow, thought Stephen. If
only he and his kind,—plausible, meretri-
cious, unscrupulous as sin,—would let the girl

alone, Peggy's father could take better care
of her than a dozen step-mothers! At which
somewhat oriental burst of fancy, the "unreconstructed widower" resumed his paper,
and applied himself to the consideration of a
threatened international imbroglio which
struck him as being far less complicated than
the particular botheration which he had on
his own hands.

Nor was it the international imbroglio
that was distracting his thoughts when, next
morning, he sat in his business sanctum, in
the city, endeavoring to weigh the pros and
cons of a projected issue of railroad bonds,
the financing of which was likely to be
offered to his house. It would have been
less annoying to forget the approximate
figure of a certain floating debt, which had
a bearing upon the proposition, because of
doubts as to Mr. Gladstone's foreign policy,
than because a little chit of twenty had come
home from a party in a state of artificial
excitement. An impending change in the
face of Europe was distinctly more important
than a heightened color in the cheek of Peggy.
Yet Peggy it was, her flushed cheeks and
flippant manner, that was at the bottom of
that lapse of memory which had obliged him

to turn back several pages in the report in question. And he was not nearly as much put out as he might otherwise have been when presently a member of a junior broker-age firm sent his name in, thus obliging him to reserve the matter in hand for later consideration

"Morning," Stephen grunted, as his caller entered.

"Morning," was Hickman's counter-grunt. After which exchange of civilities, the younger man dropped into a chair which he was at least not forbidden to take, and got to business.

"I believe you know Harold Burke," he observed, tentatively.

"Much as ever," was the indifferent re-joinder. But the watch-dog in Stephen was sniffing the air.

"Thought you might. He comes from your town."

"Yes. I knew his father. Died some years ago."

"Man of means?"

"Some," was the laconic reply. Stephen's business was to listen, not talk.

Hickman shifted in his chair, preparatory to making a fresh start.

"I called round," he said, "because I thought perhaps you might like to take over Burke's account."

"Well?"

"The market dropped so hard last week that——"

Stephen's eyes narrowed.

"Margin running out?" he inquired.

"No; not yet. But it 's on the cards, of course, and we thought, if it should come to that, and if you were a friend of the family——"

"Yes, yes; I see. What 's the collateral?"

"D & K fives. Does seem rather gilt-edged stuff for a fellow like that to be carrying; but you say his father was a man of means."

Stephen ruminated a few seconds. Then:

"We 'll take up the account if you like," he said, "and if Burke agrees. The collateral 's sound enough."

When, a day or two later, the account was made over to him, Stephen's fingers closed upon those D & K fives with a curious sense of having got his man where he wanted him. Just what he was going to do with him he would have been at a loss to say. But Stephen could always afford to wait. Meanwhile he had signified his readiness to see Burke, himself, the first time he should put in an appearance.

"Well," the broker remarked, as his new customer sat down, and glanced about the room with a slightly supercilious interest in its meagre appointments. "So you 're going to let us carry your account?"

"Glad to, Mr. Spencer. Glad to. Nothing could be more satisfactory."

"Hm!" was the compendious rejoinder. Yet, much as Stephen disliked amplification, his conscience forced him to add: "Nothing could be more satisfactory unless—keeping out of it altogether just now."

"Queer advice from a broker."

"We often give queer advice here. For instance,"—Stephen was speaking slowly and weightily,—"we usually advise our customers to let the market alone when it has the jumps."

"I should think that was just the time to catch on," the young man volunteered. He really felt sorry for Peggy's father. Such golden chances as must come his way!

"Others have thought so," was the somewhat ambiguous reply.

"Well, you see, Mr. Spencer," Burke

kindly explained, "I'm in the market to make money. You can't make money when the market's in the doldrums."

"No?"

"Nor you can't make money, if you'll excuse me for saying so, by—keeping out."

"Hm!" Stephen commented.

"You'll certainly admit that, Mr. Spencer."

"Oh, yes."

Burke reddened with vexation. If it hadn't been for Peggy,—ah, yes, and that collateral; he was almost forgetting about that in the pleasurable exercise of instructing Peggy's father,—he would have openly resented those repetitious monosyllables. As it was, he thought better of it, and kept his temper.

All the same, he couldn't spend the day listening to an old man's platitudes, and, with an ingenious reversal of his real sentiments, he remarked, as he pushed back his chair and got on his feet:

"I know your time is valuable, sir,"— adding, in a facetious vein which struck him as ingratiating,—"It's quite possible that you may have more important customers than I."

"Not at all," Stephen returned, suavely, and quite truthfully too; for it crossed his mind that this was probably the only customer on his books who was in a position to give him a bad quarter of an hour. And Burke, concluding that this dull old file was as far behind the times in manners as in methods, repaired to the main office with a sense of getting out into the swim again.

Yet when, some days later, the market began "jumping" in the wrong direction, his mind did recur to the "old file" as a rather particularly desirable father-in-law. If only that tantalizing Peggy would come to terms! What tips the old chap must have up his sleeve! What a mint of money he must be worth, if it came to that, and Peggy the apple of his eye,—as she would be the apple of anybody's eye that could once dislodge her from the parent stem. But (with a lightning change of metaphor), the little devil was skittish as the stock-market itself. Lucky for him that he had a firm hand and a steady head, or she might yet give him the slip,—she and that other gamble of which he was in equally hot pursuit. And as the passion of possession, twofold and heavy handed, gripped him anew, a certain crease,

16

which started at the left-hand corner of his mouth and made a bad angle with the jaw, showed up as the kind that frequently defaces "damaged goods."

That crease deepened perceptibly as day by day the market became more skittish. The stubborn speculator bought and sold, backed and filled, usually, though not always, at the wrong moment, and with each wild clutch at that cavorting steed, whose bridle seemed to be merely an ingenious contrivance of tape and ticker which any man of spirit might get the hang of, more collateral was required, more sinews for the struggle, and always more collateral was forthcoming.

And Stephen, from the vantage-ground of his private sanctum, watched the frantic plunges of his cock-sure customer, examined the steadily increasing collateral, and told himself that the source thereof was matter of pure conjecture. If, when the predestined crash came, something more than a fortune were to go by the board, if the upshot of all this folly should be moral as well as financial discomfiture,—well, there would at least be an end of the fallen angel business. Lucifer himself, floundering in the mud, could hardly avoid cutting an inglorious figure. And again the broker told himself that it was of course none of his business, but it *was* odd that a man of Burke's proclivities should control so many high-class securities. His father, to be sure, had been a careful investor, and no doubt Mrs. Burke had plenty of good stuff in her strong-box. But he certainly did not propose meddling in his neighbor's affairs to the extent of looking over old accounts and finding out whether it really was D & K fives and Merrivale debentures that the elder Burke had purchased for his wife when she came into her property along in the seventies. If there was one species of duffer that Stephen despised more than another, it was an inquisitive stock-broker.

Meanwhile, here was Peggy, capricious in her moods as the market itself,—a simile which, as we know, that young lady's present critic was not the first to hit upon,—and Stephen, keenly alive to the situation, was too wary an operator to invite disaster by any premature move. He would bide his time.

At last there came an evening when Peggy herself gave the signal for action, and in unmistakable terms.

Her father had been watching her from

the ambush of his newspaper, as she sat in a
low rocking-chair pretending to read *Bar-
chester Towers;* then, jumping up so suddenly that the rockers beat a tattoo on the
floor, passed into the next room and began
drumming on the piano, only to stop short
off and run up-stairs, apparently with the sole
purpose of running down again; finally
ensconcing herself in a corner of the sofa,
where she sat cutting the leaves of *Harper's
Monthly.* The engaging little boy depicted
upon the cover of that already veteran
periodical, earnestly playing cup-and-ball
with a bewildering number of soap-bubbles,
should have been a lesson to her in concen-
tration. Yet, after a few minutes, she tossed
the magazine to one side and sat there,
gazing across the room into the fire, for all
the world as if her own last bubble had
incontinently burst.

"Well?" her father queried; and there was
no need of adding, "What's the matter?"
so used was Peggy to those monosyllables of
his.

"Oh, nothing," she answered. Whereupon
the inquirer tranquilly resumed his paper.

She watched him out of the tail of her eye,
in a manner peculiar to very astute persons.

What did he find in that stupid old paper, anyway? Always the same thing. She did n't believe he would ever know the difference if the date were to be changed. And real life so intensely interesting! At which point she heaved a terrific sigh.

"Did you say anything?" Stephen inquired.

"Yes; I did."

"What?"

"I said I wished you were not so prejudiced."

"Hm! About what?"

"About any man that asks me to marry him, if you insist upon knowing."

Stephen laid down his paper.

"So he has had the effrontery to make you an offer?"

"If you choose to put it that way."

"And you?"

"Oh, I told him he need n't be in such a hurry."

"Well?"

"He says I shall come to it. He says I 've got to."

"But you have n't."

"Have n't I?" There was a droop in the girl's voice that misliked him rudely.

"Come, come," he remonstrated. "Don't be a little fool."

At that she sank back among the cushions and, flinging her arms above her head in the very abandonment of lassitude, murmured, "I sometimes think I should like to."

"Peggy!" cried Stephen, sharply. "You 're mooning, and I 'm ashamed of you!"

"Are you?" she queried, unblushingly continuing to moon. "Oh, dear! It does make it so difficult."

"Mooning?"

"No,—you. If only you liked him!"

"Then there 'd be two fools in the family. One 's enough, in all conscience."

A long silence ensued, during which Stephen, picking up his paper, endeavored to fix his mind on Mr. Gladstone's comparatively negligible embarrassments.

Presently—"Papa," she mused. "Did you ever notice your *bête noire's* eyes, the way they follow you round?"

"Yes," was the curt reply. "That 's how I first discovered that he was damaged goods."

"Funny! Now, I 've noticed them too, and that 's why I can't say no."

"You can if you try," Stephen asserted;

Peggy's Father

She essayed to pull her hand free, but he held it fast.

and his tone was so authoritative that it took Peggy back to the time before her mother died, when she used to have to mind. She rather liked it, too. It seemed for the moment to relieve her of responsibility.

She got up, and came toward him with a wavering air, half defiant, half appealing, and wholly foreign to the natural spirit of the girl.

"I think I'll go to bed," she said, and stooped to kiss him good-night. He knew she was thinking of his last words.

Detaining her for an instant, and looking straight into her eyes, "You can, Peggy, if you try," he said again.

She essayed to pull her hand free, but he held it fast. He was stronger than she; there was no denying it. Yes, he *was* the stronger. And again the sense of authority possessed her, and again it seemed to her good.

"I wish you'd make me," she said, under her breath, as, with an adroit movement, she snatched her hand away. But on the threshold she paused to call back, "If you don't—he will!" And she was gone.

And again, as on the evening of the dance, Stephen sat where she had left him, pondering the thing she had said. The fire burned low, while silence fell upon the house, and still he sat on, pondering, pondering the thing she had said: " If you don't,—he will."

He knew well enough that she never would have challenged him, had she believed in his power to deter her; that the little villain was only shifting the responsibility upon him, while keeping the game in her own hands. She had not said: "I wish you would forbid it." That would have been a simple matter, and of doubtful efficacy. She had said: "I wish you would make me!" There was something quite touchingly ingenuous about this strategy of Peggy's, instinctive refuge that it was of a mind chafing under alien subjugation. The girl simply was, yes, she was, in love. All that trash about the fellow's eyes was as sure a symptom as a ream of raptures. Peggy was in love, his Peggy, with the quick ardors of her mother, and her father's innate obstinacy,—a dangerous combination for a girl in love with a scoundrel.

Yet nothing her father could say would mend matters, so far at least as her feeling was concerned, which after all was the essential thing. For Stephen had no mind to be left with a love-lorn damsel on his hands. That would be a handful indeed! She must be cured, not coerced. She must be made to understand the worthlessness of the man. Already she knew that there was something wrong about him; so much she had herself admitted. In her eyes he was already adorned with the sort of nimbus that attaches to the Captain Kidds of romance, the Rochesters of fiction; and, thanks to a girlish wrong-headedness,—a girlish innocence, too,—she must needs own herself attracted, nay, be-devilled, by it.

"I can't say no," she had declared. He, her father, was to "make her." And as Stephen pondered her words, there moved somewhere in the back of his mind a reluctant consciousness that it was in his power to do so, by the only effective means: namely, by giving the man a chance to show himself up in his true colors. What was that he had himself said about the despised Miss Nancy kind of man? He might n't be on sale? Well, there 'd be no hitch of that sort when it came to dealing with Harold Burke. He was safe to have his price.

And what if he had? How could that affect Stephen Spencer? When had he

ever stooped to bribery and corruption? A
dubious enterprise at best, and costly too.
Why, the man was already up to his ears in
difficulties. A pretty penny it would take
to pull him out! Not that the prettiness of
the penny had any special bearing on the
case. It was on the highest moral grounds
that Stephen repudiated the idea of,—yes,
that was the matter in a nutshell,—the idea
of compounding with iniquity.

Thus did Peggy's father, usually so chary
of words, so discreet of thought even, beguile
himself with fine-sounding phrases, in defence of—what? Why, of that penny, to be
sure, that penny, to the prettiness of which
he feigned a Spartan indifference.

And, by the irony of circumstance, it was
not concern for Peggy that finally brought
him right about face. It was concern for
another woman, one with whom he had but
a bowing acquaintance; and that woman was
none other than Harold Burke's mother.

He met her on the street one day, a handsome, rather showy personage, who held her
head high. And it suddenly struck Stephen
that she would not find it easy to hold her
head like that when she knew the truth,—
when she awoke some morning to find herself

the mother of a rascal. As the thought
assailed Stephen, not in the form of words,
which may be juggled with, but as a picture,
a series of pictures, definite, convincing, as
the figure of the woman herself, to whom he
was in the act of lifting his hat, he knew for an
absolute certainty that those bonds her son
had been playing fast and loose with were her
property; and what is more, he knew that he
had known it all along.

It chanced that on the day in question
things went from bad to worse in Burke's
affairs; his margin dwindled to danger-point.
If the market did not speedily recover,
or if no reinforcements were forthcoming,
the man would be sold out: not through any
hostile action on Stephen's part, but in the
ordinary process of business routine.

The day passed, and in neither quarter had
relief materialized.

Next morning the broker sent for Burke
and, in a few curt sentences, spoke his mind.
The man behaved much as was to have been
anticipated. He denied nothing, he extenu-
ated nothing. His pose was not that of injured innocence even. He merely intrenched
himself in his right as an "operator" to be
sole judge of his own methods. As for the

securities,—assuming for argument's sake that they were the property of his mother, he must still hold himself accountable to no man. She had placed her affairs in her son's hands without reserve; she would be the last to recognize the pretentions of an outsider to intermeddle between them. However, if Mr. Spencer would feel more comfortable about it, Burke was quite ready to transfer his account elsewhere; Mr. Spencer had but to say the word.

Now this was nothing more nor less than vaporing,—last resort of a man in a bad fix; and Stephen knew that the fellow was cornered.

"Mr. Burke," he said, quietly. "My object in bringing up this matter was to pave the way to offering you assistance,—very material assistance."

For one irrational moment Burke wondered if this were Peggy's doing,—if she had wheedled her father into approving his suit.

"Have you—" he stammered; for the idea was a heady one, and it caught him at low rations.

"Yes, I have my reasons for interesting myself in your affairs. I am acting in behalf of two women,—my daughter and your mother."

At that Burke came to his senses.

"Whatever your motive may be in regard to Peggy," he began, cautiously.

"To my daughter," Stephen interpolated. "It is only as my daughter that she concerns you, sir."

That "sir" was like the first prick of the blade in the hands of a sure swordsman. It stung. Burke was not a good loser.

"If she concerns me only as your daughter," he cried, hotly, "I fail to see how my mother concerns you at all."

"Then, in the name of your mother you would feel justified in declining my assistance?"

There was a pause, during which that ugly crease at the young man's lip stood out as never before. Stephen sat, absently drumming with his fingers on the arm of his chair. He was in no hurry; he had his man.

At last Burke spoke.

"If you have a business proposition to make," he said, with carefully simulated nonchalance, "I am, of course, bound to hear it."

Upon that, Stephen drew from among the papers lying on his desk a closely written sheet,—a detailed statement, as transpired, of Burke's account to date.

"Your liabilities at close of business yesterday, Mr. Burke," he observed, running his eye down the debit column, "amounted to the sum of $27,561.34, covered, with a very narrow margin to the good, by the various securities placed with us as collateral. It is plain that unless you are in a position to redeem these securities, it would hardly stand within your option to—transfer your account."

Burke checked a movement to speak.

"Now, after due consideration," Stephen went on, "I have decided to remit the amount of your indebtedness to Stephen Spencer & Co., on two conditions. First, that you induce your mother to put these bonds, which, I take it, comprise the bulk of her negotiable securities, in charge of some business man of repute, whom you and she may select, *subject to my approval*. You can easily convince her of the advisability of the step, since she places such implicit confidence in your judgment and integrity."

The tell-tale crease at Burke's lip took on an uglier twist, but he remained silent.

"Secondly, that you subscribe to an agree-

ment which I myself have drawn up, by
the terms of which, and *in consideration of
value received*, you formally and definitively
renounce your suit for my daughter's hand.
Here it is." And with that, Stephen
produced a paper of his own inditing and,
passing it over to his customer, settled
back in his chair to await developments.

Burke examined the brief document with
needless deliberation. He knew as well as
its author, that this was no instrument to be
tested in the courts; that it was of value only
as it might affect Peggy, who alone would be
called to pass judgment upon it. Nor was
she likely to err for lack of illuminating commentary. "This lover of yours," her father
would explain, in his dryest manner, "this
precious lover of yours, who would n't take
no for an answer, has thrown you over in
return for so and so many dollars and cents.
Very well, then; either he is a renegade and
sticks to his bargain, or he is a blackguard
and breaks it. Which will you have?"

Yet, impossible as it was to blink the ugly
facts, Burke was in no mood to stomach them.
While studying the proposition in all its
enormity, he was very collectedly weighing
the risks involved in rejecting it out of hand.

The impulse to do so was so strong that his native assurance rose to it. A man's conviction of his own invincibility dies hard.

"You are perhaps not aware, Mr. Spencer," he announced, with the crude self-assertiveness which was second nature to him, "that since last evening your daughter is as good as engaged to me."

It was a home-thrust, and it hurt badly. If the tale was true, and it well might be, for Peggy herself had given fair warning, it did certainly complicate matters, in so far as it must cruelly enhance the girl's mortification at the sordid bargain of which she had been made the object.   Yet more disquieting still was the bald assurance of the fellow's tone, the insolent challenge of those remorseless eyes. The man's attitude at the moment was a revelation of the sort of power that he might exercise over an impressionable girl, giving her no rest, no respite, until there stirred within her an insidious desire to yield, there where she had so long resisted. Had she not herself declared: "If you don't, —he will"?

Well, if she had lost her head, all the more important that her father should keep his. And there was nothing in Stephen's manner to betray the harsh misgivings that galled him as he answered:

"If I really believed that my daughter were 'as good as engaged' to you,—whatever that may mean,—it would not affect my action. That paper which you hold, together with the other condition named, is an ultimatum."

"And if I reject it?"

"The alternative would seem to be obvious."

Burke stood up. He was beaten, and he knew it, but——

"I suppose you will allow me a few hours for consideration," he said, with a vain pretence at being a free agent.

"A few minutes, yes. Not a few hours. The market closes at twelve on Saturday. Think it over, by all means, however. But" —as Burke made as if to go—"here in my office. If you cross the threshold without having given me your signature, the transaction is off."

Upon that, Stephen touched a bell on his desk, and a messenger appeared.

Without further consideration of Burke's attitude, the broker asked, "Has Mr. Apgood got back from the vaults? Hm!

17

Ask him to bring me Mr. Burke's collateral. Mr. Burke is closing his account with us." And in silence the two men waited.

Burke had stepped to a side window which gave upon a narrow well. He stood staring at the panes, quite unaware that they were of ground glass, while Stephen, making no pretence of indifference, waited the coming of Apgood. A church clock in the distance was striking eleven as the clerk came in and placed a bulky envelope upon the desk.

"What's Windermere doing?" Stephen inquired casually. He could almost see Burke prick his ears.

"Forty-six and a quarter, sir."

"Hm! Quick work," was the pungent comment. "Two points off since opening." And he glanced again at Burke's ears, which as a matter of fact had remained totally non-committal. Indeed, Stephen it was whose countenance played him a trick. For, as he sat, balancing the goodly packet in his hand after Apgood left the room, a twinge of chagrin pulled his lip awry. They were practically his, these securities; he was paying for them twice over; and to what purpose? He had only to have let things take their course; Lucifer was safe to have got his mudbath, at no expense to any one but himself; while these bonds, to which Stephen already possessed the indisputable title, these bonds which were already his——

Yet, stay! Was it then his, this sorry plunder that he was covetously nosing and pawing? Gammon! Supposing he *had* paid for it! More fool he! You can't buy out Peter by subsidizing Paul. And, as if to clinch the argument, Stephen reached for a pen, squared the envelope on the desk before him and, having drawn a line through the superscription, proceeded to write above it, in his cramped but particularly legible hand, "Property of Mrs. Dawson Burke."

When, a moment later, Burke turned and crossed the room, his antagonist was in the act of depositing a stout, oblong packet in his private safe.

"I shall hear from your mother early in the week?" the broker asked, without looking round.

Whereupon Burke, giving a snarl of affirmation, seated himself, and affixed his signature to the damaging agreement as mechanically as he had examined those unremunerative window-panes.

As he flung down the pen and shoved back

his chair, Stephen came up behind him and, resting his hand on the young man's shoulder, said, gravely and not unkindly:

"You 've got your chance, Harold Burke, your chance of being an honest man—and a good son. Mind you don't miss it." And in dogged sullenness Burke walked out of the room.

"And now for Peggy," Stephen muttered, as he picked up the incriminating document and, with a rueful grimace, slipped it into his pocket. He wished he had n't got to see the child's face when the purport of the thing dawned upon her. Oh, yes, it would be an eye-opener; no doubt as to that. But Peggy's father had always been rather squeamish when it came to surgery, actual or figurative. Since there was no help for it, however, the sooner it was over the better. Accordingly, at close of business, as was his custom of a Saturday, Stephen took the Dunbridge horse-car and went home to luncheon.

As he left the car and passed up his own street, where the snow lay hard-packed under bare, spreading elm-branches, his eye was caught by an approaching figure, the only moving object in a winter-locked scene.

"Sneak!" he ejaculated, between his teeth.

The two men passed each other without a sign of recognition, but not so quickly but that Stephen caught a glimpse of a lowering face. Whether anger or chagrin predominated was not apparent, but whatever had produced that scowl, the sight of it was meat and drink to Stephen. He entered his own gate, closed it carefully behind him, and walked up the path, with a sense of being master in his own domain, such as he had not enjoyed in many a long day.

Nor did that agreeable impression lack speedy confirmation. For, no sooner had his latch-key touched the lock than the door flew open, and Peggy stood before him. She had the look of an avenging spirit— a circumstance which rendered only more flattering the impetuosity with which she flung her arms around his neck, crying:

"Oh, papa! You blessed darling! I *am* so glad to get you back!"

Eagerly, breathlessly, she helped him off with his overcoat and hung up his hat on its particular peg, and together they passed into the familiar den, swept clean to-day alike of evening shadows and of artificial lights. The temperate winter sun was shining in at the

bay window; the fire in the grate was burning
in a steady, business-like way. As Stephen
stood on the hearth-rug, spreading cold hands
to the friendly glow, he could hear the click
of silver in the dining-room, where Nora was
laying the table for luncheon, while a pleasing
suggestion of something broiling was wafted
in through the swinging pantry doors, plying
back and forth with a sound as of a flapping
sail. Hour and place seemed peculiarly
favorable for straight-forward daylight con-
fidences. Yet that incalculable Peggy, though
visibly tingling with excitement, had apparently fallen dumb. And for a second time
Stephen found himself taking the initiative
in this ticklish business.

"Did he come to say good-bye?" he
inquired, with studied composure, as he drew
up a chair, and seated himself close before
the fire.

"He did n't *stop* to say good-bye,"
was the succinct rejoinder; and, for once,
Peggy's father wished she would talk a bit
faster.

"Well, out with it," he prodded. "What's
happened?"

"He's gone."

"Gone for good?"

"Good, bad, or indifferent,—it's all one to me. He's gone!"

"Well?"

"He wanted me to marry him—to marry him right away." She was speaking fast enough now, as if eager to have it over. "He said he'd got to go away at once. He wouldn't ask me to go with him, because he had lost all his money, and had got to begin again. But if only I would marry him, if he could only know that I belonged to him, it would be something to work for, it would give him courage for the fight. He wanted me to slip away with him this very morning, and get it done. He said nobody need know until he came back for me."

"Well?"

"He was really quite pathetic, and I did feel sorry for him. Besides, I *had* half promised, and—oh, papa, I thought I wanted to do it. It seemed such an easy way of having it settled and done with, and it need n't have changed anything for a long time to come. But I said of course I could n't do such a thing behind your back."

"Well?"

"He got very much excited, and asked me if I loved you better than I loved him. And

before I knew what I was about, I had said
yes!"

"And what made you say that, Peggy?"
Stephen's voice sounded rather husky.

"Because it was the truth," she flashed.
"The moment I had said it, I knew. And
then I knew it had all been a crazy dream,
and I told him so, straight out."

"And he?"

"He got perfectly furious. He said I owed
it to him to do just whatever he wanted,
because—because——"

"Because—what?"

"Because it was through you that he had
been ruined. That Stephen Spencer & Co.
had led him on to gamble; that you had lent
him money, and made everything easy for
him, and then, when things went wrong,
you had sold him out."

The button-holing about Stephen's lips
was drawn so tight that they were barely
able to form the syllable, "Well?"

Peggy's breath came fast, and there was
that in the young eyes that made the glowing
coals look dull.

"I told him that was enough," she hurried
on. "That if he did not leave the room, I
should. And then—he lost all control of

himself, and I—" the rush of words halted.
It was in a voice, low-pitched, but on edge
with scorn and repulsion that Peggy added,
"I knew, then, what you had meant by
—damaged goods."

Stephen regarded her keenly. In an hour
his little Peggy had grown into a woman.
She could defend herself, now; she was safe.
Slowly he drew from his pocket a folded
paper, and, leaning forward, placed it with
careful exactitude on the coals, where licking
flames crumpled it to ash.

And Peggy, a trifle disconcerted by the
apparent irrelevance of the little rite,
dropped on her knees beside him, with a
view to fixing his attention. But there
was no need of that; her father's mind
had not wandered.

Looking down into her face, and passing
his hand very gently over the spirited young
head,—

"Little Margaret," he whispered.

He had rarely called her by her mother's
name, and never with that lingering accent.
The girl's eyes softened, and something
sparkled on the lashes. But almost instantly
she brushed it off and, scrambling hastily
to her feet,—for, although Peggy had shame-

lessly mooned, the real Margaret was still a bit shy of her own emotions,—

"So you see it *was* you," she declared, with a saucy toss which did not deceive anybody, "It *was* you that made me do it, *just as I told you to !*"

VIII.

THE DEAN OF THE BOARDING-HOUSE.

"A BOARDING-HOUSE is no place for a child."

Thus spoke Arabella Spencer, the dean of the boarding-house, and none had the temerity to dispute her. Even the injudicious petting of the child in question, an engaging little three-year-old answering to the name of "Dimple," was discreetly abandoned; whereupon the little tot, with an indifference anything but flattering, transferred her attention to a jointed wooden doll, some seven inches long, whose sole attire for the moment consisted in a neat crop of painted hair. If Dimple, in the care with which she was wrapping a scant bit of pink calico about the attenuated form, evinced a rudimentary sense of the value of raiment in a cold and critical world, we may be sure that she found nothing amiss in the painted hair. Who would not prefer it to the kind that got into horrid snarls and had to be combed and tweaked into order?

As the child immersed herself in maternal cares, the dean of the boarding-house, who was similarly engaged,—save that the small flannel petticoat she was cat-stitching would appear to be destined for alien offspring,— glanced from time to time, and with a grudging interest, at the little mother. No, a boarding-house was no place for a child; nor was it, superficially considered, the fitting place for a well-to-do daughter of the Pratts and Spencers. A stranger, learning of the eminent lineage of Arabella Spencer, might well have asked what untoward fate had brought her to this pass, though for the initiated the key to the riddle was not far to seek. "My grandfather built this house," she took pride in stating; "my father owned it, and my mother lived in it for upwards of fifty years." And, if in an expansive mood, she would add, "I myself was born in the room I now occupy." What wonder if, with such claims to precedence, she was early accorded the deanship?

It was one of her fellow boarders, the late Professor Calder, who had conferred upon her this titular dignity, and in nothing was her gratification at the amiable pleasantry more apparent than in the zeal with which, both before and after his death, she was ever ready to proclaim the profound erudition of the scholarly recluse. From youth up Arabella had been noted for a tenacious loyalty, and her friends were wont to point out that at the age of fifty she had yet to change either her name or her nature. She was to-day the same excellent, opinionated personage she had given evidence of being while yet in her cradle, and she was still Arabella Spencer.

Let it not be inferred, however, that she was therefore an old maid. That was an obloquy which no granddaughter of Old Lady Pratt had had the hardihood to incur. One or two, indeed, had postponed the fateful step almost to the danger limit; but before she went hence, that unswerving champion of the domestic hearth had the felicity of seeing the most recalcitrant of her children's daughters gathered into the blessed fold of matrimony.

Arabella, to be sure, had shown no signs of recalcitrancy, barring a preliminary revolt against the necessity which society imposes upon a woman of changing her name.

"Say what you please, grandmother," she had declared, with the easy finality of

youth,—it was the very day on which she had
signalized her entrance upon young-ladyhood
by the donning of an elaborate thread-lace
veil, becomingly festooned across the rim of
her poke-bonnet as she now tossed it back in
the interest of free speech. "Say what you
please, there is something *galling* about it.
As if it did n't matter what a woman's name
was!"

"Did n't matter!" quoth old Lady Pratt,
glancing shrewdly at the mutinous young
eyes, black, like her own, but as yet singularly
unlit of wisdom. "I should say it did matter.
Jest you wait and see."

"Then you did n't like giving up your own
name!" was Arabella's too hasty conclusion.

"Like it? Of course I liked it! And I
guess Kingsbury's full as genteel a name as
Spencer, too! But from the fust hour that
your grandfather—" A faint flush stained
the sound old cheek. "But there! Jest you
wait and see."

As often as Old Lady Pratt found herself
caught in any allusion to the romance of her
life, which the passage of years had been
impotent to dim, she would take refuge in the
little phrase, "But there!" It held a world
of meaning on her lips.

Now neither did Arabella have long to wait, nor was she ever constrained to "see," for by an incredible freak of fortune her very first suitor—and consequently her last— bore the cherished name of Spencer.

"I declare for 't," Old Lady Pratt exclaimed, when Harriet stepped over to acquaint her with her daughter's engagement, "ef 't wa'n't for soundin' irreverent, I should call it ill-judged of Providence to *humor* the girl so!"

"Well," Harriet rejoined, with uncompromising frankness, "I guess that 's as far 's the humoring can be said to extend. Joseph seems to be an unexceptionable young man, but I can't truthfully claim that he 's a commanding personality." It may be observed in passing that years of opulence had greatly enriched Harriet's vocabulary.

"I knew it," the old lady chuckled. "It was the name that fetched her!"

"Either that or the statistics," Harriet assented dryly, and with an ironic recognition of her prospective son-in-law's one distinguishing trait.

For although Joseph Spencer, a mediocre lawyer, and already at thirty middle-aged, was guiltless of any scientific apprehension of

statistics, he had the sort of mind that revels
in figures. In fact, it may be questioned
whether it would ever have occurred to him
to offer himself to Arabella, had she not
chanced, in an unguarded moment, to mention
the exact number of gallons that go to make
the annual water-supply of the city of Lon-
don,—an item which, as he very well knew,
she had gleaned that same evening from the
Dunbridge Weekly Chronicle. But, indeed,
what more could the most exacting have
demanded? The poor girl lacked the requisite
data for computing those gallons herself; and
Joseph, recognizing that fact, was joyfully
ready to accept the mere enunciation on her
lips of a sum mounting into eleven figures as
a revelation of the unsuspected scope of the
female intellect. From that hour he knew
that he had found his affinity.

And what if the determining factor in
Arabella's action had been an equally flimsy
one? What if Old Lady Pratt was right,
and it had been the name that "fetched her"?
Young people are subject to strange delusions
in this most critical of all adventures, and the
glamour of a name has played its part ere now
in many a more exalted alliance than poor
Arabella's. One thing at least may be as-

serted: that having once made her choice, and in perfect good faith, no shadow of regret was ever known to tinge her words or actions. She took her Joseph as she found him, and it is but fair to admit that she found him quite innocuous.

For, aside from the master-passion of his life, to which his wife soon became aware of playing a distinctly secondary rôle, young Spencer might have been fairly described as a negative character. And when, after some ten years more of assiduous figuring, he achieved the final and not unimpressive negation of a premature demise, Arabella, whose mourning partook of the tempered fervor which had formed the high-water mark of their marital relations, went home to the fine old house of her grandfather's erection, where she soon settled down into a very congenial life with her excellent mother. Matrimony had been to her little more than a period of stagnation, only fleetingly stirred by the coming, and, sad to say, the going, of an only child. For the little creature, twice a Spencer, had died on the day of its birth— too early, as intrusive sympathizers were informed, for her to have become deeply attached to it. Whether this cold-blooded

18

attitude was genuine, or assumed in self-defence, none could tell. Certain it is, however, that the dead level of her marriage, lacking as it did even the animating element of overt discord, had produced in her something akin to atrophy of the affections; so that her strong but limited nature had come to centre more and more upon names and places, to the exclusion of any vital human interest. Even the death of her mother, which, occurring before that vigorous dame had attained her eightieth year, threw them all off their reckoning, left the daughter quite mistress of her feelings; and it was not until the decree went forth in family council that the old house must go, that the iron entered into Arabella's soul.

In vain did they point out to her the deterioration of the immediate neighborhood which must soon render the place unavailable as a residence for any one with sufficient means to maintain it—in which category Arabella herself was unhappily not to be reckoned. She only knew that it was the old home, the home to which she was bound by every fibre of her being; and she fought, tooth and nail, against its profanation. But alas, she was to learn, as many a doughty conservative has done, that those primitive weapons are of small avail in a single-handed encounter with Progress. Before her eyes, and with her own enforced connivance, the sacrifice was accomplished, and the property delivered over to the spoilers, who made no secret of their intention of cutting up the superfluous land into house-lots. I think the most humiliating act of Arabella's life was the affixing of her signature to that iniquitous deed of sale.

For days following her overwhelming defeat, she shut herself up in the great lonely house,—where the very servants seemed like ghosts of the past,—wandering restlessly from room to room, sliding her hand along the cool mahogany stair-railing, turning with her foot, though it was midsummer, the circular brass "register" whose high polish she had always gloried in,—shedding veritable tears over the fragrant shelves of the linen-closet, so soon to be denuded of their housewifely store. As day by day she nursed her bitter grievance, it came to look as if she might never again be on amicable terms with her recreant kindred.

Happily for the cause of good feeling, however, she was spared the crowning indignity of actual dislodgment; for, even as she was on the verge of ejection, news reached her that the old homestead was to be turned into a boarding-house. The crisis was acute, and she wasted little time in pros and cons. None of her family, to be sure, had ever lived in a boarding-house; but the thought of their impending "disgruntlement," far from giving her pause, only lent a pleasing zest to the sacrifice she was resolved upon.

"Yes," she announced, with admirable nonchalance, "I have n't got to move out after all."

"Not move out?" echoed her brother Richard, who, having solicited an interview on a matter of business, had unwittingly exposed himself to the shock.

"No; I 'm going to board with Mrs. Wadley. I 've engaged mother's chamber."

The blow was delivered quietly, but with telling effect, and Richard did not attempt to conceal his discomfiture.

"You mean to say that you 've engaged to live in a boarding-house, without consulting any of the family?" he was so ill-advised as to ask.

"There was no one in the family to consult —of whose judgment I had any opinion," she asserted, yet with the unruffled calm of one conscious of having the situation well in hand.

"It 's not a matter of judgment," he declared testily. "It 's a matter of fact. In the first place, you 've got income enough to have a house of your own. Not anything like this, of course, but——"

"I am aware of the exact figure of my income, Richard."

"Then it 's going to be noisy and disagreeable here for a long time to come. There 'll be building going on, and——"

"I 'd rather have that in my ears than on my conscience," she interposed, with unmistakable point; and Richard, perceiving that she was in anything but a conciliatory mood, wisely desisted from further argument. He had a hot temper of his own, and he was not sure just how much of a drubbing he could take without hitting back. Moreover, he loved his sister and, if the truth were known, he found himself secretly applauding her spirit.

But all were not as tolerant as he, and for a short space the family was up in arms. Her eldest brother, James, after spending as much as fifteen consecutive minutes in an attempt to shake Arabella's determination, declared that he had no patience with her; only, as James had never been known to have patience with anybody, that did n't so much matter. Aunt Edna, the soldier uncle's widow, who had accepted too many benefits first and last at the hands of her rich sister-in-law to feel quite pleasantly toward the family, gave it as her opinion that you never could tell where one of Harriet's children would break out; while even Uncle Ben, that kindliest of wags, remarked with something bordering on asperity, that the girl might as well be a cat and done with it—to stay prowling round a house after the folks had moved out!

Only her younger sister, Lucy,—who had been blissfully in love with her architect husband since the day that he had entered into her heart by way of the Gothic tree-vistas of Elm Street,—only Lucy did justice to her sentiment about the house.

"Grandpa built it," Lucy would explain, with an artless sententiousness all her own. "A builder's work, you know, is really a part of himself; and Frank and I think it lovely of Arabella to feel as she does about it."

And Arabella, heeding neither cuffs nor kisses, stayed on in the ancestral mansion, undaunted by desolating changes within and without. The good Mrs. Wadley did her misguided best to vulgarize the stately interior, while the new owners lost no time in dividing up the half-dozen generous acres into small house-lots, to be promptly disfigured by a mushroom growth of cheap and tawdry dwellings. The terraced lawn in front was thus thrice encumbered, the sightly gardens at the rear were ruthlessly invaded and obliterated, and the old house itself stood crowded to suffocation among the interlopers, despoiled even of its last vestige of a driveway, and accessible only by a footpath leading from the side street. Within one short year, as calendar years are reckoned, during which Arabella had suffered untold scourgings of the spirit, the great desecration was accomplished.

It was now seven years since this befell, and even as the vandals had been powerless to budge the old house from its proud eminence upon the uppermost terrace, so Arabella, too, had held her own, and from being merely the self-appointed guardian of ancient dignities, had come to be recognized and deferred to as dean of the boarding-house. Hence it was that when she pronounced a boarding-house to be an unfit place for a child, no voice was raised to dispute her.

If, after that, conversation seemed inclined to languish, there was nothing unusual in the circumstance at this evening hour, the only hour of Arabella's day when it was her habit to "mingle" with her fellow boarders. There was a conclusiveness in the dean's dicta which not infrequently operated as a check on social intercourse.

Half-a-dozen ladies were gathered in what was once called "the long parlor," now sadly abbreviated by reason of a partition thrown across the middle, directly beyond the stately Corinthian pillars, which, thus robbed of their significance in the architectural scheme, made a not very impressive appearance. The little girl had established herself on the floor between the two front windows, just where one of the long pier-glasses used to rest on its marble slab, her straight little legs sticking out in front of her at an exact right angle with the small upright back; and Arabella seemed to remember that once upon a time, in fact at about the period when the pier-glasses were installed, she too had possessed the enviable faculty of maintaining that difficult position. She glanced furtively at the child, still immersed in sumptuary affairs; and presently, when general conversation had somewhat revived, she drew from her work-basket a roll of white galloon braid, and snipped off a half-yard of it.

"Little girl," she called abruptly, "you 'd better come and tie this round your doll to keep her clothes on."

Arabella's principles would not permit of her addressing any human being, of whatever degree of insignificance, as "Dimple," nor yet could she bring herself to use her mother's name of Harriet, which the child's sponsors were understood to have bestowed upon her. Harriet, indeed! this offspring of a flighty, inefficient mother, turned loose upon a boarding-house!

"She must be taught common decency," Arabella remarked to her next neighbor at the centre table; and Miss Tate, one of the dean's warmest adherents, earnestly endorsed the sentiment.

Meanwhile, the nameless one picked up her small person from the floor and approached the dispenser of toilet requisites with un-disguised interest. It was the first time the tall lady with the shiny breast-pin had ever spoken to her, though Dimple had often felt those observant eyes upon her. As the child put out a confiding hand for the proffered gift, Arabella hesitated an instant. How could that futile paw be expected to perform so intricate a feat as the tying of a bow-knot?

"Here, I'll fix it for you," she said, brusquely; and yet the movement was not ungentle with which she took the wisp of wood and cotton from the little hand and deftly executed the small task.

As she handed back the object of her solicitude thus reclaimed to decency, the child gave vent to her feelings in a gleeful hop and bleat as of a gratified lambkin, which was really far more expressive than any conventional acknowledgment would have been. But Miss Tate, intoxicated by Arabella's condescension of a moment ago, needs must become didactic.

"What have you got to say to the kind lady?" she put in, and thereby blundered badly. For Arabella prided herself upon never "looking for thanks."

Nor were matters at all improved when Dimple, poking her jointed darling under the very nose of the lady with the shiny pin, lisped, "Kith Dolly!"

"Nonsense, child," Arabella protested,

Arabella

" Kith Dolly ! "

really abashed by the suggestion, and pushing the preposterous manikin away.

But, "Kith Dolly! Kith Dolly!" the little thing persisted, while Arabella firmly resumed work on the flannel petticoat. Upon which, unable to control her wounded feelings, that absurd infant set up a most heart-rending wail, to which doleful accompaniment two incredibly large tears came welling up in the round blue eyes, and spilling over on the round pink cheeks.

This was really too much, and the dean of the boarding-house was on the point of adopting repressive measures, when again Miss Tate blundered.

"You are a very naughty girl, Harriet!" she expostulated severely.

Arabella took instant umbrage. She scarce knew which was more to be resented, the use of that honored name in accents of reproof, or the meddling of an inexperienced spinster in a matter so plainly outside her province. For suddenly, and with a queer, exultant thrill, Arabella remembered that she had once been a mother. After all,—poor Miss Tate!—how could she be expected to understand a child?

"She does n't mean to be naughty," the

dean of the boarding-house pleaded, with a
pitying tolerance for the too zealous martinet;
and there, before them all, she took the dolly
in her hand and unblushingly kissed it.

Upon which the child, in an ecstasy at
having got her own way, proceeded to push
her advantage still further, and lifting her
little face, "Kith Dimple!" she commanded.

Then Arabella bent her head, intending to
administer a noncommittal peck, such as she
kept about her for the little Pratts and
Spencers that abounded in the family. But
as her lips touched the soft cheek a quick
pang seized her, and there awoke in her heart
something that had slumbered there for nigh
upon thirty years,—something that she had
supposed dead and buried long ago. And
again a strange thought crossed her mind,—
that if her own baby had lived it might have
had a child like this. Not a very wonderful
thought, perhaps, but it gripped, and Arabella
was not used to that sort of thing.

Shaken out of her habitual composure, she
hastily gathered up her work and prepared to
leave the room, quite ten minutes in advance
of the accustomed hour.

"Run and play, little girl," she admonished, with a crisp decision curiously at vari-

ance with the disconcerting thrill that possessed her; and the child, content with the victory she had so lightly scored, trotted back to her post between the windows.

When Arabella, bidding the ladies good-night, had made a dignified exit, there was an immediate outbreak of comment.

"Well," snapped Mrs. Edgecomb, as soon as the rustle of skirts had ceased on the stairs, "I should like to know who's spoiling that child now!"

"I confess that I was glad to see Mrs. Spencer unbend," Mrs. Treadwell admitted, in her comfortable way. "She's as good a woman as ever lived, but I must say she's always seemed to me just a little mite stiff."

"She's never stiff with me," Miss Tate intimated, with a fatuous simper. "But then, I suppose I'm on more confidential terms with her than some."

"Eh? What's that? Confidential terms?" piped up old Mrs. Inkley, in her rasping falsetto. "There wa'n't never anybody on confidential terms with Arabella Spencer. I've known that girl sence before she was born, 'n' she's close-mouthed as her own bed-post!"

"She's open-handed enough, anyway,"

Miss Tate temporized, discreetly changing her tack. For Arabella's liberality was matter of common knowledge which even a pre-natal authority could not well gainsay.

"I do wish our dear dean might get to taking an interest in that child," kind Mrs. Treadwell purred. "The mother seems to be well-meaning enough, but——"

"What is it she's 'round after so much?" asked Della Robin, who liked to know things.

"I should say she was 'round after Ed Lambert, far as I can judge," Mrs. Edgecomb opined. "She's forever buggy-riding with that fellow, or going to Comic Opera with him, the way she's done to-night, when she'd better have stayed at home, putting her baby to bed."

"They say young Lambert's going on the stage," Miss Tate ventured, taking heart of grace to re-enter the conversation.

"There ain't no stages nowadays," rasped old Mrs. Inkley, who never seemed to hear anything unless there was a chance to contradict, the which she had a fatal propensity for discovering in Miss Tate's most harmless statements.

"She means the operatic stage," Mrs. Treadwell interposed soothingly. "He's got a real good voice, you know. His father sang in the Orthodox choir."

"How long has she been a widow?" queried Della Robin, once more yielding to a fitful thirst for information.

"A year and a half. And it leaves her soul-alone in the world; for her folks are all dead, and, as far as I can make out, he never had any from the beginning."

"What did he die of?" Mrs. Edgecomb demanded, in the tone of a Pinkerton detective, who will brook no evasion.

"Why, he was in the sardine business, and she says he was lost on a down-east freighter, off the coast of New Brunswick."

"I hope he was," was Miss Tate's somewhat startling comment. "That is, I hope she is n't mistaken, or rather,—I was only thinking,—supposing she was to marry again, you know, like Enoch Arden's widow,—only she was n't a widow, either, was she!" and, hopelessly entangled in a wordy web of her own contrivance, Miss Tate fell abruptly silent.

"Well, no!" Mrs. Treadwell laughingly agreed. "I should say she was rather particularly *not* a widow!" And the conversation, having thus strayed into the higher realms of literature, became so much less animated that the more studiously inclined found themselves free to return to their evening papers.

And all this time the "little girl" was prattling innocently with her dolly, paying no heed whatever to the discussion of her parents, which, truth to tell, was couched in terms far transcending her comprehension.

Arabella, meanwhile, arrived in "mother's chamber," lighted her drop-light, which glowed softly through the porcelain transparency of its pretty, six-sided shade, and, seating herself in her favorite chair by the table, breathed a sigh of satisfaction. Here at last she was on her own ground, safe from intruding fancies. She glanced about the fine old room, where each piece of furniture stood in its accustomed place as in her mother's day, and her eye was caught by a small mahogany armchair over there by the fireplace. A capital little chair it was, of excellent design and workmanship, and boasting a seat-covering embroidered in cross-stitch.

As she picked up her sewing, on which she had been somewhat hindered by the little incident of the galloon braid, she found herself thinking how she used to enjoy sitting in that little chair, until it grew too snug a fit.

The seat-covering represented a pair of picka-ninnies, one of them playing the accordion, the other cocking an appreciative ear to listen. It had been some time before she could bring herself to do them the discourtesy of sitting down on them; but later, when she found that they never seemed to mind, she had come to the sapient conclusion that little black boys in cross-stitch were not so sensitive as the other kind. Funny little boys! They had n't changed a bit in all these years.

The flannel petticoat, on which she was making excellent progress, was not so en-grossing but that her mind was free to roam.

It seemed as if almost any child might like to sit in a chair like that, she thought; why not that little girl down-stairs, whose doll —really, the creature must not be allowed to go naked any longer! And, at this point in her meditiations, Arabella laid her work down, and, rising, made a bee-line for the piece-bag which hung on its hook in her dressing-room. Ah, here was just what she wanted,—a bit of flowered silk, reminiscent, but cheerfully so, of her girlhood.

Squandering no time on those sentimental considerations which cluster so thickly about a piece-bag, she put back the other neat rolls

19

of silk, and, with an intensely practical air, returned to her seat beside the drop-light. Here she picked up her scissors and began cutting up the dainty remnant into breadths and biases, by the side of which the baby's petticoat, victim again of unmerited neglect, looked for all the world like a Brobdingnagian garment. Eagerly she twisted and turned the morsel of silk, nimbly she plied her needle, fashioning a marvellous little frock such as only a seven-inch pygmy could make use of. And such were the exactions of her task that the mantel-clock had quietly but firmly mentioned the hour of ten before ever she found leisure to straighten her back.

As she subjected her completed handiwork to a searching scrutiny, which, however, brought no flaw to light, "Mother always said I was a capable needlewoman," she told herself. But that was disingenuous of Arabella, for she well knew that her mother's approbation was not what she was just then aiming to deserve.

And when, the next afternoon, the small chair was once more in commission, its little occupant rapturously engaged in arraying Dolly in the fairy frock, Arabella sat tranquilly hemming the Brobdingnagian petticoat

as if she had no other interest in life. She
believed in letting children alone, and nothing had so pleased her in the behavior of her
little beneficiary as the matter-of-course way
in which she had received the fairy offering.
Indeed, if the truth were known, it had
seemed to the child quite as natural to accept
gifts at the hands of the lady with the shiny
pin who had kissed Dolly, as at the hands of
the mother who kissed Dimple herself when
she happened to think of it, which was getting
to be less and less often.

For Dimple's mother, as may have been
inferred, was allowing herself to be a good
deal monopolized by that same Ed Lambert,
who, though not a stage-driver, was a famous
whip. She was a pleasure-loving creature,
and she never wearied of driving, in what
she regarded as the height of "style," behind
the smart trotter that Ed handled so well.
The young man's tongue was a valiant one,
too, and his bold, masterful eyes were more
eloquent still, and—well, he was quite de-
liciously in love with Dimple's mother. He
was going "on the road" in February, with
a Gilbert and Sullivan opera company,—he
had secured an engagement to sing a minor
part in *Pinafore*, which was sure to lead to

something better,—and he was ardently in-
sistent that she should marry him and come
along too. Only, there was Dimple, quite
another order of pinafore,—an operetta of
the little widow's own, in fact,—and one that
somehow did not seem to fit into the programme at all. And so Dimple's mother
felt it her duty to seize upon every opportunity of telling Ed how she adored Dimple,
and of how she could never take any step to
the detriment of the child; and this obliged
her to spend so many hours a day in his
society that Dimple found herself reduced
to very low rations in the matter of kisses.

Meanwhile, Dimple's own little affair was
progressing quite as trippingly as her mother's,
as indeed it deserved to do. When she was
not playing out-of-doors (such a poor little
contracted "out-of-doors" as the old place
now afforded!), she was like as not to be
found in Mis' Pensey's room,—her own
attractive corruption of an august cognomen!
And not only had she achieved a new and
engaging title for Arabella, but she herself
was no longer put off with the far too generic
appellation of "little girl."

It came about in this wise. She was taking
a walk with Mis' Pensey one day in late

October,—an unusual indulgence, since Arabella was a bit shy of being seen abroad in compromising company,—and, as they were traversing the quiet thoroughfare of Green Street, the child gave one of her bird-like chirps, articulate in this instance as "Pitty house!" Whereupon Arabella, glancing up, beheld a turkey-red curtain fluttering at an open window, and became aware that it was Old Lady Pratt's house that had been thus singled out for commendation. She stayed her step a moment. It did look pretty, the tidy old house with its fresh white paint and green blinds, its neat grass-plot and the garden-beds bordering the walk. It had been in good hands since it went out of the family, faring far better than her own home had done, and now it was again placarded, "For sale." Who would buy it, she wondered,—this house, also of her grandfather's construction, where her forbears had lived and died. She was glad to hear it called a pretty house, though she knew well that it was the gay curtains that had caught the baby fancy.

As they resumed their walk, "Pitty house!" the child insisted, with the cheerful reiteration whereby she had learned to compel assent; and Arabella, looking down at the little thing, trudging along so contentedly at her side, answered gently, "Yes, it is a pretty house, *Harriet!*" The thing was done so casually that the child paid no special heed, though from that hour she answered to the name. But to Arabella it marked the lowering of an irksome barrier which she had not quite known how to cross.

Yet all this time,—and time was travelling fast,—while one after another her defences were going down before the soft assaults of her ingenuous little adversary, Arabella was far from admitting to herself the true measure of her subjugation. She was getting rather fond of the child, no doubt; and she certainly was as little trouble as a child could well be. But even if she had been troublesome, it was no more than right that somebody should take an interest in her, poor little thing! She thought it might be well to teach her her letters—there seemed to be no likelihood of any one else doing so. She wondered whether she could lay her hand on the primer out of which she had learned her own. She was to take tea with Frank and Lucy that evening, and it happened that Lucy was storing a box of her books that ought to contain it. She would go over early and see about it.

It had got to be midwinter by this time, and all the world was on runners,—the snow beaten down to a solid crust which nothing short of a February thaw would loosen. Arabella, walking home from Lucy's at about nine o'clock, escorted by her architect brother-in-law, thought how exhilarating the frosty air was, and the gay jingle of the sleigh-bells, and the moonlight glittering on the snow; and it never once occurred to her to trace her good spirits to the well-thumbed primer that she held in her hand.

They stood a moment at the front door while she got out her latch-key. The half-grown moon which was dipping into the west shone in under the piazza-roof, striking full upon the lower panel of the door; and as Frank took the key from her hand, with his little air of gallantry,—a foreign importation which she had never got quite used to,—"I don't wonder you stuck to the old house, Arabella," he remarked. "That's the finest front-door in Dunbridge."

Such a tribute would ordinarily have been deeply gratifying to her, but she was thinking of something else just then.

"Yes," she assented, rather abstractedly, while she pulled off her gloves, and noticed

how smooth the cover of the primer was
worn. "It's a very good door, but it wants
painting." And with that she bade him
good-night and passed into the house.

Almost on the threshold the news met
her: there had been an accident on the Mill-
dam—a runaway sleigh coming up behind.
She had been in young Lambert's cutter.
There was no time to turn out. The pole
had struck her in the back.

Was she much hurt?

Oh, worse than that. It was all over an
hour ago. Ed Lambert was beside himself,
poor fellow; but he was not in any way
to blame. They had brought her in at
about six o'clock. She had never recovered
consciousness.

And the child? Where was the child?

"We've moved her little bed into your
dressing-room," Mrs. Wadley explained. "We
thought she'd sleep quieter there than if
I'd took her in along o' me, as I'd ha' been
glad to. I hope she won't make you too
much trouble. She must ha' been asleep
when I come away a few minutes ago. She
did n't say nothing."

But Arabella had passed swiftly up the
stairs, and had opened her door, very, very

softly,—only that her heart was beating so loud that she trembled lest it should wake the child.

She had closed the door behind her, and was cautiously making her way across the room, when a wee, remote voice from over by the chimney-corner arrested her. Turning sharply, she beheld a strange and seizing apparition. There, in her accustomed place in the little armchair, just in the path of the moonlight, sat a small white wraith, shivering a bit—for the thin cotton shift was never meant for such service—waiting for Mis' Pensey.

"Mumma's deaded," the wee voice whimpered. "Mumma's deaded."

In an instant Arabella had her in her arms, and was folding her in the long, fur-lined cloak she herself wore.

"You precious baby!" she murmured brokenly, as she bore the pitiful little mourner across the room and, seating herself in her own mother's high-backed invalid-chair, essayed to comfort her. "You precious baby!"

But, "Mumma's deaded," the little thing grieved. "Poor Mumma!"

"Yes, darling, yes. But it does n't hurt

to be deaded.   It means just going fast asleep
like little girls do, in their soft, warm beds."
And she wrapped her ever closer, tucking the
cold little toes deep into the good warm fur.

Was it some dim, fleeting hint of the Great
Mystery that had penetrated to the baby
intelligence?   Or why then did the soft fur
fail to console?

"Dimple feel bad," the wee voice sobbed.
"Dimple feel bad!"

"There, there, Dimple!"   It was the first
time that name had ever passed those
fastidious lips; but so much was due the
"deaded" mother in that hour.   "Don't
cry! She must n't cry! Mis' Pensey 'll take
care of her to-night."

And crooning meaningless words of tender
baby-talk, she held the child close and warm
until it slept.   Then, as the clinging form
relaxed, and the catching sobs were hushed,
she fell to pondering the strange wind of destiny that had driven the little waif to her
sheltering arms.   And she no more questioned its meaning than she would have
questioned had it been her own baby, or her
baby's baby, nestling there in utter helpless-
ness, like a spent dove—spent and affrighted
in the rude buffetings of its little gust of grief.

And when the child, sleeping fast, was safely tucked away in its white bed, Arabella drew up a chair and placed herself on guard beside her precious charge. Hour by hour she sat, erect and motionless, prolonging her vigil deep into the night. Now and again her thoughts would turn to the young mother, from whom she had always held herself sternly aloof, coldly disapproving; and with a sorrowful compunction she would recall certain appealing traits, scarcely noted at the time. A quick, upward glance of the eyes, a ceaseless, ineffectual play of the fingers. There had been an odd trick of ending each phrase with a rising inflection, as if craving assent to a tentative statement,—an air of indecision, as of a rudderless cockle-shell adrift on the waters of volition. Arabella, who held fast to the doctrine of non-interference, did not even now believe that it had been in her power to steady that frail bark on its wavering course, but she found herself remorsefully wishing that she had been just a trifle friendly with the foolish young thing. And there, in the midnight quiet, she entered into a solemn compact with herself never to let the little one forget her mother; to cherish every gossamer thread of memory in the baby consciousness till, striking root in that sweet soil, it should flower into a fair and sacred image.

Sitting thus, drawn in upon herself, Arabella had not noticed how cold the room was growing, till suddenly a sharp chill struck her, and she rose to fetch the cloak that she had laid aside. The movement changed the direction of her thoughts, restored her to her normal mood of practical efficiency. As she returned to her post, and, stooping, drew the coverlid more closely about the softly breathing form, her mind reverted with a thrill of pleasure to the little house in Green Street. What a pretty home it would make for the child—the old house, with its funny nooks and crannies, its queer stair-landings, and the gay turkey-red curtains which it should be her very first concern to provide. What a pretty grass-plot for a child to play about in; and the garden-beds!—there should be a special corner for her to dig in, and they would have plenty of the double daisies, pink ones and white, that were always in such a hurry to blossom.

And the old home? The home to which she had clung with such fierce pertinacity all these years? As the dawn quickened in the little room, Arabella looked through the doorway into the great chamber beyond, thoughtfully considering each familiar feature of the dignified interior. What was it, after all, but a contrivance of wood and plaster that had served its turn, and would serve its turn again, for other occupants? For herself, the eloquence of material association had grown strangely dumb; the dead past, in so far as it was dead, had lost its magic. And as she leaned above the child, listening to its quiet breathing, as she gently touched the little cheek, soft and humid with the sweet warmth of sleep, she knew that it was not for the sake of her own baby, nor of the baby that might have been, that she was to gather this little creature to her heart of hearts, but for love of the child itself.

And a few weeks later, when all legal formalities had been consummated,—when the house in Green Street was hers, and the child was hers, beyond peradventure,—then, and not till then, did she apprise.her astonished family of her new departure, meeting remonstrances and congratulations alike with the initial argument, which to her thinking covered all possible ground for criticism: "A boarding-house is no place for a child."

And when the flurry of comment was safely weathered, there came a quiet evening, in the calm of which she could contemplate with just the right degree of wistful regret the dear old chamber so soon to be abandoned to strangers.

The child was playing about the room, making the most of the few minutes remaining before the inexorable bed-hour,—indulging Dolly, too, in one last gambol. Suddenly she glanced over at Arabella, whose thoughtfulness may well have taken on a semblance of melancholy. Laying Dolly down in the little chair, the child stood a moment, gravely studying this new aspect of her beloved friend. Then, very quietly, she drew near, and, with a quaint movement of sympathy, laid her little hand on Mis' Pensey's knee.

Touched by the gravity of the little woman, Arabella lifted her to her lap, and for the first time, and with the solemnity of a baptismal rite, accosted her as: "Little Harriet Spencer."

Whereupon that incalculable infant, airily brushing aside the momentous ceremony, looked straight up into Mis' Pensey's face, and, with adorable perversity, lisped: "Kith Dimple!"

And Arabella, baffled and disarmed by the sheer audacity of the little sprite,—beguiled too by a love surpassing the love of names and places,—bent that obdurate neck of hers, and meekly did the bidding of the child.

IX.

THE DANDER OF SUSAN.

SUSAN LEGGETT was sound as a nut at sixty. Not that sixty is any age at all, so far as that goes. Susan's grandmother, Old Lady Pratt, of delectable memory, would have called it the edge of the evening. But it was something, even at sixty, never to have an ache or a pain, and to be able to read the Dunbridge *Weekly Chronicle* without glasses. To be sure, one knew pretty well beforehand what was in the *Chronicle*, so that was no great feat; especially as they had n't begun printing with mouse-colored ink at that period.

Susan's detractors said that the reason she kept so young was that she was always having the entertainment of making other people lose their tempers without ever losing her own. But her partisans, who were greatly in the majority, averred that she never said sharp things behind a person's back, as indeed, where would have been the fun? For Susan was essentially dramatic. She loved setting character in play; it was like throwing a stick to a terrier.

Her husband, the Professor of Christian Ethics, had resigned his chair seven or eight years ago, because he imagined himself an invalid. Susan, having come into her share of the Spencer property at about that time, and being anxious to get back among her own folks in Dunbridge, had readily fallen in with this notion, though once the move was made, she stoutly denied that there was anything whatever the matter with him; which might have been disconcerting to the professor, only that he was used to Susan. He admired his wife immensely, and thought that she had a remarkable mind.

Of all the advantages attaching to her change of residence, none was more highly prized than the frequent opportunity of treating her brother James to the unvarnished truth, and then using her fine mind in an effort to discover what could have disturbed him. Susan was by no means devoid of tact; but, like her "real thread" lace, she did not wear it "common."

20

She was calling at her brother's one day, when Nannie, her sister-in-law, pleading a headache, excused herself and left the room. James and Susan were invigorating personalities, but taken together they sometimes formed rather too powerful an astringent for a sensitive organism like Nannie's. Her defection was viewed with pitying tolerance by Susan, who did not however feel called upon to exercise a like indulgence toward her eminently robust brother.

"You know, James," she remarked, with unflinching sincerity, "it's all your fault, as I've told you time and again, Nannie's being such an invalid. First you don't let her lift a finger for fear she'll tire herself, which is enough to make a gibbering idiot of any woman; and then you keep her nerves on edge by blowing out at her every five minutes about nothing."

"Blowing out at her?" was the indignant protest. "I never blow out at her! Never blow out at anybody!"

"There, there, James; don't get all wrought up, just as I'm leaving you." And, as she rose to go, "How's Benny doing now?"

"How's *Ranny* doing now?" James retorted viciously. For Ranny was Susan's only child, and there were rumors about Ranny.

These had not reached Susan, however; so she was able to reply with telling emphasis, "Oh, Ranny has never given us a moment's anxiety," and to leave the room with her head in the air. Susan was a short woman, not to say stout, but at mention of Ranny's name she had the faculty of holding her head so high that one involuntarily looked for stilts.

James meanwhile kept his seat, a smouldering eye upon the departing chignon, which was quite as provocative in its way as the ringlets of yore. He and Susan had been near enough of an age for fraternal amenities; and as often as not, when she referred to the golden days of childhood, as she occasionally did, being of a sentimental turn, this was the picture that arose in his memory: a small boy in a sputtering rage, and a startled little girl, a size or two smaller, with a deservedly rumpled head-piece.

"How 's Ranny doing now!" she repeated, as she turned her steps homeward. "I declare, there 's no lengths James won't go when he 's out of temper. How 's Ranny doing, indeed!" While as for Benny,—

well, she certainly hoped he would not commit any more excesses, though if he did, she was too good an aunt not to wish to know all about it.

But what did James mean about Ranny? That was really what was gnawing at her consciousness all the time that she was simulating concern for Benny. What did James mean by that peculiar echo of her own significant inquiry?

The cousins were not far apart in years, but they had never had much in common. How should Ranny have much in common with a boy who was known to be dissipated? —a word which Susan spelled in italics, but pronounced *sotto voce*. Her Ranny, her only child, upon whom every care had been lavished that Christian Ethics could devise or parental devotion bestow. She did not believe he had ever had a glass too much in his life; and as for cards, he hated the sight of them,—would n't even take a hand at euchre in the family circle. While Benny, poor boy, the youngest of nine,—of course his mother had had neither time nor strength to bring him up carefully. Really, a large family was a great mistake.

There had been a time when, if Susan had

not been at bottom a thoroughly amiable woman, she would have hated her sister-in-law, whose babies used to come along so regularly that they might have been made a feature of the Old Farmer's Almanac; while she, Susan, had waited nearly fifteen years for Ranny. When the boy did arrive he was but a puling infant,—and our forbears knew what that queer little word meant, if we don't. It was thought in the family that the name, Randidge Leggett, Junior, which was instantly clapped upon him, might have proved something of a facer for so young a child. But that was soon mended. For when, at a tender age, he was brought to Dunbridge and solemnly introduced to all the magi and magesses of the clan, Old Lady Pratt, without a moment's hesitation, addressed him as "Ranny." Upon which he was said to have ceased puling and chirked right up.

To-day, when Susan arrived at home, she found the professor mousing among his papers in an aimless way that was growing upon him, now that he was out of a job. He glanced up at his wife as she entered, and willingly relaxed his efforts. It always did him good to see Susan come in. She was so brisk and hearty and wholesome. When she fretted because she was not tall and stately, like her sister Arabella (which she frequently did, merely for the pleasure of drawing him out), he would assure her that long-necked women were formed for poets to write verses about,—though the careless fellows sometimes neglected to do so,—while the roley-poley kind were made to be loved. Was it any wonder that Susan accounted her husband a profound thinker?

"Well, my dear," he inquired, "been cheering up your neighbors?"

She came over and dropped a kiss on the top of his head before replying. It had been her habit from time immemorial. Perhaps that was why she was the only person who seemed not to have observed that he was beginning to grow bald. As the professor would have put it, "The attrition of a frequently repeated process tends to blunt the perceptions." He used such erudite phrases in conversation with his wife, for, whether she understood them or not, she might always be depended upon to think that she did.

As she performed the customary rite, he got hold of her gloved hand and called her "my love." This he invariably did when he pressed her hand. Nor was he conscious in so doing of any attrition of the faculties.

"I 've been to see Nannie," she announced, sitting down on the other side of the big study desk, and drawing off her gloves. "James was in a shocking temper. What do you suppose he asked me?"

"I 'm sure I can't imagine."

"He asked me how Ranny was doing! Now, professor, what do you suppose he was driving at?"

"Perhaps he had heard of Ranny's promotion."

"Ranny's promotion? What do you mean?"

"Why, Ranny has just been in to tell us. He says they 've moved him up a notch, and,"—he eyed her apprehensively,—"he asked me to tell you, so I have to, my dear, —he may have to go west."

"Never!" cried Susan, springing to her feet. "Never! He shall throw the whole thing over before he goes west."

"I was afraid you might feel that way. Of course we should miss Ranny."

"Miss him? Why, I would n't have him go west to be President of the United States!"

"He would n't have to," the professor interpolated.

"Go west? Go west? Where is the boy?"

"He said he should n't be in again until after we had gone to bed."

"He 'll be in before *I* 've gone to bed. You may rest assured of that! Why, Randidge—" and she stopped, with a little gasp,—"do you suppose he was *afraid* to talk to me about it?"

"Well, my dear, you *are* pretty decided in your views, and—Ranny appears to be pretty decided himself in this instance. In fact, it struck me,"—and the professor began blinking through his glasses in a way he had when his brain was under its own steam, rather than towing in the wake of a brother savant, —"it struck me that he was rather particularly pleased with this opening,—for every reason."

But Susan, in hot pursuit of her own thought, missed the implication.

"There 's no need of his staying with the Stickman Company at all, if they put such conditions on his promotion." She had sat down again, and it was evident to the professor that she was about to use her remarkable mind. "Any one of his uncles could

give him a new start; James might certainly think of something,—though I don't
know that I could ever bring myself to ask
a favor of him, after the way he spoke of
Ranny just now."

"But, my dear," the professor interposed,
with pained insistence, "I was about to say
that what the boy seems to want is to—"
he hesitated, but there was no help for it,—
"to get away."

"Randidge!"

As Susan spoke the word that was the
Alpha and Omega of all she loved, she sank
back in her chair, incapable of further
speech,—and the professor knew what that
meant. Ranny, her Omega, wanted to get
away. To get away from home, from his
father, from his mother,—to get away!
Their only child, that they had waited for so
long! Their one chicken! No, it was too
much! And Susan, the brisk, the cheerful,
the hearty, broke completely down.

Then the professor got on his feet and
came over to her and, perhaps with a vague
reminiscence of past favors, essayed to kiss
the top of *her* head. But his glasses were
dangling on the string, and he found himself so suddenly confronted with a bunch of

apocryphal roses, that he was obliged to content himself with patting her shoulder and saying, "There, there!" which did just as well.

Then Susan looked up through her tears. "*You* won't desert me," she implored, clutching blindly at the sheet-anchor that had never failed her yet.

"Desert you?" he protested. "Desert you!"

And, as was ever the case in moments of conjugal fervor, his brain was fired with the familiar fiction that he had never loved another, and he found himself impelled as by automatic action to murmur something to that effect. What matter if there lived one or two elderly ladies who could have told a different tale? What mattered they, since they were clean forgotten! And so he comforted Susan, and cheered himself, with that immediate and unstinting devotion which is so much better than historic accuracy.

But when bedtime came and no Ranny, she would not let him share her vigil, but sent him off, in the well-founded assurance that, being an avowedly light sleeper, he was safe not to be disturbed by any echoes of the battle-royal for which she was preparing.

And when the house was quiet, Susan sat down on the top stair and waited. She could not have told why she chose just that conspicuous and uncomfortable situation, unless with some far-reaching strategical design. But there she sat, full-panoplied for the fray. And yet, while she knew that there was a struggle before her, she felt in no combative mood. Rather was she singularly open to gentle influences. That was because she was thinking of her boy, which always made her heart soft. And indeed, for all her martial aspect, never was there a heart more prompt to soften than Susan's own.

She had turned down the gas in the upper passage-way, leaving the entry below brightly lighted as usual. The house was still warm, in spite of a bleak November wind outside, for the professor had but just banked down the furnace. Pleasant odors of geranium and heliotrope came floating up from the wire stand in the dining-room, while the ticking of a placid old clock, taking quiet note of the passing seconds, swelled to the slow stroke of eleven. The sense of home was very strong. Surely Ranny could never hold out against it. He would only

have to look and listen—and smell—to feel
that here was where he belonged.

Good boy! It was as Susan had assured
her brother; he had never given them a
moment's anxiety. She had often said that
if she had had a dozen children she could
not have loved the lot of them as she loved
Ranny. He was so exactly what she would
have wished him to be,—though there was
no denying that she had been compelled to
revise her specifications from time to time.
She had fancied, for instance, that she
wanted him to grow up tall, and of imposing
carriage; but when he turned out short and
stocky she saw that it gave him a singularly
manly, trustworthy air. She had imagined
that he would inherit his father's scholarly
tastes; but when he begged off from college
and chose a business career, Susan was the
first to declare that that was the thing for a
man in a big growing country like this. And
even when he developed a marked obstinacy
of disposition,—Susan called it strength of
will,—she perceived how much it was to the
advantage of a man to know his own mind.
From the beginning she had accepted Ranny
as the Lord made him, concerned only to
perform aright her supplementary task of

keeping his manners and morals straight; for, despite her cheerful commentary on the surface foibles of her kind, Susan had a fundamental respect for inherent character and tendencies. Here, however, in this present crisis, was no question of such weighty matters. This deplorable caprice of Ranny's,—it was, it must be, fruit of some light impulse, lightly to be checked.

As the placid clock ticked off second after second, she told herself that she was really taking things too seriously. Ranny had no doubt felt flattered by the promotion, and for once his excellent judgment had been at fault. But as for his going west,—going west! And at the fatally reiterative phrase Susan clasped her hands together until the knuckles showed white. She would yield in everything else, but not here. On that path she felt herself a very rock of resistance. It seemed to her that no locomotive ever built could get past her if it were bearing Ranny away. She had a grotesque vision of the whole westward-bound traffic blocked by her stout person, immovable, indestructible, in its adamantine purpose.

The clock struck twelve; he must soon be here. And a sudden craving for the sight of him stirred her to impatience. Ah there he was! How often had it happened that he came just when she most wanted him! And she held her breath as the latch-key turned in the lock, the big door opened, and Ranny stepped inside, a short, close-knit figure, shutting the door and making it fast with a quiet decision of movement not suggestive of a pliable disposition.

As the young man turned to put out the gas, the light struck full on his face, and Susan's nerves, strained already to severe tension, vibrated to the shock. The boy's usually self-contained countenance was alive and alight as she had never seen it, not even in those rare moments of expansion which only his mother had shared. What could it mean, this look of exaltation, of strong emotional up-lift? She rose to her feet, prepared to take his secret by storm.

At sound of the movement he glanced up and saw his mother standing there; and swiftly, as in conscious self-defence, he turned out the gas. But not so quickly but that she had seen his face fall. A sickening reaction lamed her will. He had come in with the look of a young conqueror, and at sight of his mother his face had changed.

The mask of darkness that fell as the light went out had been no more effectual than that which his will had summoned at the same moment, against his mother.

"Why, mother," he exclaimed, "you up? Anything wrong?"

Then Susan descended the staircase, leaning heavily on the balustrade, and coming up to him said, "No, Ranny. There's nothing wrong. I only thought I should like to kiss you good-night."

"Dear little mother! How nice of you!"

But though he kissed her, dutifully enough, his words had not the true ring.

And so ended Susan's first engagement with the enemy that she could not see, that she could not locate, of which her very scouts were afraid. And worsted for the moment, not by the errant son outside there in a hostile world, but by the mother in the innermost depths of her, she crept to her bed and passed a sleepless night.

But not for nothing had Susan husbanded her reserve fund of tact for great occasions, and never did it stand her in better stead than in the watches of that sleepless night, from which she arose with her plan of campaign distinctly mapped out.

Stepping to the front door with Ranny after breakfast, as was her daily custom, she said quietly, "You'll not decide anything hastily, will you, Ranny?"

"No, mother," he answered, surprised and touched by her forbearance.

"Just when would it be if you go?"

"Not before January."

"Oh well," was the cheerful rejoinder, "that's a long way off!"

And upon that she gave him quite the same kind of kiss as usual; while the professor, witnessing the little scene from his seat at the breakfast-table, fell to winking his eyes and assiduously wiping his glasses.

But to-day Susan had no time for the indulgence of emotion, and no sooner had she got the ordering of her household off her hands than she made a bee-line for James's store. She found him in his private sanctum, running through his mail, and, had she but guessed it, confidently anticipating her visit. For brother and sister had exchanged too many home truths first and last, not to be on terms of excellent understanding.

"Now, James," she began, without preamble, and planting herself at his elbow, "out with it. What did you mean by asking how Ranny was doing now?"

"Mean?" he repeated, beginning to sharpen a pencil, and breaking off the point. "Why, I was only hitting back."

"Then you *were* hitting back. I thought so. Now—what do you know about Ranny?"

"Mainly what his mother has told me," he answered, protruding his lips in sign of craft and deliberation.

"Come, James, don't prevaricate. You meant something."

But James seemed quite absorbed in his whittling.

"Do you know anything about Ranny that I don't?" she demanded.

"How should I know what you know?" His penknife was toying perilously with the attenuated point it had achieved. To relax his attention meant disaster.

"James!" The supplicating mono-syllable struck home.

"Well, Susan," he admitted, with a shrug, "since you insist. It's something that pretty much everybody seems to have got wind of, except you and Ran."

Her hands were so tight-clasped by this,

21

that one of the fingers of her glove split
down the seam.

"Do you think that is right?" she asked
quietly.

"No," cried James, tossing the pencil
to one side, regardless of the point, "I 'm
blessed if I do!"

"Then, for pity's sake, tell me!"

He was looking out at the neighboring
chimney-pots.

"It 's a girl," he answered.

"A girl?   Good heavens, James!   But
Ranny 's nothing but a boy!"

"That won't help you any."

"But he 's too young."

"Stuff, Susan. He 's older than I was
when I got married. We did n't think it
young then."

"Who is she?   Do I know her?"   Her
voice was grown monotonous.

"You would n't be likely to."

"Is she—respectable?"

"I guess so."

"Guess so?   James!"

"She 's a working girl. They 're usually
respectable."

"What does she do?"

"Waits on table in an ice-cream saloon."

But Susan never flinched.

"Where?" she asked, in the same dull, level tone.

"On Marlowe Street, next the theatre."

"Do you know her name?"

"Not all of it. They call her Biddy."

And still she kept a steady front.

"How did you find out about it?" she asked.

"Well, Aleck Pratt met them driving together a week ago; and the girls saw them at the cathedral at some musical shindy; and they 've been rowing up-river. Mary Anne's boys almost ran them down under the willows one day last August. It 's always Sundays. Guess they 've been going together for a good six months."

"And nobody told me!"

"I suppose they kind o' hated to bell the cat."

"James!"

"Oh, I 'm not excusing them, nor myself either; though I did n't know a word of it till Tuesday, and I 've been trying to get the spunk to break it to you. For of course it 's got to be headed off, and the sooner the better."

James rather prided himself on his family pride.

"But how did everybody know who it was?" she persisted, driving hard at the point, like a seasoned cross-examiner.

"Oh, it's a place the young folks go to for an ice-cream of an afternoon, or after the theatre."

"After the theatre? A young woman! For she is young?"

"Presumably." Then, with a keen look at his sister, "Going to do anything about it?"

"Do anything!" The challenge brought her to her feet. "I rather think I am going to 'do anything'!"

"What are you going to do?"

"*I'm going to get an ice-cream!*"

"Good!" he cried, springing to his feet. And as he held the door open for her, "I'll bank on you, Susan, when once you get your dander up!"

And Susan, strong in the "dander" of that brotherly encomium, marched straight for the "Ice-cream Parlor," as it called itself, which already her imagination was painting in lurid colors. She was a bit taken aback to find it merely a quiet, decorous place, with rows of marble-top tables, mostly unoccupied at this hour, and a bevy of tidy waitresses gossiping in a corner. As the stout, elderly customer entered and took her seat, a prettyish little person with freckles, detaching herself from the group of girls, came down between the tables and stood at attention.

"Bring me a chocolate ice-cream," Susan commanded, endeavoring to look as if such were her customary diet at this hour of the day.

"There's nothin' but vanilla so early in the mornin'."

"Then bring me vanilla!"

Susan loathed vanilla and all its works; but that was neither here nor there. Cold poison would scarce have daunted her in this militant mood.

And when the initial sacrifice was accomplished, and she was valiantly imbibing of the highly flavored concoction, Ranny's mother set herself to a systematic study of that group of girls. At first the half-dozen potential adversaries looked to her exactly alike, and one and all she regarded with impartial antagonism. But presently she found her attention concentrating upon a certain tall, showy blond, of stately bearing and masterful address, still further endowed with a rich brogue,—the only genuine thing about the hussy, Susan told herself, taking vindictive note of each unlovely trait which made the girl conspicuous. And that the maternal instinct, now keenly on the scent, should lack no confirmation, there straight-way arose an agitated whisper of, "Look sharp, Biddy; it's your turn!" And behold the Biddy of her worst forebodings, bearing down upon a youth in tweeds, who had just seated himself at one of the tables, and taking him in charge, with an air of competence which left no doubt in Susan's mind of the girl's sinister identity. She recalled, with a shudder, Ranny's fatal predilection for great bouncing partners, away back in dancing-school, when, to his mother's un-speakable chagrin, he was forever leading out the tallest bean-pole of the class. Yes; all signs and portents converged upon that stately siren; and as Susan grasped their ominous significance, her dander rose to boiling point, driving her brain in a dozen directions at once.

"So you would propose offering her money?" the professor inquired, in his leisurely, speculative tone, when she had sprung upon him her whole arsenal of high-pressure conclusions.

"To be sure. What else can we do? Money is the only possible bait for a creature like that."

Hm! Susan was undoubtedly right about it. And what a picturesque way she had of expressing herself! Only—might not the hook have to be heavily baited? The professor, whose youth had known the spur of necessity, was not always able to share his wife's exuberant indifference respecting the power that makes the mare go.

"If only her demands be not exorbitant," he ventured half-heartedly.

"What if they are?" was the gallant rejoinder. "You would n't have the hussy put a low price on Ranny!"

And that night Susan slept a sleep so confident and so unbroken, that morning was upon her in no time.

At the earliest possible hour, and wishing that she might have the incredible luck of attracting the siren to her service, she repaired to the scene of action. But again the little waitress of the previous day came forward, this time with an engaging smile of welcome.

"We 've got chocolate ice-cream this mornin'," the girl announced, pleased as if catering to an honored guest.

"How nice of you to remember what I liked," said Susan, glancing up into the friendly little face, which seemed all the more attractive for its piquant spatter of freckles.

"I always remember what folks like." The unconscious disclaimer was pronounced with a slight brogue,—a mere lilt, as compared with the siren's challenging accents,— but slight as it was, it touched a spring, and Susan's thoughts were off and away.

Her intrepid fancy had just arrived at the point when she should confront the enemy, a check for a large amount in one hand, in the other some sort of legal quit-claim for Ranny, when a much over-dressed young woman made a rustling exit from the room, and Susan's ear was caught by the delicate brogue of her own little Hebe, bubbling over with, "Say, gurrls! did ye mind the hat on her? Right on top of her head, where anny-body could see ut! Now would n't yer thought she 'd ha' put a thing like that under the table?"

And as the girls broke into suppressed

Susan

Susan's ear was caught by the delicate brogue of her own little Hebe.

titterings, "Ach, go 'way wid ye, Biddy!" the siren cried. " 'T ain't a patch on my new chapeau!"

Susan's heart contracted with a quick misgiving. So that was Biddy too, the dear little one who had remembered that she preferred chocolate! She hoped to goodness that that was not Ranny's Biddy,— that honest little human girl with the sweet voice and the spirited, sensitive face! At mere thought of an antagonist like that, Susan's dander dropped to zero.

"How many Biddys have you here?" she inquired, ostentatiously fumbling in her purse for change, while the little Biddy waited.

"Only one. I 'm the only Biddy o' the bunch."

"But I thought they called that tall one Biddy."

"Her? Oh, she 's Liddy."

"And you are Biddy," Susan repeated, still managing not to find that illusive coin. "And pray what is your other name?"

"Molloy." It fell on the ear like a note of music.

"Biddy Molloy. How pretty!" was the involuntary comment.

"Do you like ut? Maybe ye're Irish yerself?"

"Oh, no!"

"Well, it's no disgrace," quoth Biddy, with a little toss. The protest had been a thought too spontaneous.

"No, no. I didn't mean it that way. But, don't you think we all like to be what we really are? Now, you wouldn't want to be a Yankee girl; would you, my dear?"

"I use n't to," was the candid response. "But now"—and she sighed wistfully— "I don't know."

Then Susan knew, with a knowledge as different as possible from any fantastic theories of tall girls and competent sirens, that this was Ranny's Biddy; and deeply dejected, yet curiously consoled, as well, she cashed her little ticket and went her ways.

To-morrow was Sunday, and when Ranny slipped away to his poor little fool's paradise, he never guessed what solicitous and tender thoughts were following him. It was Indian summer weather, and Susan could fancy the two young people—how touchingly young they were!—rowing, up-river, where Mary

Anne's boys had once come upon them.
All day long she was haunted by a picture
of their little boat, passing under the willows,
Ranny at the oar, Biddy paddling an idle
hand in the water. She saw it all as vividly
as if she had been standing on the bank.
She saw the reflection of the boat in the
tranquil stream; in their faces the reflection
of an honest, natural love, such as all young
things have a right to,—a love that had come
to flower in the sweet out-of-door life, in
the Sabbath stillness, or quickened and up-
lifted on the strains of great cathedral
music. For Susan was imaginative, in her
own homely way, and the casual touches in
James's report, which had passed unnoticed
at the moment, fitted now into Ranny's little
love-story, as a tune will fit the verse it was
written for.

As the beautiful Indian-summer day wore
on, poor Susan, dramatic, sentimental, soft-
hearted, hardly dared look her unsuspecting
husband in the eye. And yet his counsel
tallied closely with her own inclinations.
For the thrifty man, only too ready to agree
that this was no case for bribery and corruption, urged upon her the necessity of getting
to know the girl better, of winning her confi-

dence, and thus studying how best to circum-
vent her. And, contrary as this programme
was to Susan's frank nature, the initial steps
at least were intimately alluring. On nothing
was her heart so set, indeed, as upon getting
to know Ranny's Biddy.

The enterprise bade fair to be an easy
one, for there was something about the child
so alive, so expressive, so individual, that
she could not set a plate of ice-cream before
a customer without some small, unconscious
revelation of herself. A trig little hand it
was that performed the humble task, and
nicely tended, too. Susan had a feeling for
hands; her own were rather pudgy.

"Are your father and mother both Irish?"
she asked, next day, vainly striving to feel
herself the relentless inquisitor it was her
business to be.

"Yes; they was Irish. But they 're both
dead."

"Oh!" Susan grieved, with instant sincerity. "When did they die?"

"Whin I was a baby."

"You poor little thing! And who brought
you up?"

"Me aunt."

"Are you living with her now?"

"No; she's dead, too. But I gets along."
Clearly Biddy was not looking for pity.

"How old were you when she died?"

"Fifteen; big enough for a job. I'm
seventeen, now," she added, with the
pardonable pride of maturity.

And, as question and answer fell, brief
and incisive, Susan perceived that Biddy—
the Biddy she must get to know—was already
emerging, clear-cut as a little cameo.

"And before that you were at school?"
she persisted.

"The last year I was takin' care o' me
aunt."

"She was ill all that time?"

"Yes; it was her heart." And the girl's
voice dropped to a pitiful note as she added,
"She suffered awful."

"But you helped her bear the suffering,"
said Susan warmly; and from that hour they
were fast friends,—which did not help matters in the very least.

That Biddy had no lack of friends among
her special customers, was patent to any
observer. It gave Ranny's mother a turn
one day, when a great calf of a boy had the
impudence to twitch the girl's apron-string.
But, "None o' that," laughed Biddy, serenely

adjusting the loosened knot, "or I'll have ye put out o' this!" Whereupon the youngster blushed and grinned and looked a hundred foolish things.

That same afternoon, however,—it was only Tuesday,—Biddy showed another side, a new phase of that vivacious temperament which she had so well in hand. The tables were nearly all full, when the girl stepped up to an unprepossessing person in a "sporty" necktie, and waited his order. The fellow saw fit to speak so low that Biddy was forced to bend her head, which she did with manifest repugnance. What he said was inaudible to Susan, keenly alert as always, but the effect was electric. Straightening up, the girl flashed back, "I guess I'm too busy to wait on you!"

As she turned away in tingling scorn, the competent siren, already come to seem as chimerical as her sisters of ancient lore, went sailing across the room, and took the discomfited gallant under her protection.

At last, on Thursday,—just one week it was, one anxious, futile, poignant week, from the day James put that fateful question about Ranny,—the professor was brought, much against his will, to expose himself

to the seductions of ice-cream at an ungodly
hour and, ostensibly at least, to bring a
trained mind to bear upon the situation.
Did Susan have a sneaking hope that he too
might succumb to Biddy's artless charm,
that he too might own himself baffled and
at a loss? If so, she had for once misread
the open book that was her husband's
mind.

"Well, dear, and how do you feel about it
now?" she inquired anxiously, as they passed
out into the busy city street, and wended
their way to the horse-car, arm in arm,
—an unblushing anachronism among the
up-to-date populace.

"Feel about it!" he repeated, so gruffly
that she could hardly credit her ears. "I
feel that you 've got to come to an understanding with that girl, and be quick about
it too, or *I 'll not answer for Ranny!*" As
if anybody had thought of answering for
Ranny, by the way.

Then Susan knew that matters were
serious,—that her husband was bracing
himself to take a stand; and she trembled
at thought of the consequences. For, like
many another tractable man, the professor
had his rare periods of mutiny, when he

became irritable, dogmatic, yet fatally in-
effective.

They were sitting, as usual at dusk, before
the study fire, trying to look the Darby and
Joan they could not feel to-night, when
suddenly the professor broke the silence.

"Susan," he declared,—and his tone
was so accusatory that she felt her courage
shrivel up as in a killing frost,—"Susan,
you are in love with that girl, yourself!"

It was her own conscience coming to
speech on his lips, and she dared make no
denial.

"Perhaps I have been foolish, Randidge,"
she faltered. "But the little thing is so
pretty, and so plucky, and so alone!"

"Not so much alone as she had better be!"
he asserted harshly; at which, conscience or
no conscience, Susan was up in arms.

"Randidge," she cried, "how can you
be so unfeeling?"

"I'm not unfeeling," he insisted, grown
suddenly didactic and authoritative. "Quite
the contrary; I am feeling deeply. But my
eyes are opened, and I see things as they
are,—things that you, in your lamentable
soft-heartedness, are unable to apprehend.
I see that you are playing fast and loose

with a very critical situation. Here is our son, our only son, exposed to one of the gravest dangers that can beset a young man on the threshold of life,—an ill-assorted marriage—marriage with a young person,—" Susan was holding her tongue by sheer force of will, recognizing the justice of her husband's contention, recognizing her duty to Ranny, yet conscious of a climbing revolt that had nothing whatever to do with reason, —"marriage with a young person," he was saying, "an ignorant, underbred young person, who would be a drag upon him all his life. And just because she has a pretty face and a taking way with her,—I will admit that I observed that trait in her myself,—but just because of these skin-deep attractions, you are weakly sacrificing your own child, his happiness for life, rather than take the most obvious measures for saving him."

"No, Randidge," Susan interposed, with a slow, fierce self-control. "If you want me to agree with you, you must put it differently."

In the heat of conflict they had not heard the latch-key, nor the closing of the front door,—Ranny was always quiet in his

22

movements,—nor were they aware of his approach, as he halted on the threshold behind them, arrested by the tenor of their talk. This was his concern; he had a right to play the eavesdropper.

"I tell you, Susan," the professor went pounding on, "she is a girl of low extraction, and has lived all her life in a demoralizing atmosphere. Working in a public restaurant of an evening, exposed even by day to such rudeness as you yourself described to me, walking the street at midnight, subject to still worse affronts, living by herself, with no one to see to it that she leads a decent life——"

There was a menacing light in the eyes of the listener on the threshold, and his hands were clenched till the knuckles showed white, precisely as his mother's were doing, over there in the firelight. But Susan broke in just in time.

"Stop, Randidge," she cried peremptorily. "Stop just where you are! I'm ashamed of you! Yes, I'm ashamed of you! To throw it up against that brave young thing that she lives the life she is obliged to live, the only life that is open to her, with no one to protect her, no one to guide her, no

one to love her! Has n't she as good a right
to all that as any other girl? Has n't she
a warm heart, and a sweet soul, and the
courage of a little soldier? Is n't she witty,
is n't she kind, is n't she good? What more
do you want in a young girl?"

"But, Susan," the poor man cried, vainly
trying to stem the flood he had rashly let
loose, "her low origin, her lack of education!
Why, she can't even speak grammatically!"

"Speak grammatically!" Susan retorted,
ruthlessly pouncing on the anti-climax.
"Neither did my Grandmother Pratt speak
grammatically; and that 's why we remember what she said! There was some flavor
to her sayings! What 's the good of everybody talking just alike, as if we were a lot
of poll-parrots, huddled together in one cage?
And what are we, anyway, you and I? I 've
never heard of any coronets hanging on our
family trees, nor any laurel wreaths either!
What 's my family? What 's yours?" And
now Susan had slipped the moorings of a
lifetime. "You were nothing but a farmer's
boy, with your own way to make, and that 's
exactly what Biddy's father was in the old
country! What have all the women of
my family done, more than love their hus-

bands, and bring up their children the best they knew how?   I 'd like to have you show me a sweeter, better girl than our Ranny's little Biddy, to do just that!"

"Mother!"

It broke like a great sob across her words, and as the professor looked around, dazed and defeated, there were Ranny and his mother, locked in each other's arms, as it were, carved out of a single block, Rodin-fashion; only there was n't any Rodin in those days, that anybody ever heard of.

Susan was the first to break that rapturous spell.

"Oh, what have I done?" she cried, as one who wakes from a bewildering dream.

"Done!" the professor echoed, settling back in his chair, and thanking Heaven that it had not been his doing.

But in Ranny's face was the look she had seen but once, and this time it was all for his mother.

X.

SHIPS IN THE AIR.

"MARK my words," said Emerson Swain, "if Hazeldean thinks there's anything those French army experts don't know about ballooning, he's simply got a bee in his bonnet, and the sooner he finds it out, the better."

The Swains were passing the college recess with Hattie's parents, Mr. and Mrs. Ben Pratt. Young Ben and his wife, Alicia, having dropped in for a Sunday call, the moment seemed propitious for a candid consideration of the one perplexing member of the family, and it was felt that the last speaker had contributed materially to the discussion. Such an utterance from such a source certainly merited attention, for Emerson, having served three years in the Civil War, where he had acquired a game leg and the title of Colonel (he had promptly dropped the latter, but had kept what he could of the other), was the family authority on matters military.

"That 's pretty much the way Hazeldean himself goes on about those siege balloons," was young Ben's dispassionate comment; "he says they 're no better than great blundering bumble-bees."

"My little brother got stung by a bee one day," Alicia remarked; "quite a lump came on his forehead."

Alicia's conversation resembled nothing so much as the piano - playing of a person who does n't know when he is getting his bass wrong, if only the tune tinkles. Perhaps that was why one could already trace hints of the crow's-feet which time would soon begin engraving at the corners of her husband's humorous blue eyes.

"It 's all my fault," Hazeldean's mother declared, in a tone of mingled remorse and apprehension; "if it had n't been for that dream I 'm forever dreaming, of flying down-stairs and circulating round under the ceiling, Hazeldean might never have got flying-machines on the brain."

"Yes, Martha," her husband chuckled, "we all know you 're a high-flyer. It 's

only a wonder your children have turned
out as well as they have. Eh, Emmy?"

Emerson Swain grinned, as he always
did when his father-in-law called him "Emmy," and thanked heaven that he had married into such a pleasant family. If Ben
teased you, you might be fairly certain that
he liked you. His wife, for instance, he
loved with all his heart, which in his case
was saying a good deal; hearts being, as his
mother, Old Lady Pratt, was fond of asserting, Ben's "strong suit." But he could
never let her foibles alone; and of all the
teasable phases of Martha's character, none
was more perennially diverting than this
particular vagary of her dreams. The vision
of his wife's substantial person, always scrupu-
lously attired, and of inviolable decorum,
floating nonchalantly over the heads of her
fellow creatures, never lost its charm for Ben.

Hattie, meanwhile, who was sitting on the
old satin ottoman, balancing a preternaturally
solemn baby on her knee, was still intent upon
her husband's confident pronouncement.

"I don't see what's to prevent Hazeldean
setting up a whole swarm of bees in his
bonnet," she observed, "now that Uncle
Edward has left him all that money."

"But that's just the mischief of it, Hattie," her husband demurred, "I consider that he has come into his fortune at a most inopportune moment,—precisely when he was experiencing a recrudescence of his unfortunate hallucination."

Hattie cocked her head knowingly and, addressing the solemn baby, remarked, "Those are lovely long words, are n't they, toddle-kins? But if we take to croaking they'll think we're jealous."

At which juncture Hazeldean himself strolled into the room and, with a casual nod to his brother and Alicia, dropped down on the ottoman, shoulder to shoulder with Hattie.

"Did I interrupt?" he inquired, glancing from one to the other of the little assemblage, which appeared about as unconscious as a rocking-chair whose occupant has precipitately left the room.

"Not at all," chirped Hattie. "We were merely discussing the Franco-Prussian War."

"Hm! I see. So that's why you all looked as if you had eaten the canary."

"Minnie Dodge says it's cruel to keep a canary," Alicia threw in. "She says birds were made to fly about."

"A fact which few persons would appear to have observed," was Hazeldean's thoughtful rejoinder. Having delivered himself of which, he relapsed against the pudgy cushions, and endeavored to insert a finger into the tight little fist of his small nephew.

Hazeldean Pratt would have been a striking figure in any company, but nowhere did his personality stand out more sharply by contrast than in his own comfortable family circle. Lolling there on the ottoman, to be sure, his superior height was lost upon the observer, while his strongly idealistic brow and searching eyes, bent now upon the youngest scion of the stock, were less in evidence than usual. And yet, the stooping shoulders, the fixed gaze at that irresponsive morsel of humanity, the complete absorption in an enterprise of no moment, all bespoke a temperament of alien intensity. Hattie herself, for all her liveliness of disposition, was a restful personality by comparison.

As their mother glanced across the room at the little group on the ottoman which, despite the fashions of the early seventies, had about it a curious touch of elder art, she inquired, "Have you seen grandmother to-day, Hazeldean? It 's her birthday, you know."

"No; I 'm on my way there, now."

"Hope it don't make you dizzy to go so fast," his father remarked, placidly shifting to starboard the bit of slippery-elm which he called his "lubricator."

Hazeldean, whose index finger had at last effected a junction with his nephew's coy little palm, did not at once reply. But as the tiny hand relaxed, for all the world like an opening rosebud, and Hattie took jealous possession of the soft pink petals, he straightened himself and, lifting his long length from the seat, observed, "You know we 're all travelling along at the rate of nineteen miles a second." Then, as he crossed the threshold into the entry-way, and picked up his hat, "Funny, is n't it?" he called back, "that we never seem to get there!"

"Get where?" asked Alicia.

But the closing of the heavy front door was the only answer vouchsafed her very pertinent inquiry.

For Hazeldean was already sauntering down the path in the deepening twilight, pondering the thing he had said. He glanced up at the first star of evening, burn-

ing still and serene to mortal eye as if it
were not rushing through space at a fabulous
rate of speed. Hazeldean loved the stars
in their courses; they were the mighty prototype of all flying things.

"If I had said five hundred and ninety-
six million miles a year," he reflected, as he
passed through the gate, and bent his steps
in the opposite direction from his grandmother's house, "it would n't have conveyed
any idea to their minds. But we can most
of us count up to twenty." Then, with a
quick turn of thought,—"And up to
twenty, I reckoned that I could fetch it
myself."

The fact that the young man had turned
in the opposite direction from his goal was
no sign that he had relinquished it. He had
his own way of doing things, even to so
simple a matter as going to pay his respects
to his grandmother. And to-night, before
confronting the sybil of the family, who
was in a quite peculiar sense his own sybil,
he wanted to do a bit of thinking out there
in the starlight.

From boyhood up, this offshoot of an
eminently common-sense family had pursued
the will-o'-the-wisp of a flying-machine;

not a good, honest, puffy balloon, mind you, that should have the law of gravity, or, more properly speaking, the law of levity, in its favor, but something in the nature of an automaton, designed to rise in the air, and propel itself hither and yon in open defiance of those well-established laws. Such a notion was, of course, too apocryphal to be taken seriously, unless when the youngster had chanced to break a collar-bone or damage his Sunday breeches in the cause; and by the time he was fairly out of his teens, his easy-going people were only too glad to believe that he had given over such child's-play for good and all.

He had now been for several years connected with a patent-solicitor's office, where his natural bent for invention was proving a not inconsiderable asset. And here he had been witness of so many futile efforts in one or another field of mechanics, he had seen so many fiascos, incurred, too, by men of greater originality than himself, that his disillusionment touching his own ability had been complete. He was as firmly persuaded as ever that the day of the flying-machine was not far off, but equally convinced that he was not the man to work out the problem. And thus rid of a serious handicap, he bade fair to become a useful average member of society.

In fact, the young visionary was probably never in a more normal frame of mind than on the evening, a year or more ago, when he first met Miss Hester Burdick, the new grammar-school teacher, at his grandmother's house. Certainly he could have given no better evidence of good sense than was to be discerned in the promptness with which he fell in love with that admirable young woman, who, for her part, had already shown herself equally discriminating by falling in love with Hazeldean's grandmother. The young school-teacher was boarding next door with her cousins, "the Doctor Baxters," and she and Old Lady Pratt had struck up a great intimacy.

As Hazeldean strode along in the starlight, with quickening step, his mind reverted to that first sight of Hester, holding a skein of worsted for Aunt Betsy, who was smiling, with a pleased sense of companionship, while the girl's eyes rested upon the clear-cut features of her hostess, among which one could almost read the thought that had just found terse expression. Old Lady Pratt had looked up brightly as her grandson entered, saying:

"Come in, Hazeldean. I want to make you acquainted with Miss Hester Burdick. She's a nice girl, and likes old ladies."

From which moment Hazeldean found himself in the highly unconventional position of being the declared rival of his own grandmother.

An unsuccessful rival, alas, for within the year he had twice suffered rejection. The last time had been a few days after his accession to fortune, when, if ever, his suit would have seemed likely to prosper.

A curious thing about that fortune, by the way. No one but Hazeldean's mother could conceive why, if one nephew was to be singled out for favor, it should not have been Edward, the youngest, who had been avowedly named for his uncle. But Martha, happy in the advantage of having been born a Hazeldean, understood that it was the family name that her brother, having only daughters of his own, had rejoiced to see perpetuated. She knew that his ideas, like hers, were generic rather than specific.

"Queer, ain't it?" Old Lady Pratt had remarked to Ben, apropos of his brother-in-law's will, "the satisfaction some folks appear to git out of a family pride they can't p'int to any particular reason for? Now the Hazeldeans come of good stock enough, like the rest of us, but I ain't never hearn tell of any on 'em settin' the river afire; hev you?"

"P'raps it's the brilliant matches they make," Ben ventured. "There's Edward, married money, and Martha,—well, she drew me! Ain't that enough to make any family feel kind o' perky?"

Thanks then to a family pride denied a legitimate basis, Hazeldean found himself possessor of a fortune denied a legitimate use. For, since Hester would n't have him and his fortune, of what possible good was either?

It was just as he had arrived at this deadening conclusion that a thing happened which infused a very explicit meaning into life. If he could not be off with the new love, he could at least be on with the old: a reversal of the usual order which struck him as original, if not altogether consolatory.

He had been the first to put in an appearance at the office one morning, now some three weeks since, when a man entered who introduced himself as Hiram Lane. He

looked about forty, and was soberly, not
to say shabbily, clad. As he took his seat
and proceeded to untie a roll of papers,
Hazeldean was struck with a certain con-
trolled alertness of countenance and gesture.
He experienced an instant conviction that
here was a man not in the same class with
the average client. When the stranger
spoke, his low, incisive voice, his diction,
spare but trenchant, lent authority to his
words. The total impression was one of
balance and significance.

"My name is Hiram Lane," he stated.
"I wish to patent a certain contrivance, a
link in the sequence that will eventually
lead to aviation as distinguished from
ballooning."

There was no apology in Lane's attitude,
no defiance. He was sure of himself and
indifferent to criticism. And something of
his quiet confidence subdued the rising tumult of Hazeldean's brain, and enabled him
to reply with answering composure, "It's
something I have always believed in."

"Good," said Hiram Lane. "Then let's
get to work."

For an hour the two men busied themselves with drawings and blue-prints, with

technical terms and scientific computations.
Hazeldean's chief entered, saw that he was
in good vein, and refrained from inter-
fering. Other clerks arrived and got to
work, other clients came and went, and
Hazeldean and Hiram Lane were still at
it.

At last the latter glanced at the office-
clock, sprang to his feet, and rolled up his
papers, with the same curt energy that
characterized all his processes, mental or
otherwise.

"Time's up," he declared. "Shall you
be here at the same hour to-morrow?"

"Yes," said Hazeldean, with like brevity,
which betrayed nothing of the tumult that
was rising again. And, an instant later,
his client's heels went ringing down the
corridor.

Lane came again next morning, and after
that at irregular intervals, always leaving
at the same hour. He was evidently not
master of his own time. Hazeldean was
conscious of no curiosity about him, personally. There were so many people whose
business and social status was all there was
to them, that he had not the slightest wish
to label and catalogue a shining exception

23

like this. He only thanked his stars that
the man had crossed his path.

And it came about that as day by day
his faith in Hiram Lane's enterprise grew,
Hazeldean's faith in himself grew also. He
had not been an addle-pated visionary,
after all, he told himself to-night; his idea
had been sound. That he had lacked the
skill, the originality, to put it into execution,
that was a mere detail, which in no way
affected the issue at stake. And besides,
there were other ways of furthering a good
cause than by actual leadership. We couldn't
all be captains, we couldn't all be fighting
men, even. But—and suddenly his mind
was crossed by the familiar phrase, "sinews
of war." He halted, there in the path,
as if his name had been called. Sinews of
war! Money! That money which he had
despised, because Hester would none of it,—
the money that had come to him by a caprice
of fortune. Why, he was an able-bodied
man, a competent bread-winner! He was
as capable as his brothers of earning his
own living. What should he want of a
fortune? And with a firm step, he started
off again, headed now for his goal, in more
senses than one.

The stars were gathering fast. How quietly, almost imperceptibly, they appeared,—as quietly as a thought does. And yet, so constant were they in that flight of theirs, that by them and by them alone the mariner was safe to steer his course. Well, here was a thought to steer by, and what a thought! Was ever such a use found for money? Some folks bought stocks and bonds with theirs, and vegetated on the income. How stupid to do a thing like that with it!

Again he glanced skyward, where the constellations were already standing out in their ancient order. There was the moon, too, not yet at the full, just sailing clear of the housetops. And here was his grandmother's gate. He wished he had not timed his visit when Hester was almost sure to be there. She was tantalizing, distracting. He could n't keep his wits about him when she was by; he was too busy feeling things. Uncomfortable things, too. In some moods the very sight of her, the sound of her voice, was like a stab. What had a man with a good, working thought in his head to do with feelings, anyway? No, he did n't want to see Hester to-night.

And yet, when presently he stood on the threshold of the little sitting-room, and she was not there, a worse stab caught him than the sight of her could have dealt. Perhaps Old Lady Pratt sensed his discomfiture, though he got out his birthday congratulations very creditably; for,——

"Hester's been and gone," she remarked, as he took Aunt Betsy's hand, which felt like a pad of dough after his grandmother's claw-like grip.

"Has she?" he echoed vaguely.

"Yes; she has. You're too late."

He knew better than to protest that he had come to see his grandmother. In face of those sharp eyes, indeed, he could not even in his own mind keep up the little fiction. So he let his case go by default.

"Do you calc'late to go through life jest too late?" she persisted, with considerable animus.

"Too late or—too early," he amended, trying, not very successfully, to force his mind back from Hester to that other matter which required a long future to its unfolding.

He had seated himself and, picking up an unwieldy photograph album, he chanced upon a recent libel on his grandmother, wherein her keen physiognomy had been so ruthlessly denuded of the smallest modicum of character that he felt himself for once almost a match for her. Her actual voice, however, dispelled that pleasing illusion.

"Have you given her up?" she inquired.

"She has given me up."

"What makes you let her?"

"I 've asked her twice," he smouldered. "If I keep on nagging her, she 'll get to hate me."

"Well," was the crisp rejoinder, "I ain't so sure but that 'd be a step in the right direction." And, shrewdly studying the young man's countenance, she fell to wishing that there were more of the stout fibre of resistance in his composition, against which a robust hate might brace itself.

Old Lady Pratt desired this match ardently. She felt sure it would be the making of her grandson, and equally sure that all the girl needed was to be waked up about him. Hester had certainly begun by liking him; indeed, no one could be quite indifferent to Hazeldean at first blush. He was too individual for that, though his natural advantages were, to his grandmother's thinking, disastrously nullified in the general

scheme of him. Even as his good looks were
too frequently lost in a slack bearing and a
tendency to stare at nothing, so his undeni-
able intelligence had hitherto missed fire.
His ideas were rarely driven home. Morally,
too, he lacked a healthy assertiveness. He
could attract, but failed to hold, and Old
Lady Pratt had watched, and perfectly
understood, the flickering out of Hester's
interest. A girl of her calibre might well
demand something more definite to tie to
than a pleasant disposition and a glancing
intelligence.

That intelligence, however, had not missed
the point of the old lady's remark.

"Yes," Hazeldean pondered, " 't were
something to be level to her hate."

"Hm! That 's poetry, I suppose," she
scoffed, while her knitting-needles clicked
and glinted a brisk protest; for Old Lady
Pratt, like many of her contemporaries,
kept her Sabbath from sundown to sundown.
"Now, what you need to cultivate is prose."

"There 's plenty of it lying round loose,"
he returned dully.

"So there 's plenty of earth lyin' round
loose," was the quick retort; "but 't aint
goin' to do you any good unless you git your

own plot 'n' till it. What are you aimin' to do with all that money o' yours?" she inquired abruptly.

The question so suddenly propounded was a challenge, and he rose to it, clean quit of his preoccupation. His thought was there, that thought that he was to steer by. The glance that met his grandmother's inquiry was not the familiar one of facile enthusiasm. It was definite,—aggressive. As his interlocutor put it to herself, there was backbone in his eye. And backbone, in any locality, was Old Lady Pratt's fetish.

"I 'm thinking of turning it into sinews of war," he replied, with quiet emphasis.

Yes; he looked self-sufficient, and for the first time in his grandmother's recollection. Supposing he did do something rash with his money, so he came out a man! Old Lady Pratt was no despiser of property; she had lived too long for that! But it was not her fetish. And so, in deference to the thing that *was* her fetish, namely, character, expressed in terms of backbone, she said, very deliberately:

"Well, Hazeldean, the money 's yours, 'n' it 'll do you good to live up to that. You

kin tell 'em I said so, if you 're a mind to,"
she added, with a twinkle.

The look of self-sufficiency intensified.
He sprang to his feet, and, seizing the wiry
little hand, "Grandmother," he declared.
"You 're the only one of them all that can
see round a corner!"

"P'raps that 's because I 've turned so
many on 'em," she suggested. "The eighty-
ninth to-day, Hazeldean."

"And you 're looking ten years younger
than Aunt Betsy, this very minute," he
averred, warmly.

"I know it," she admitted, with a little
smirk of gratified vanity. Then, moved
to quick compunction,—" Poor Betsy!
P'raps I 'd oughter 've let her wear a false
front, after all!"

When, a few minutes later, Hazeldean
passed out into Green Street, which lay
before him, a network of shifting shadows,
there was Hester Burdick, still abroad, a little
Scotch-plaid shawl thrown over her head,
her face upturned in the moonlight. He
stood an instant, watching her approach.
What was that his grandmother had said
about making the girl hate him? It might
be a step in the right direction? Well, so it

would be,—in the direction of getting rid, once for all, of that foolish, senseless hankering that kept him mooning around, wherever and whenever she might be looked for. He had not paid her an honest call in a month now. But he had been scheming to meet her, and telling himself that he hoped she would not be there. Well, there should be no more of that. He would confront her now, squarely and fairly, and fairly and squarely he would ask her again, and make an end of this miserable shilly-shallying.

He met her, just as she reached the Baxter gate.

"I 've been taking a roundabout way home from your grandmother's," she volunteered; "It was such a lovely evening."

"Yes; it 's a great evening!" and, placing his hand on the gate, he held it firmly closed.

"But I 'm just going in," said Hester, waiting for him to make way for her.

"So was I. But I find I like it better outside."

"As you please. But I 'm afraid you 'll have to let me pass."

"I 've been letting you pass for ages," he averred doggedly. "This is a hold-up."

"Really!" with an instinct to run for cover. "Then why not come inside?"

"Not I. There are folks in there. But I 'll come as far as the piazza, if you 'll play fair."

"But I 'm not playing."

"Nor I!"

She perceived that he was not to be put off.

"Very well; then come," she said resignedly; "it 's silly to stand out here talking riddles."

He knew that he could trust her, and he opened the gate. As they approached the steps he laid a detaining hand on her sleeve.

"Hester!"

"Ah, don't!" she protested, hurrying up the steps. He was not in the habit of calling her by her Christian name, but that was not what she minded.

They were standing on the piazza now, in a sort of cat's-cradle of trellised moonlight.

"Hester!" he implored.

She stiffened.

"It 's no good, you know. I thought you understood that."

He pulled himself up.

"I did, in a way; but I wanted to make sure."

She flushed a bit.

"I 'll make an affidavit if you wish," she proffered, not without a touch of pique.

"No; I 'm willing to take your word for it."

He loved her and craved her, inappeasably; yet, in the very moment of denial, he was conscious of a curious satisfaction. Steel had struck steel between them for the first time; the mere clash of it was tonic.

"Did you stop me expressly to say that?" she asked, distantly. For, in truth, his manner was anything but flattering.

He did not answer at once. He was thinking how well she looked with that little square of shawl over her head. For all her haughty air (she had never found it worth while to be haughty with him before), that little shawl made her look so human, so lovable! The kind of head-gear it was that was worn by the wives of laboring men,— those plain women that just love a man without thinking, because they can't help it, and don't want to. He thought that if he could snatch that little shawl from her head, and button it in under his coat, he might make that do.

Perhaps he looked predatory, for, with a half-distrustful air, she edged toward the door.

"I really must go in," she said.

At that, he threw off his preoccupation.

"Then it's quite settled?" he asked; and he forced himself to ask it quietly.

"Quite. I'm glad you find it such a relief."

The shawl had slid to her shoulders, but she did not notice.

"It *is*—an immense relief"; and he eyed the shawl, that was slipping, slipping, down her shoulders. "There's something I've got to do and"—with a swift movement he caught the shawl as it fell—"and now I have a free hand. Good-night."

With a bound, he was at the foot of the steps, while she stood above him in the clear moonlight, reaching out an imperious hand.

"Give me my shawl!" she commanded.

But from somewhere off there in the dark came the preposterous answer, "I consider it mine!" And he was gone.

"Well, I never!" she gasped, as, with tingling nerves and heightened color, she turned and went into the house.

Hester Burdick had been loved before;

she had once, in an elemental moment, and to her undying chagrin, been kissed. But never before had she been robbed. It was detestable—she was sure of that—but it was a sensation. It waked her up. Ah, wise Old Lady Pratt!

And Hazeldean strode along homeward, the little shawl buttoned tight in under his coat, literally hugging himself over his ill-gotten booty.

Yet, arrived at last in his own room, which was squared off with patches of moonlight, he pulled out the little shawl and regarded it critically. After all, it was nothing but a shawl! He was afraid he should n't be able to make it "do," after all. With a rueful grimace, he tossed it upon his desk, which stood by one of the moonlit windows, and turned to light the gas. The match-box had been misplaced. Glancing about in search of it, his eye fell upon that bit of Scotch-plaid, which lay in a round heap, a small break in its contour suggesting that it had once framed a face.

With a choking sensation of fierce pain, he dropped into the chair by the desk and, gathering the soft folds in his hands, buried his face in them. So he remained for several minutes, motionless. But when, at sound of the supper-bell, he raised his head, his features were set in firm lines, and the moon, at gaze, found nothing there to gratify its romantic predilections.

Those firm lines were already beginning to feel very much at home in Hazeldean's mobile countenance when, the following Saturday, he made his offer to Hiram Lane. He had thought the matter out very soberly, and the proposition was couched in terms of business commonplace. If the young capitalist had never before experienced quite the sense of exultation that stirred his blood as he made the offer, neither had he ever been quite so completely master of himself.

"You know what you are about?" Lane had demurred. "You know the chances of failure?"

"Yes."

"That it must be a matter of years at best? That you and I may not live to see the end?"

"Yes; I know."

They were in Lane's lodging, a great barn of a room in a cheap suburb, cluttered badly with grotesque contraptions of wire and

cane, of canvas and oiled silk. A very fair
apology for a chemist's laboratory, ranged
on rough shelves in one corner, lent an air
of scientific reality to the establishment,
further emphasized by various workman-like
drawings and tabulations spread out upon
a deal table. But in all the room was no
faintest suggestion of creature comfort.

Lane was seated on a high stool, nursing
his knee, and eying his pet model,—a crude
but extremely ingenious affair, no more
resembling the modern "flyer," to be sure,
than the formless embryo resembles the
plant in full flower. And yet—the germ
was there, and both men knew it.

"It's a one-sided sort of partnership,"
Lane observed. "You'll never see your
money again; you *may* never see any results
at all. But—the fact is, you're the only
chap I've ever run across, who had the
gumption to catch on, and—I think you're
entitled to lend a hand."

True fanatic that he was, the man honestly
believed himself to be conferring a favor;
wherein Hazeldean, in the magnanimity of
his soul, fully concurred.

"Very well," he said. "We'll call it
a partnership, and some day——"

"Some day, we 'll show 'em the way to Mars!"

With that, Lane jumped down off his stool, wrung Hazeldean's hand, severely but briefly, and then began, with technical exactitude, elucidating the advantage of a slight readjustment of the new model which he was contemplating. Neither of them dwelt further upon the financial aspects of the case, until just as Hazeldean was leaving, when he said, "It 's understood then that you draw upon the First National, as required, to that amount."

"Yes," Lane agreed; adding, with a strong note of feeling, "and I draw upon you, personally, for something that no money could buy."

A close hand-grip sealed the bond, and Hazeldean, walking home over the long bridge, carried with him the sensation of that hand-grip, and felt that here, too, was something that no money could buy.

He was walking, shoulders squared, head well set back, as he had recently contracted the habit of doing. The keen autumn air, the metallic blue of the sky, the in-coming tide, the brimming river-banks, all conspired to heighten that sense of vigor

Hazeldean

Presently his attention was arrested by a flock of gulls,
flecking the cold, dark bosom of the stream.

and well-being that follows upon decisive
action.

Presently his attention was arrested by
a flock of gulls, flecking the cold, dark
bosom of the stream. They were in restless
motion, and he watched them with kindling
interest. Yes, they were rising, see! and
circling in the sunshine, now in light, now in
shadow, as they wheeled and turned. What
more natural than that flight? What more
glorious? They rose higher, and turned
up-stream. As they flew directly over his
head, his eye, following them, was caught
by a figure on the other side the bridge. It
was Hester Burdick, out for her favorite
walk. He lifted his hat, and she inclined
her head, coldly. They had not met since
the robbery. The sight of her, walking
there in the common daylight, the chill of
her indifferent salutation, brought him back
from his flight of fancy with a dull reaction.
What business had he with that shawl of hers?
How could a grown man have been guilty
of such tomfoolery! The thing must be
returned, of course. "Now I have a free
hand," he had said. Well, here was the
test. Only—he would not brave it yet;
not until Lane had taken the preliminary

24

steps toward cutting loose from other work, and beginning operations on a larger scale, thereby clinching the contract, and putting the terms of it beyond discussion.

And during that interval Hazeldean's sense of personal efficiency expanded and took distinct shape. It found expression most of all in the handling of his daily work. He felt the vital necessity of vindicating his action before the bar of his own judgment at least, and this could be done in but one way: by approving himself independent of those artificial props which he had so cavalierly rejected. In the process, he found himself acquiring a sense of mastery, not only of business detail, but of his own powers, his own grip on life. He spent less time than heretofore with Lane; he did not greatly concern himself with the inventor's doings. All such matters were delegated once for all to the acknowledged expert. His own job was to establish himself in his own line.

And at last, when he felt that he had the situation well in hand, he took the little shawl back to its owner, speculating as he did so upon the chances of her consenting to see him.

She had no choice as to that, for she opened the door herself. At sight of him her countenance changed, and she did not invite him to enter.

"Are n't you going to ask me in?" he inquired. The question sounded more a demand than an entreaty.

"My cousins are playing cards in the parlor," she temporized.

"But there 's the dining-room."

He was struck with admiration of his own hardihood.

"I am correcting compositions in there," she objected.

But she stepped aside, and gave him grudging admittance. The parlor door stood open, and they could see the players, studying their hands in deep absorption.

"I pass," quoth a voice with a grievance.

"Order it up," Dr. Baxter announced. And the game went on.

They seated themselves on opposite sides of the dining-table, which was covered with a red-checked cloth on which were spread her papers and a blue pencil. The light from the chandelier, touching her hair to bronze, left the features somewhat in shadow, head and shoulders silhouetted against a background of turkey-red curtains. The *chiaroscuro* of the total effect was subtly disquieting, so at variance did it seem with the girl's singularly open, straightforward nature. Happily, however, his errand was a definite one; he need have no traffic with moods and tenses.

"I have brought you back your shawl," he announced, without preamble, drawing from his pocket a small parcel, carefully wrapped in tissue paper. He had not smoked a pipe in his own room for a week past, lest the odor should contaminate those sacred folds—a needless sacrifice, by the way, since, truth to tell, Hester rather particularly liked tobacco-smoke.

"You are quite sure you are through with it?" she inquired, with a pardonable indulgence in satire.

"Not exactly that, but things have changed since I—annexed it. I should n't feel justified in keeping it any longer."

"Indeed!"

"No; I have n't the right even to think of you any more. I 've burned my bridges."

"And you can't swim?"

The little fling sounded just a trifle forced.

"Not that particular stream. But"—

with a sudden flash—"I may come flying across, one of these days."

"So, you 've gone back to that, have you?"

No, Hester was not herself to-night. Her speech, like her face, was in *chiaroscuro*.

"In a sense, yes. But not on my own account."

"Riddles again!"

And, upon that, she fell to tracing blue arabesques on a stray half-sheet.

"Not at all. It 's plain as a pike-staff. A man I know has the brains, and the originality, and the persistence and the self-abnegation, every quality, in fact, except capital."

"Ah!" She glanced up quickly, while the careful arabesques went askew. "And you?"

"I am going to supply that."

Since it was a kind of general obloquy that he was inviting, he might as well face the music here and now.

"Your uncle's legacy?" she inquired, in a tone that was studiously non-committal.

"Yes."

"All of it?"

"As much of it as he may need."

"And you call that burning your bridges?"

"Most assuredly."

"What bridges?"

"The bridges that don't lead anywhere. The bridges that ought to lead to"—he looked her full in the face—"to you!"

"Ah!" she breathed again. "Won't you tell me a little more about the man you 've burned your bridges for?"

"I have n't burned them for a man; I 've burned them for an idea."

"Tell me about the idea."

And Hazeldean told her, simply and concisely, without exaggeration, about the great idea to which he had pledged a fortune. He talked so well that she could comprehend the gist of his argument, and he perceived the clearness of her comprehension.

"It may be many years," he admitted. "We may none of us live to see it. But some day, some day, the thing will be done, and —every little helps."

"Does any one know, any one but me?"

"Nobody, yet. But, of course, I shall be obliged to tell my folks. It will be pretty rough on them, I 'm afraid."

"Rough on them? They could n't be so narrow!" She had pushed back her chair. Her face was plainly visible now; her speech wholly spontaneous. "They must see, they must feel—" But here she put sudden compulsion on herself, and fell silent.

"Hester!" he cried, leaning forward across the table. "You can see it that way? You can feel with me about it? And yet—" He sprang to his feet with an impatient movement.

"And yet?" she echoed, unfolding the shawl from its tissue wrappings, and absently resting her cheek against it.

He was not standing the test, and he knew it. With a sense of wrenching himself free, he said abruptly, "I 'll go now, and leave you to correct compositions in peace to the end of the chapter, on one condition: that you come out on the piazza, and give me absolution, just where it happened. I 'll go, honor bright, if you 'll do that."

"Well, if you offer such an inducement," she jested, tossing the little shawl over her head, in token perhaps of amnesty, as together they passed out into the chill evening air.

There was only starlight to-night; only the stars in their courses looked down upon that provocative little shawl. He almost wished she had n't thrown it over her head;

that little shawl that made her look so human, so lovable, so like those plain women who loved a man without thinking, because they could n't help themselves.

"It 's a big good-bye for me," he was saying, with a stricture at his throat that really hurt.

"On account of the burned bridges?" she queried, under her breath.

"Yes," he said, firmly and finally; "on account of the burned bridges." And he took her hand in parting.

"I 'm glad you 've burned them," she observed, striving hard for the purely conversational tone. "I always hated that money of yours."

"Hated it?"

"Yes, and the things you said about it, and about—us. They sounded such castles in the air."

The shawl had fallen back from her head, and her face showed clear and frank in the starlight. There was a dawning sweetness in it, too, a sweetness that Hazeldean had divined from the very first, though never until that hour had his eyes beheld it. But he kept himself steadily to the issue in hand.

"And *ships* in the air?" he urged. "You would rather hear talk of *them?*"

"Yes; only—it's not the talk, either. It's what you've done. It's so—real!"

He had both her hands now, and his eyes held hers.

"Hester!" It was as if he were conjuring her to a confession of faith; "Hester! You do believe, you really do believe—in it all?"

And she answered quietly, almost solemnly, yet with that in her voice which was a confession of more, far more, than faith:

"Yes, I do believe that we shall live to see your ships in the air come true,—*you and I!*"

XI.

THE PASSING OF BEN.

ON the day Martha died, Ben laughed. It was not the harsh outbreak of a man distraught with grief; it was just his own quiet, deep-throated chuckle. And Ben and Martha had been a united pair.

"Why, father," his daughter Mattie inquired, anxiously. "Are n't you feeling well?"

"Oh, yes; I 'm feelin' well enough,—for an old man; but not so well 's your mother, Mattie. She 's feelin' better 'n she 's felt for a long while, I 'll be bound."

"But what made you laugh, dear? You laughed just now, you know."

"Oh, I was thinkin' of somethin' she said to me the day we got engaged. That was nigh upon fifty year ago, Mattie." And this time the old man heaved a profound sigh.

"Yes, I know," said Mattie, very gently. "But if I were you, I would n't do it again. Folks might misunderstand."

"Your mother ain't goin' to misunderstand. Should n't wonder if she was laughin', too. The same things always did tickle us both,—me 'n Martha."

Ben's accent had been inclined to sag a bit on the final "a" in his wife's name, though it never came to anything worse than a hint of backsliding. For Martha, whose sense of propriety was highly developed, was the last woman to suffer the indignity of being called "Marthy." In all the larger concerns of life she had dutifully and joyfully looked up to her husband, who, truth to tell, was her beau-ideal of manly virtue and wisdom,—and surely no one was better qualified to judge of Ben than she who had wintered and summered him for "nigh upon fifty year." But in what she regarded as her own province, namely, in such non-essentials as speech and deportment, dress and household economics, her word was law.

"There never was a man so hen-pecked," Ben would aver, with the perennial relish which attaches to a joke that has been

many years a-ripening. Whereupon Martha
would make pretence of direst dudgeon, sure
to set his small eyes twinkling,—those blue
eyes that looked for all the world like own
brothers to her turquoise set, most highly
prized of the famous Hazeldean heirlooms.

A homely, humdrum pair these lifelong
lovers had been.

And now Martha had passed over to the
other side, and Ben must e'en bide his time
until his own passing should be accomplished,
—that passing which in his private thoughts
he regarded as having begun on the day
when Martha loosed her hold and fell asleep.
It was not in his kindly, tractable disposition to embitter the allotted interval with
vain repinings, to pick a quarrel with that
good friend of his, the order of nature, to
which he owed such countless blessings.
Martha had simply got tired and gone early
to bed, and presently he should slip off
his boots and follow after, very softly, so
as not to wake her. And then, in a little
while, it would be morning.

Meantime, here were all the children up
and about. How tireless the young folks
seemed!

The winter which followed upon Martha's

death was a grim season; yet in the very inclemency of the weather, which was chill and surly rather than boisterous, Ben found his own consolation. For Martha was safe from its evil consequences,—Martha, for whom such weather as that had spelled neuralgia.

"She used to be liable to headaches," he would say. "Real bad ones. Ain't it good to think she 'll never hev any more?"

And when the fire crackled on the hearth, and Mattie's youngest (whom his mother would bring in, as one less fortunately endowed might have proffered a bunch of roses or a hot-house peach) crowed with delight at the gleaming andirons Martha had taken such pride in, the grandfather would shake his head, in pity rather than in sadness, as he mused, "Poor little chap! He can't remember his granny!"

From the first, Ben would not hear to making his home with any of his married children; and Martha's children, as was to have been expected, had one and all proved to be of "the marrying kind." They might come to him when so minded; the old house could stretch itself a bit for the grand-children,—and for the great-grandchildren, too, since these latter appeared to be taking time by the forelock. But as for abandoning his own fireside, that was out of the question. Besides, as he took a sly pleasure in stating, "Martha 'n' I would n't uv liked it. 'T would uv been a real trial to us to hev an outsider settin' round, lookin' on at all our little tiffs, 'n' pretendin' they was n't noticin'."

"But you and mother never had any tiffs," young Ben (aged forty-seven) would protest.

"Now, Ben, don't you be runnin' away with the idea that your mother had n't any sperit, jest cause she 'd learned to put up with my aggravatin' ways."

"Of course she had spirit," Ben admitted, with a grin. "I guess we youngsters found that out! But I don't know 's I ever saw her fly out at you."

At that, a broad smile would overspread the old man's face, and he would remark, "P'raps you wa' n't so very observin' in those days, Ben. 'T was along in the middle forties."

At which Ben junior would feel extremely young and inexperienced, and fall to wondering how much an infant in long-clothes really did take in of its parents' moods and tenses.

Not that he and Alicia were addicted to what is popularly known as "words." Indeed it would have taken a more "aggra-vatin' " husband than old Ben himself to fall out with her. As Old Lady Pratt used to say,—for, thanks to the accident of longevity, that shrewd observer of her kind had been privileged to see her grandson introduce this refreshing variant into the family circle,—"Alicia can't hold her mind still long enough to take offence."

And since Ben senior was possessed of a quizzical vein which Alicia rarely failed to titillate, it was to his eldest son's house that he most frequently found his way,—especially of a Sunday afternoon, when the young folks were to the fore. There were six of these, and the smallest was named for Martha.

She was a sprightly little five-year-old, who had come along so far behind the others, —twins, the last invoice had been, and boys into the bargain,—that she was regarded as a sort of afterthought in the family, not to be taken too seriously. A canny little afterthought it was, that fully understood

the advantages of its position, and in no
instance more fully than in the easy subjugation of "Gamps,"—its own particular
appellation for this most biddable of
"grown-ups."

That little Martha, any little Martha,
should be a prime favorite with old Ben was
a foregone conclusion, but it is pleasant also
to record that the partiality was in a high
degree reciprocal. The moment the old
gentleman's step was heard in the passage-
way, she would come capering and chirping
about him, and no sooner was he established
in the big leathern armchair (declared to
"fit like a glove"), than the little monkey
was climbing over his rotund person, confidently searching his pockets for lemon-
drops or peppermint lozenges, or paying
flattering attention to those side-whiskers
which Martha had never let him change
the cut of since their wedding-day.

And old Ben, fondly tracing a resemblance
to her granny in the vivacious little pick-
pocket, would wonder what on earth was
to be done to get those pretty eyes set
straight. They were just the color of
Martha's, and the twinkle was there that
had ever answered to his own. But alas,

the pretty eyes were crossed, so that the twinkle that was meant for him would go astray, and alight on some irrelevant object. And old Ben fretted,—fretted more about those vagrant twinkles than about his own bereavement. Naturally, too,—for was he not perfectly sure of seeing Martha again in a few years at the most? while he was growing daily more apprehensive lest he should not have a good report to give her of her little namesake's eyes, the early righting of which she had had much at heart.

At last Ben screwed up his courage to do what he had been ever chary of doing,— namely, to interfere, by word or hint, in other folks' affairs.

"Don't you think, Alicia," he asked one day, in a studiously conversational tone, "that it 's about time little Martha's eyes were attended to?"

He addressed this quite incendiary remark to Alicia, rather than to Ben, because the mother seemed entitled to first considera- tion in such a matter. And Ben junior, pull- ing comfortably at his pipe, was only too thankful to be left out of a discussion, the fate of which, at Alicia's hands, was easy to predict.

25

"Little Martha's eyes?" the latter echoed pleasantly. "Oh, I don't know. They 're so cunning! They always remind me of that joke about the little cross-eyed bear; a pun, you know, on cross—I 'd—bear. I—apostrophe—d."

"Yes, yes. But about little Martha's eyes." And this time a touch of special pleading was not to be suppressed. "They 'd ought to be attended to, you know."

"Oh, I never fuss about them; you ask Ben if I do. I just dress her up pretty, and curl her hair, and—I wonder now, if I ought to have it cut. Some say it grows better if you keep it short while they 're young. So I let Flossie's grow out, and I kept Lyssie's short, and I don't see but they 've acted about the same. If only Flossie's——"

Thus Alicia rippled happily on, while two pipes dispensed fragrance in the room, and two pairs of blue eyes, with exactly the same indulgent smile in each, followed the curling smoke-rings. Ben senior, glancing across at Ben junior, could see no promise of effective support in that quarter, as indeed why should he? A man can't be expected to take sides against his wife, especially where

the children are concerned. A pretty how-
d'ye-do there would have been if he had
undertaken to poach on Martha's preserves!
Only,—Martha was Martha, and always
knew what was best for the children. And
old Ben's thoughts drifted away to the safe
haven of Martha's perfections where, for the
time being, her little namesake's one defect
was forgotten.

Not for long, however, for the old man
was never many days without a sight of
those twinkling eyes that could n't twinkle
straight. He got into the way of purloining
the child, sometimes for a day or two at a
time,—an act of depredation readily con-
nived at by the vested authorities.

"I suppose it helps him to forget," was
Alicia's cheerful comment.

They were standing at the window, she
and Ben, watching the first fluttering flakes
of snow, that would soon have wrapped the
gaunt earth in a sheltering coverlid.

"Helps him remember, *I* guess," Ben
amended.

"As if he needed anything to help him
remember! I 'm surprised *at* you, Ben.
Why, it 's only two months since your
mother died, and he so fond of her! And

I'm sure *I* can remember, *perfectly*, that Swedish cook we had, the year Walter was born. I can even remember the scar she had under her left eye. I used to wonder whether she had been dropped into a fiord when she was a baby; nurses are so careless with children. Only, come to think of it, I don't suppose she had any nurse. Poor folks don't. And you *will* allow that your father and Sarah take better care of little Martha than any nurse ever did. So I don't see why he should n't have her come to stay with him just as often as he likes."

"Nor I," was the peaceable rejoinder. And as Ben stooped and kissed his wife, just by way of sealing the compact, he thought to himself that her cheek was as soft and sweet as ever it was. And when she brushed the kiss off, he remembered that that was exactly what she did the first time it happened, unconsciously inviting a repetition of the little ceremony. It was all very much to-day as it was then, only that somehow the repetition got omitted. For, really, one is n't quite so young and foolish as one used to be.

And after all, the point was gained,—the point which nobody had thought of disputing,—that the grandfather should have just as much of little Martha as was requisite either for remembering or forgetting.

And so, as the season drew in, and the snow piled itself high in the front yards of Bliss Street, the old man might often be seen passing up his own board-walk, between shining walls of winter's masonry— and Tim's—a chubby little figure trotting by his side, a gay little voice out-chattering the English sparrows, only recently come to town.

"What makes the snow stand up?" the little voice piped one day. "It lies down, over to our house."

"Get's kind o' tired over there, I s'pose, with so many boys and girls racketing 'round."

"Why don't Gamps have so many boys and girls yacketing 'round?"

"Used to hev. But they all stood up and walked away."

"I know. My daddy was Gamps's little boy. What made my daddy walked away?"

"Well, I guess he wanted to go 'n' keep house with little Martha's mother."

"Like Sarah keeps house for Gamps!" This with a sudden hop of blithe intelligence.

"No, little Martha, no! Like Gammy kept house for Gamps."

The small hops ceased, and the childish gait became staid and thoughtful.

"What made Gammy walked away?"

They had come to the piazza steps. Old Sarah would open the door for them; she was sure to be on the lookout, good soul! Yet, somehow, Ben was n't in such a hurry to see the door open as he used to be, and his foot lagged a bit.

"What made Gammy walked away?" And the scarlet mitten, imprisoned in a big hand, grew distinctly restive.

"Well," he answered, slowly, as they started to mount the steps. "We got thinkin' 't was about time we took a little journey, Gammy an' me. And seein' 's Gammy was spryer 'n Gamps, she jest went on ahead to make things comfy."

"Nice Gammy!" quoth little Martha, approvingly. Upon which the scarlet mitten found itself so tightly squeezed, that its owner shot a quick glance upward, surprising a look in the old man's face that even a child could understand. Wherefore, from that time on, "nice Gammy" it was, in little Martha's vocabulary.

"Well, Sarah," Gamps would say, as the front door opened. "Here's little Martha, come to stay the night. S'pose we 've got a cubby-hole we could stick her into?"

"Yes, sir," Sarah would reply, with dignity. "The spare room's aired, *and* het, accordin' to orders." For Sarah was a servant of the old school, and knew her place,—besides seeing to it that other folks kept theirs.

And Ben would think how, bye and bye, when Sarah had got the little thing tucked away in the huge canopy-bed with the flowered calico flounce, he would go up and bid her good-night. And somehow it did n't seem quite so long—the time to come before that grand good-morning that was to be the signal for starting life all over again.

And as Sarah was disappearing down the passageway,—for it was the grandfather himself who unbuttoned the little coat and pulled off the shiny rubber-boots,—he would like as not call after her: "How about a taste of that quince preserve, Sarah?" Adding, as little Martha's eyes danced sideways, "Yes, the nice, sticky kind, that Gammy put up."

And presently, when they sat at table,

the gentle old man and his lively little guest, he would say, gravely, as he helped her to another bit of quince, "I don't know what we're goin' to do when these preserves Gammy made give out."

Then old Sarah, who understood him as nobody else did, would emerge from her retreat in the pantry to observe: "I reckon there's plenty of it left to last out our time."

Whereupon old Ben would cheer right up,—not because of the abundance of Martha's quince preserve, but because of the limit implied in the cunningly chosen phrase, "our time."

Yes, old Sarah understood him better than any one; for had she not served him and Martha "hand and foot," since Hazeldean was a baby? And now Master Hazeldean's eldest was at the Institute, educating for a mechanical genius,—or so Sarah understood.

"The old gentleman keeps up very handsome," she would say to Hazeldean's wife, her special confidante since the defection of the mistress. "But I can see him hankerin'."

And quick tears would spring to Hester's eyes, usually so steady and so unclouded.

For she had once nursed her own husband through a critical illness, and she knew something of the horrible hurt that she had but narrowly escaped.

And yet, although she longed to comfort the lonely old man, she was quite aware that he craved no sympathy that she could give. He would rather chuckle over Alicia's inspired nonsense, or applaud Eddie's wife, as she taught her lord the most elementary *p's* and *q's*, than avail himself of the store of tenderness and good sense that made of Hester such a tower of strength in her own little world.

"Yes, Martha," he used to admit, in the happy days when Martha was by, to teach him *his p's* and *q's*, "Hester's a good girl, there never was a better. But she don't hit the funny-bone."

"Now, Ben," Martha would protest. "She's got more fun in her little finger than Alicia and Fanny have in all their anatomy."

"Like's not, like's not. But it's the anatomy that tickles! I tell you, Martha, —well, Mar*thar* then, if you will put on airs, —I never'd hev thought of fallin' in love with you, if you hed n't hed your comical

side. Now don't go flarin' out about it
—unless you 're a mind to!"

"Flare out!" Martha would retort, with
unutterable scorn. "I 'd as soon flare out
at a feather-bolster!"

Whereupon, Ben would shake his sides, and
resolve to be "aggravatin' " some more.

But all this was long, long ago, and now,
Martha having given over being comical
(just for a short space, let us hope), he had
to make the best of little Martha, who did n't
care a button how her name was pronounced,
and whose bright eyes were so needlessly
"comical," that they set all his theories
at naught. And he, whose aim in life it
had become to keep everything up to
Martha's standard, must needs suffer a
blemish in the child that bore Martha's
name.

As long, however, as he seemed to be the
only one to be put out, he tried to possess
his soul in patience. He fretted, to be
sure, though strictly in private, over Alicia's
little cross-eyed bear, but it growled so
sweetly, and hugged so satisfactorily, to say
nothing of the engaging trick it had recently
adopted of punctuating his encomiums
upon Martha with "nice Gammy," that

he had little real difficulty in making the best of it.

Then, of a sudden, all was changed. For, in the twinkling of an eye, in the twinkling, alas, of little Martha's eye, the old man discovered that he was no longer the only one to be put out about it.

The catastrophe was indirectly due to one of Alicia's inspirations. The child had been for a year past at a private kindergarten, happily engaged in making mud-pies (only that they called it clay), singing nursery rhymes a trifle off the key, and inadvertently imbibing a few rudiments of knowledge, when one day her mother chanced to hear it asserted that the kindergarten failed to stimulate the initiative. Precisely what the phrase signified, Alicia would have been at a loss to say. Since, however, there appeared to be a desideratum not provided for in the mud-pie curriculum, and since she was naturally desirous that her child should enjoy every possible advantage, it came about that the beginning of the Easter term saw little Martha summarily advanced from kindergarten to primary school.

Now the schoolhouse stood just around the corner from Bliss Street, and Ben, who was at home a good deal, now that he was leaving the business more and more in the capable hands of Ben junior, found himself anticipating many an agreeable windfall as a result of the projected change. Accordingly, on a certain Monday in April, when he had been out in the garden superintending the spading of Martha's currant bushes, he did not wait for Tim to knock off work at the stroke of twelve before turning away and sauntering round to the front of the house, where he stood waiting to see the children go by. For this was little Martha's first day at the primary school.

Ben's sight and hearing were remarkably good, and scarcely had the shrill babble of young voices reached his ear, than he espied a solitary little figure, vanguard of the troop, running full-tilt around the corner. Smart little thing, sure to be the first, coming to tell Gamps all about it. He made quick time down the path, and was at the gate before her.

"Well, well, little Martha! Got here first, did n't ye? Gave 'em all the slip, like a little—Why, bless my soul, what 's the matter?"

For now that she was close upon him, he could see that the round cheeks were flushed and tear-stained,—scored with dreadful little gullies, that had scarce had time to dry.

As he caught her up in his arms, "He said I was crossed-eyed," the child wailed. "He said little Marfa was crossed-eyed! And he sticked his finger out!" With which heart-rending jeremiad, she hid her face in Gamps's neck, and burst into tears,—he could feel them there, wet and warm under his collar, and ah, how he could feel the pitiful sobs shake the little form, held close against his own.

"There, there," he coaxed, while a veritable lump gathered in his throat, and the old eyes grew moist. "Little Martha must n't cry. She must n't cry! It makes Gamps feel bad!" And so moving was the appeal that, with a mighty effort, the sobs were checked, while a small hand stole up to Gamps's cheek, lest perchance a really-truly tear might have got itself caught in the whiskers.

But the kind old face was very stern, and a hot anger mingled with the pain of it all, —anger against naughty boys in general, and dilatory grown-ups in particular,—as he set the child on her feet, and led her around to the rear door, so as not to have to bother with the latch-key.

Arrived in the familiar sitting-room, where the knobs on Martha's work-table beamed at him from out their accustomed corner, and Martha's "rocker" stood ready to set itself going at the slightest provocation (he would often brush against it on purpose), he sat down and, lifting the child to his knees, essayed to comfort her.

"There, now, that 's better, ain't it?" he pleaded earnestly. "As if we cared tuppence about bad little boys, you 'n' me! And we 'll send 'n' tell mother that little Martha 's goin' to stay and get her dinner with Gamps. Should n't wonder if Sarah would let us hev some o' that squash pie she made yesterday, 'n' that Gamps could n't eat up all by himself, 'cause it was so big, —unless the mice hev got it," he added, craftily.

And under these friendly blandishments, little Martha soon plucked up her spirits, and was all animation again, exactly as Gammy used to be when the sun came out after a storm. And "quicker 'n a wink," she had jumped down and run trotting off to Sarah, ostensibly to get her face washed, but really to make sure that the mice had n't "etted up" that squash pie over night,— mice being notoriously greedy.

Yet, an hour or so later, when her grandfather followed her into the hall, where she had bustled on ahead to put her things on, he found her down on the floor, looking at herself in the looking-glass under the pier-table,—that looking-glass that Martha used to depend upon to tell her whether her skirt hung right. For Martha was very particular about her appearance, and never could bear to have anything in the slightest degree "out of kilter." And here was her little namesake, peering into that same mirror, with pretty eyes most wofully out of kilter.

"Hello!" the old man cried, determined to think no ill of the coincidence. "Playin' hide 'n' seek?"

But a funny little voice, quite unlike the usual gay chirp, inquired, "*Is* little Marfa's eyes cross-eyed? *Is* they?"

"Well, s'posin' they was?" he answered, gallantly, as he picked the child up and led her back into the sitting-room. "What do we care? I guess they're *pretty* enough for anybody, 'n' I guess they *see* sharper 'n most folks's."

"But he sticked his finger out!"

"Guess he was jealous!" By this time he was seated, and had her on his knee again. "Yes, that was it. He was jealous. I bet he was. Listen, little Martha; what kind of eyes did *he* hev?"

"Blue,—just like Gamps's."

"There now, what did I tell ye! That's jest what's the matter. Why, little Martha's eyes are black, like Gammy's, 'n' they was so pretty that if it had been anybody but Gammy, Gamps would uv been jealous too. Nobody wants blue eyes, if they hed their choice!" This, in a tone of disparagement calculated to make a blue eye blush.

And again little Martha took heart of grace, which set her small tongue wagging, and her small feet pattering, and sent her presently back to school, armor-proof against a regiment of "sticked out" fingers.

But old Ben found scant comfort in his own transparent sophistries, and scant toleration for a state of things that Martha, his Martha, would have made short work of. And again he took his courage in two hands.

"Yes, I guess you 're right," young Ben admitted, with the cautious rectitude which made him the admirable man he was. "I guess you 're right. We shall have to see if we can't bring Alicia round to it."

They were walking home from church, father and son, Alicia having stayed behind to teach her class in Sunday School. And for once Ben senior was not tempted to speculate as to the modifications a Bible story might be expected to undergo in its passage through the curious refracting medium of her brain.

"I dunno, Ben," he demurred. "I 'm afraid I ain't very sanguine about this bringin' Alicia round. Don't you think mebbe you 'd do better to—well, to *assert your authority?*"

"Same 's you used to?" young Ben was mean enough to suggest. But then, when a man is put to it he can't always choose his weapons.

Old Ben stiffened.

"I don't see the connection," he said; and he spoke so sharply that the son knew he had gone too far.

"I beg your pardon, Dad," he cried, quickly. "It 's *not* the same thing,—I know

26

that, well enough. But, somehow, I don't like to be the one to hurt Alicia's feelings."

"No, of course not," his father assented, more than mollified by the implied tribute to Martha. "A man don't."

"She'd mind a thing like that from me more than from anybody," young Ben explained. Adding, rather shamefacedly,— for he was Yankee to the core of him and intensely shy of sentiment,—"I suppose she's really more fond of me than you might think for."

"I know she's fond of you," old Ben testified, warmly. "And she's a dear little woman, too. Do you know, Ben," tucking his hand confidingly under his son's arm, "your mother used to say I liked Alicia best of the three. But—I never owned to it before."

And young Ben, in his turn immensely gratified, got hold of the kind old hand and said, as they parted company at Hazeldean's door, where the grandfather was expected to Sunday dinner, "Don't you get to worrying, Dad. We'll bring her round, yet."

But it was not this cheerful prognostication which lingered in the old man's mind when, later in the day, he was walking slowly, with bent head, on his homeward way. It was those other words: "I don't like *to be the one* to hurt Alicia's feelings."

"No, a man don't," old Ben said to himself. "A man don't. But *who else is there?*" And straightway his heart sank, at the ominous presentiment that came creeping over him.

But he soon threw it off. How could he ever have thought of such a thing, arrant coward that he was when it came to meddling in other folks' affairs! You can't teach an old dog new tricks, and he reckoned that few old dogs ever got to be his age! To be sure, if Martha had been there, Martha, who never failed to rise to an emergency! That would have been a different color of a horse. How high-handed she had been that time, back in '49, when he was badly bitten by the California gold craze. With what spirit she had brought out her ultimatum! He could hear her yet, as she declared, "Very well, Ben. You 'll do as you 're a mind to. But just as sure as you send a single dollar of your good money on that wild-goose chase, I 'll have my hair cut off short, every spear of it! You see if I don't!"

He laughed now, at thought of his
consternation.

"And she 'd hev done it, too," he chuckled,
as presently he stood looking up at her
"picter," that "picter" he had persuaded
her to sit for shortly after that, just in case
anything ever *should* happen to those glossy
black braids. Yes, she would have done it
fast enough. And all to save his making
a fool of himself with a couple of thousand dollars. While here was her own little
namesake, poor lamb! Why, Martha 'd
have *cut her head off*, rather than a little
child should suffer such a wrong,—a little
Martha, too, a little Martha Hazeldean
Pratt! Catch *her* putting up with any such
nonsense!

Dear, dear, it did seem to be growing
harder every day to do without Martha!

Meanwhile, spring had blossomed into
summer; Gammy's nasturtium vines were
a riot of color that set little Martha's eyes
dancing every which way. The Dunbridge
schools, from primary to high, were closed
for the season, and still there was no sign
of Alicia's being "brought round." Only
once had the grandfather approached her
on the subject when, to his dismay, she had

burst into tears and left the room,—Alicia, who could n't hold her mind still long enough to take offence! This was so extremely disconcerting that it was some days before the aggressor could bring himself to speak of the incident to his son.

Young Ben was deeply chagrined.

"Too bad," he said. "Too bad! And it 's not a bit like Alicia. Seems as if her nerves were all unstrung over it. Should n't wonder if she 'd heard something that frightened her."

"But there ain't really anything to be scared about?" They were sitting in Martha's grape-arbor, safe from interruption.

"I know it; I know all about it. I did n't tell you at the time, because nothing came of it, but I went so far as to have the child's eyes examined by Dr. Rumrill, the great oculist in the city, and he said it was a very small matter, and might as well be done any time, now. I think that 's what upset Alicia so,—my going ahead like that, without letting her know beforehand."

"And he says it would be a small matter?"

"Yes."

"And it might as well be done any time, now?"

"Yes. But then, there's Alicia. I'm really afraid she'd get sick over it. Do you know Dad," he went on, as he knocked the ashes out of his pipe, preparatory to taking his leave. "I sometimes think that if mother were alive she'd know what it was best to do."

Old Ben pulled several times at his pipe before replying. Then, "I've often thought that," he said, soberly.

And from that hour, that hour in the grape-arbor, where husband and wife had so often taken counsel together, it seemed as if Martha herself had assumed control, so plain did everything grow.

First came a timely epidemic. A case of measles broke out in the family, nice, comfortable measles that never hurt anybody yet, and little Martha was sent to stay with her grandfather, just to get her out of harm's way. And one by one, or just overlapping, like shingles on the roof, all the older children came down with it; and it went particularly hard with Walter, who was his mother's idol. So that by the time it was over, poor Alicia was so wan and thin, what with nursing and worrying, that her husband declared that there was nothing for it but

to carry her off to the seashore for a fortnight's change of air.

And when she wanted to take little Martha
with her, everybody seemed positively inspired to say, no, she must leave all her
cares behind her. And young Ben said
it was their first honeymoon in twenty
years, and he was n't going to go snacks
with anybody. And, thus diverted, Alicia
asked him, did he remember how they were
sitting on the beach at Old Point Comfort
on their real honeymoon,—well, then, on
their first one,—and a little girl about
half as big as Martha was playing round in
the sand, and a lady asked if it was their
little girl, and they had been quite indignant,
—just as if they looked like old married
folks! And Ben said that would be exactly
the way of it, if they took little Martha
along; no matter how young and frisky
they might be, people would think they were
old married folks. And somehow it got
itself settled that little Martha was to stay
with Gamps, and promise not to eat green
pears, while Flossie kept house for the big
children. Nobody seemed to have planned
anything, but there it was, all arranged.
And it must have been that somebody

had brought it about, and why not Martha? So thought old Ben, at least; for he was getting to be something of a mystic in his modest, homespun fashion.

And not a word had ever passed between the two Bens, not a word, or the raising of an eyebrow, that could incriminate them in each other's consciousness. And old Ben wondered.

"Now, don't let little Martha wear upon you, Dad," young Ben had admonished, when he came to say good-bye. "And if anything goes wrong, *you can count on me.*"

"Don't know what should go wrong," the old man answered, with elaborate unconcern,—for he was bold as a lion, now that Martha had taken control. "Unless she stubs her toe on her own impudent little nose!"

"Yes, yes; I understand! And, I say, Dad," Ben called back, as he left the old man standing in the doorway, a small figure beside him, throwing handfuls of kisses after her own daddy, "*I appreciate!*"

Well, of course he appreciated. Very proper that he should. Were n't they going on their honeymoon, he and Alicia? And were n't they lucky not to have any of the small-fry tagging after them? No, not a word had been uttered on either side that could incriminate anybody.

And now the honeymooners were off, and the doctor would be here to-morrow, the doctor and the nurse, and it was time little Martha was let into the secret.

And again it seemed as if Gammy were in control. For every word the old man said went straight to the right spot.

Oh, yes, little Marfa would like of all things to have her two eyes look the same way, "like other little girls's."

"For you see," Gamps explained, mindful of the virtue of consistency, "Cross-eyed eyes are all well enough, but they ain't in the fashion jest now, any more 'n poke-bunnits, like what Gammy used to look so pretty in, ever so long ago. But she would n't be wearin' 'em now, 'cause they 're out o' fashion."

"What kind of a bunnit is Gammy wearin' on the journey she 's goned away on?" This was a very complicated proposition for little Martha to formulate.

Ben tried to imagine something in the way of a halo for those glossy braids, which had never turned gray, like common, every-day hair does; but somehow he could n't fetch it.

"Mebbe they don't wear bunnits up there," he hazarded. "It's like playin' in a garden I guess. You don't want a bunnit in a garden."

"An' lots of flowers?"

"Yes, lots of flowers, that smell sweet, like the ones little Martha 'll hev to smell of when her eyes are all tied up for a little while, just to git rested after they 've been—" he paused for a word.

"Made over?" she chirped. "Like muvver's party dress she tooked away wiv her?"

"Yes, that 's it. All made over pretty, like mother's party dress. And there 'll be a kind lady in a funny white cap, like the fairy godmother in the story-books, to help take care of little Martha. Only Gamps and Sarah 'll always be round, to make sure that the fairy godmother don't carry her off to fairy-land."

And so the old man wove his pretty fabric of fact and fancy, and when he perceived that every word he said went straight to the right spot, he never for an instant doubted to whom the credit was due.

And next day, when Dr. Rumrill had

departed, rubbing his hands with satisfaction over a good job done, and the little figure, with bandaged eyes, lay breathing quietly under the influence of a gentle anodyne, and the nurse whispered, "It was the loveliest operation I ever saw," old Ben slipped down into the kitchen to tell Sarah,—seeing that there was nobody else to tell,—and I think that if that worthy dame had been one whit less particular about remembering her own place, and keeping other folks in theirs, he would positively have hugged the good woman for sheer joy.

"My stars and gaiter boots," cried young Ben a fortnight later, when he and Alicia, returned from their honeymoon, found Gamps and all six of the children assembled on their own broad, low-built porch. "What ever has happened to little Martha?"

"They's in the fashion," piped a gay little voice. "Gamps an' me, we had 'em made over, jest like muvver's party dress that she tooked away wiv her!" And she came dancing down off the porch, and pulling at her mother's skirts. For Gamps had said, "Be sure you kiss mother first."

"Why, Ben!" cried Alicia, turning white and "trembly" under the seaside tan. "Why, Ben! What is it?"

"Don't ask *me*," was the innocent protest. "This is the first *I* 've heard of it."

Alicia stood stock still, her hand on the child's shoulder.

"It was n't you that had it done?"

"No such luck," he asserted, stoutly. "Never knew a word about it till this blesséd minute. But, thank the Lord,— and Gamps,—it 's done!"

Alicia looked doubtfully from one to the other of the little group, and then she looked down into the dancing eyes of the child, on tiptoe there in front of her. The air was electric. Every one, down to the twins, felt a sense of expectancy. Only little Martha was quite unconscious.

Pulling at her mother's sleeve, "He said little Marfa must kiss muvver first," she admonished.

At the word, Alicia caught up the little creature and kissed her again and again,— lips, cheek, eyes, but the eyes again and again. Then, as the child broke loose and sprang into her father's arms, the mother moved slowly, waveringly, up the path. Boys and girls all stood back, like people in a play, leaving the grandfather in a mercilessly exposed situation. Slowly, very slowly, Alicia moved toward him, still with that doubtful look in her eyes.

The old man flushed crimson, and his lip trembled. It was a moment to try the stoutest heart. But he stood his ground.

"Well, Alicia," he said.

Only for an instant did Alicia hesitate, while she glanced in her bird-like way from Ben to his father, from his father to Ben. Then her face cleared, and, with a queer little catch in her voice, "I'm not sure, Ben," she jested, "I'm not sure but I like him *best of the two!*"

That broke the ice. In a quick burst of feeling, that was well worth waiting for, she flung her arms about the old man's neck, and clung there, laughing and crying.

Really, old Ben's collars had a rough time of it, first and last.

That was the high-water mark in the passing of Ben, that passing which he always reckoned as having begun on the

day Martha went away. A cheerful passing
it was, cheerful with no forced effort, no
hard-won philosophy. It was like the passing of day, when the sun is setting in a clear,
quiet sky, with here and there a freakish
cloudlet to catch the light. Neighbors,
kindred, children's children, all partook
of the gentle benediction of a nature un-
spotted of the world, yet touched with a
quaint humanity, whose foibles were but as
whimsical cloudlets, shifting, gleaming, shim-
mering to the last.

And since children delight in pretty
whimsies, where malice has no part, and
since they feel safe and happy when wrapped
about with love, what wonder that the old
man's chief companion in those latter days
was a little child,—a child that bore Martha's
name, and in whose young eyes, clear and
straight now as any in the land, lurked a
dancing light which they seemed to have
caught from Martha's own.

And a little child she still was when that
tranquil passing was accomplished.

Did old Ben die, like other folks? No
doubt he did, for he was no saint, to claim
translation. But that is something nobody
seems to remember about. They only know

that for yet a little while he walked with Martha, in an ever closer intimacy, and that now, though no longer seen of men, he is walking with her still.

FINIS